All at Sea

by Lembit Opik

Bretwalda Books, Unit 8, Fir Tree Close, Epsom, Surrey KT17 3LD
info@BretwaldaBooks.com
www.BretwaldaBooks.com
ISBN 978-1-910440-37-7

Printed and bound in Great Britain by
Marston Book Services Ltd, Oxfordshire

All at Sea

by Lembit Opik

Chapter 1:
All aboard

Given that our ancestors emerged from the ocean, it's curious how many people shudder at the prospect of finding themselves all at sea. For seasoned mariners, cruise ships offer an opulence beyond compare and - perhaps in deference to some vaguely recalled memory of our evolutionary past - a genteel communion with humanity's oceanic origins. For others, it's hell on water; a twilight zone between life and death - the last refuge for those who have tired of this mortal coil, but haven't got round to actually dying properly yet. Such a mix of sentiments reflects the endless capacity of the human mind to draw entirely contradictory conclusions from identical facts.

Nestled amongst the other carriers in Southampton's sprawling and impressive sea docks, all the emotions and behaviours which make humanity so endearing are present in a great, grey, steel clad cathedral known as the Continents Terminal. A giant, echoing basilica with the architectural appeal of a tin of lager, these premises are the property of the Atlantic & Gulf Line. The structure is the starting point, wherein all the conversations of voyagers combine into a single, tidal throng of words.

There's a hierarchy of experience here. You can tell the seasoned voyagers from the cruising virgins. Elements of the madding crowd display bewilderment at 'check-in,' where they surrender their baggage uneasily to insistent stewards. Others address the hard pressed staff as if greeting old friends. Still others, weary from their long and tedious motorway ordeal shuffle silently forward, as if the only possible outcome of this whole business will be disappointment.

Dockside, preparations are well advanced for the departure of a medium sized cruise liner. As passengers drift along the covered walkway which leads them to the carpeted comfort of Deck 5, beneath them on the quayside endless pallets containing obscenely exquisite fayre are being loaded through a hole into the bowels of the ship. These are vital provisions for the pursuance of the primary collective on-board pastime: weight gain – a seaborne phenomenon as difficult to avoid as breathing.

The bow of the vessel proudly announces her identity: the Spirit of Dogger V, so named as the fifth flagship of the line since the first wooden craft creaked her way to far flung ports in 1862.

The original Dogger primarily distinguished herself as a reliable transport for the conveyance of entrepreneurs and their families between London and Africa. However, her most infamous voyage was also arguably the line's first foray into pleasure cruising - albeit on a charter basis - along the coast of the great African continent. This ill-advised escapade was an act of pretention by a ludicrously wealthy British landowner, Sir Cecil Howard, who determined to take himself and a select party of friends and associates along the east coast to observe the 'primitive culture of the indigenous residents at close quarters' and from the comfort of the vessel.

The expedition did not end well. Half of the party spent the majority of their time below decks suffering a recurring case of food poisoning. It got worse. After a foolish and alcohol-fuelled moment of madness, Sir Howard commanded the hesitant captain to moor the vessel in untamed territory. Pompously marching ashore to inspect, and to an extent deride, what he reportedly called 'the nude people,' he was to suffer an ultimate ignominy of his own, being abducted and boiled to death in a cauldron by the indigenous tribe. Their decision to consume this nosey and voyeuristic Englishman was doubly ironic, given the community's strong dietary preference for fish. An entry in the Captain's log records that the tribe subsequently suffered chronic vomiting and diarrhoea after their gruesome dinner. It is clear that any such report would be very hard to corroborate, and as such, the Captain's attempt to give the hapless Brit something of a posthumous last laugh has to be treated with great caution. All we do know is that later generations of the tribe did recall the incident in spoken lore as the 'The Feast of the Inquisitive Long Pig,' though information of the intestinal consequences of Howard's end have not survived the passage of time.

The present day Spirit of Dogger V is a far cry from the creaky vessel of yore. A full 888 feet from bow to stern, she is capable of handling almost any sea state, and her stabilisers ensure at worst an uncomfortable rather than an unsafe passage, whether faced with a perfect storm in the Atlantic or a high wind in Jamaica.

In keeping with the traditions of the Atlantic & Gulf Line, this vessel is captained by the oldest skipper in the fleet, a gentle responsibility requiring little more than the prudent application of respect for the sea, and an infinite display of patience towards the unremitting demands of the clientele which this venerable ship attracts. The Captain is thus expected to divide his time equally between duties on the Bridge and the Promenade Deck, where it is conventional for him to spend time listening to genuine complaints of veteran cruisers, as well the vapid bleatings of those hoping to convert gripes into generous compensation packages - which can then be spent on subsequent voyages. A third category is intent on securing a place on the Captain's Table. These sycophants are the least offensive, though the most wearing, of those he must treat with deference.

Perhaps rather unkindly, this final captaincy is known internally by the Line's employees as either the 'Dog Leg' – or amongst the less reverent and cheeky younger staff as 'Dogging.' For most, it is a melancholy sail into retirement. For Captain Bladder, it can't be over soon enough.

Captain Bladder is not a young man. He has spent his entire working life at sea, initially in the British Navy, followed by a long and successful career transporting sheep from New Zealand to British ports. He frequently speaks of those days in fond terms, citing his consignments as 'a most edible kind of passenger,' a personal quip he makes in full knowledge of the consumption of the ill-fated Sir Howard. But it's true. He reminisces about the lamb carrying days as a far cry from the obstreperous herds of bipeds with whom he must now contend. Captain Bladder does nevertheless have a coping strategy – grumbling. His muttering commentary is both prodigious and consistent, but the rules of the sea prevent him from any significant grumpiness when in the public eye. This only serves to deepen his suppressed resentment of the 1,850 guests who regularly overwhelm his professional life for up to 104 consecutive days at a time.

This afternoon, Bladder is on the Bridge, looking mournfully down at the rain soaked quayside. He watches as the usual cacophony of vehicles rolls up, depositing bemused first timers and salty repeat old timers next to the warehouse within which the pre-boarding formalities continue.

'80 so far,' he mutters laconically. Bladder has taken to counting the number of electric wheelchairs. He has long believed that the number of these devices on board is directly proportional to the misery he will experience during the tortuous months of the world cruise, which invariably begins and ends at this very terminus. First Officer Ward looks at the Captain impotently. He knows from experience that there is nothing to be said that will cheer Bladder up. But he tries anyway.

'Cheer up Captain. At least we won't have those two from the Caribbean. You know, Mr and Mrs Major.'

Without looking away, lest he miss a scooter or wheel chair, the Captain responds dolefully.

'Yes we will. EVERY cruise has a Major of some sort. Some world cruises have two. Or three... or even four once. Oh and if they're from different battalions – 'Bladder sucks in through his teeth and suddenly looks at Ward – 'then, do you know what they do?' The First Officer shakes his head expectantly. 'Then they fight each other.' The Captain turns back to count for electric wheelchairs. 'And for some reason they always seem to complain about the kippers.' This observation silences the First Officer who recalls a physical assault which occurred one morning between a petulant retired colonel and a steward who had committed the unforgivable crime of confusing kippers with haddock in milk.

We leave the Captain to his counting and glide out through the entrance to the Bridge and along the corridor. Down the stairs we go to Deck 5, where crew are welcoming the motley collection of guests onto the vessel. 'Welcome back,' they say, aware that to those who have not been on board before this serves as a form of flattery, and to those who have sailed with the Dogger in the past, it's a confirmation of their status as valued guests.

We pass carefully by the arriving couples, and along the gangway, between the singletons in search of love or alcohol – or both - till we arrive in the terminal itself. Here the masses are forming orderly queues, patiently directed by smiling staff, who long ago learned the art of finding true joy in marshalling strangers into order. Each individual is required to fill in a form to confirm they have enjoyed rude health in recent days, without vomiting, nausea or uncontrollable bowel movements. Each dutifully confirms that this is so, regardless of the reality, for who in their right minds would forego the cruise of a lifetime for the sake of a humiliating confession? After all, they reason, even if they do start feeling peaky, they'll be within 30 seconds of a toilet for the next three months. And so the passengers sign up, sign in and hand their credit cards to the check-in staff, thereby entering a 'cashless' society where anything as vulgar as 'money' has no place – and where one is excused the irritation of having any idea how much you've actually spent. And then it's off to the gangway, to embark with hand luggage, dreams and whatever personal bacteria may sneak on-board within stomachs, a little secret like the countless litres of undeclared booze.

But, what's this? Here is a man remonstrating with a member of the X-Ray staff!

'Now pay attention, young man, the machine makes me feel ill. Do you speak English? I assume from your expression that you are following this. Now, I know a thing or two about nuclear things, but I can't say more than that – I was in the army you know. And I will not go through THAT machine.' This is the Captain's nemesis – the inescapable and ubiquitous military man, whose path will inevitably collide with Bladder in unpredictable but invariably provocative ways. His wife – introduced only ever as Mrs Major - looks on, having long ago surrendered unimportant disputes to his vast ego, and having no doubt that, regardless of the outcome, this altercation will be added to his endless list of dinner time anecdotes. Incredibly, Mr Major's protests bear fruit, and he is subjected to a cursory hand search before being courteously directed to the check-in. Mr Major reflects his sense of victory in the swagger of his step.

Outside the terminal, we spy an unusual vehicle amongst the cars – most driven by offspring depositing their aged parents to the pavement. Behind two taxis arriving from the station, a long white limousine draws up. This can only contain one particular duo – the honeymoon couple, married yesterday and whisked off through the kindness of their parents to enjoy the first weeks of their married life on the Spirit of Dogger V. They emerge with perfect hair and limitless bags, for she requires a comprehensive wardrobe in keeping with the vanity which goes with her two dozen years. Her newly betrothed partner for life, Douglas, has a vast array of his own luggage, containing clothes and unspeakable toys which he hopes will not show up in the security search. They look pensively at the arriving hoards, desperately seeking signs of others their age, and spying none.

'Do you think this is altogether wise,' Susan asks her spouse absentmindedly.

He gazes at the shuffling queues, the sticks and the motorised scooters.

'Yes, it's going to be great,' he says unconvincingly. A historian by trade, the scene reminds him of the retreat from Moscow, but with old people and electric wheelchairs instead of the Wehrmacht and tanks.

Over at the check-in desk, an elderly gentleman is having what appears to be a coughing fit. He convulses repeatedly, spluttering and wheezing until staff drift towards him pensively.

'I'm fine, I'm fine, he stammers following a great expellation of air. He shakily hands over his health form which confirms he's never felt better. The check-in assistant accepts the form and, entirely for her own interest, makes a mental note to check if Mr Grainger is still alive in 104 days.

And still they come. The husbands and wives, the families, the same sex couples, the changeover staff arriving to relieve those released at last from months at sea. The passenger manifest is a melting pot of Britishness, as committed to sea life as they are to pulling out of what they still refer to as 'The Common Market.' It is significant that no French or German travellers are scheduled to board. Long ago the North Atlantic & Gulf line abandoned marketing this vessel in these particular countries. The Spirit of Dogger V did not fare well with such a combination of guests – tensions spilling over to breaking point more than once during shuffleboard matches, the guests talent competition and, most violently of all, during the 'syndicate quiz' events in the Billabong room. These days, the Dogger is treated as a last vestige of unreconstructed Colonialism, its inhabitants basking in the universal use of English and the pleasingly traditional presence of staff from the Indian subcontinent.

Up in the Bridge Bladder has reached a watershed figure.

'One hundred and two. That's a lot of wheelchairs. It's going to be like the M25 in rush hour on the Promenade Deck.' Then his mood momentarily lifts. 'She looks fetching. That woman there, with her new husband,' and he turns to Ward. 'I doubt they've done their research. I bet it was a wedding present. They'd better not go on the Promenade Deck – they'll get run over.'

'Yes sir,' responds First Officer Ward. He is confident the new mister and misses will be pretty much guaranteed an invitation to the Captain's table, only because there is no obvious way to invite the girl on her own.

In the 104 days between now and their return to Southampton, the Captain will speak to any guest who wishes to commune with him. He'll do it with a smile, and share one of six stories he repeatedly tells to the delight of the guests. And then he will return to the Bridge, and sit on the port side. He will pretend to look out for dolphins while really looking back to a time his intercontinental compliment of frozen lamb made no complaints about anything – and when the most politically incorrect thing he could do was to ask for the mint sauce.

Chapter 2 :
I spy

'Ladies and gentlemen, this is your Captain speaking, and may I say what a... delight... it is to welcome you aboard the iconic Spirit of Dogger V for what I know will be the cruise of a lifetime for all of us... or at least for you. Whether you are with us for just one leg of this world cruise, or for all of the 104... wonderful... days, I am sure that my outstanding team of officers and staff will do everything in their power to ensure you have a magnificent experience on board this fine vessel. We are just making the final preparations for our departure from Southampton, and as the... outstanding... Chief Engineer winds up the rubber band and makes sure everything is in order, may I make a request of each of you to attend the safety demonstration in your allocated muster station. This is for all of our safety and while I am, er, fairly sure nothing will happen which is going to require the application of these emergency procedures, it is important that you do familiarise yourself with them. After that, can I suggest you join our Great British Sailaway Party on Deck 12 at the back with our, er, outstanding entertainments staff. And how about getting yourself a gin & tonic – and why not make it a large one. So, once again, on behalf of all of us here on the A&G line's flagship vessel, welcome aboard Dogger and I'll speak to you again a little later once our world voyage is under way.'

The Captain takes his finger off the microphone button. He sighs. Ward looks at him a little pensively.

'What's wrong Captain?'

'I spy trouble. I mean, I've never understood it. This is just so unusual. Why would people want to spend one-hundred-and-four consecutive days - all in a row - aboard a ship if they're not being paid for it?' The question catches the First Officer Ward off guard.

'Er, well... they obviously DO want to. We're totally full again.' The Captain is staring down at the quayside, watching the last of the preparations by shore staff who ARE paid to hang around the ship. Ward makes a second effort to find purpose in the situation. 'Captain, perhaps it's because, they,' Ward's words tail off. He asks himself if he would come on board if he weren't being paid and furrows his brow. 'I don't know, Captain. Perhaps they, because they, um, perhaps they like it, sir? Perhaps this is what they like to do?'

'Yes. This is what they actually do like to do. But, to me, Ward, that is like saying in my spare time I like to do the same thing every day, while sleeping in a confined space with the same people and having absolutely no chance of escape. Doesn't that strike you as at all odd? If that's what they like, why don't they just find a way to go to prison for a few months? At least that has the added benefit of involving a potentially enjoyable crime at the start. And it's free. And I'm told,' says Bladder turning to Ward with purpose, 'that they even teach you a skill these days. Like road surface repair or, I don't know, shoe making. Do they still do that in prison? Or is that just in Dickens?' Bladder looks away again. In the tone of a barely muttered lament, he sighs, 'all they're going to learn on board our ship is to gaze in wonderment at the animals their cabin staff have fashioned from a bathtime towel. And then there's the art of carving an ice sculpture – which none of them will ever do. And some of them will go to dance lessons for the fat and infirm. And they'll all go to talks on how to live with gout, which a large proportion of them will have acquired by the end of the voyage. Because we pride ourselves in killing them softly by plying them with a ludicrous abundance of rich food.' Unlike the Captain, the First Officer likes people.

'Um, I don't really think it is that odd. I think most of the passengers are quite normal, actually.'

Just as Ward has said this, the Captain points down at the promenade deck. They observe two young men stagger into view with plastic beakers of lager in their hands, making contorted faces at each other and apparently attempting to do a two man Conga along the front portion of the deck. The Captain turns towards Ward with a certain amount of smugness. 'Ward, does that strike you as normal? Really? REALLY? And what on earth are those two lads doing on this ship anyway?' Ward feels somewhat wrong-footed by the lunging likely lads down on deck.

'Well – no, I can't explain it sir. Maybe they're the entertainers?'

'I accept they are entertaining, but doing a two man Conga is hardly going to bring the house down for three months, is it?' The Captain returns to his main theme. 'Maybe it's the environment which makes them go mad. For a start, what normal human decides to have 104 consecutive dinners with the same people? I mean, I've seen marriages break up because the wife has insisted on having an evening meal with her husband a few times a week. This lot seem capable of talking about the day's events with the same people every day, even though they've all experienced the same day's events. And in my experience, most of them have an average repertoire of around three jokes. What do they talk about the rest of the time? DO they compare notes on their developing gout? And what sane man would expect to be entertained in the same theatre every day for fifteen weeks? Those two clowns down on the deck might as well be the entertainers for all the difference it makes. And then there are all the wedding renewal vows – just for something to do. I mean, how many times can you marry the same person before it begins to feel ironic?'

'Well, Liz Taylor married Richard Burton eight times.'

'NO'! exclaims Bladder turning on Ward with surprising vigour. 'She was married eight times. But she married Richard Burton only twice.' Now, Bladder looks like a man reminiscing. 'I met her once. On a cruise ship. She was with Burton as it happens.'

'I'm genuinely impressed, Captain. What were they like?'

'She was flighty but charming. He, on the other hand, was a cad. A lady called Debbie Reynolds was there too. Delightful woman. Delightful and troubled. Which rather goes to prove that cruise passengers become mad at sea or, as in the case of Taylor, are mad already and go to sea to surround themselves with water as a consequence. It's a sort of inverse form of rabies.'

While Ward is in awe of the Captain's celebrity encounter, the First Officer doesn't share the Captain's cynicism.

'Actually, I think it's quite romantic.' The Captain swings round again, clearly getting even more exasperated by Ward's naivety.

'This is your first full world cruise on board the Dogger isn't it, Ward? Well, let me tell you that you'll have a very different view of these things by the time we get back.' The Captain's voice changes to an altogether more sinister and haunted tone. 'These world cruises bring out the very worst in a man – the greed, the selfishness, the gluttony. I've seen it break relationships like matchwood.' He bends his wooden ruler for dramatic and precarious effect. He narrows his eyes. 'It can corrode the very soul of a saint. You'll see. And who has to pick up the pieces of all those broken relationships, those ruined souls? We do. It's us Ward. Us.'

Ward is rather taken aback by this monologue. He knows that part of the Captain's depression is the sure knowledge that he will enforce a self-denying ordnance of courtesy and abstinence from gin for the duration of the cruise. For the Captain, his occasional glass of champagne mocks his taste for the hard stuff and he wrestles with having a little or none at all. Because he only has champagne at receptions which he himself must host, it has developed a negative association. Bladder's exhaustion at the hands of guests, when all he really wants to do is sail, has become a grand maritime form of aversion therapy which has robbed him of his drinking days.

'You did use the word outstanding four times in your commentary, by the way, Captain. And I agree with you. It's a fine ship, a fine crew. So, it could be worse.'

'Yes, a fine ship indeed, but HOW could it be worse? We're at the top of our game on this vessel. We could be transporting soldiers to war, or lamb to Britain, or anything to anywhere for the betterment of society. Instead, what have we got? 104 motorised scooters and wheel chairs. Countless veteran complainers. A Major or two somewhere, seeking to declare war on the cabin steward or the French. They'll all be down there, all getting ready to pass judgement on the food, the décor, the blocked toilets which will be their own fault for trying to flush something like a pair of underpants or a coat down the loo. I even had one fat woman who flushed it without getting up and the vacuum system sucked her guts out. And you know what she did after we patched her up? She insisted on going round showing everyone a picture she had taken of herself in that compromised state.'

'A selfie?'

'A what? I don't know what you call it, but, yes, she took it herself, so if that's a shelfie, then that's what it was. Selfish more like. Thought she was the centre of attention for the rest of the cruise. Kept telling people she'd had DIY liposuction. Awful woman. She even had a copy of her revolting photo printed out and framed for me. She gave it to me on the last day of the cruise.'

'What was the picture like?'

'Disgusting. Like a cross between the 'before' picture in a Weightwatchers advert and a close up of processes in a sausage factory. And this, Ward, is what we have to look forward to. For 104 days. And we have to take it all.'

First Officer Ward nods politely and remembers that the horny dancer from High Liners troupe was supposed to get on again today. He wonders if the flirtations they had on one of A&G's other ships – the Spirit of Biscay – will continue. Ward realises that the Captain has finally finished his morose monologue and finds reason to escape from the Bridge.

'Excuse me Captain, I'll just go and check on the safety drill preparations.'

Jack and Jane Jitters have never cruised before. They're standing in their cabin staring out at the balcony. They're both from the Ardoyne district of Belfast in Northern Ireland. This is only their second departure from the British Isles in all the years they've spent together. The first involved 'a job' Jack had to do. In his earlier days he had taken a keen interest in various troubles facing the province. But those days are gone and his skills were in great demand after the signing of the peace accords. He spent his remaining days working in the fireworks trade. Everyone agrees he is one of the best in the business, partly because he tends to make his own.

'Oh, Jack, I'm not sure I like this. Look at all that water,' she says in her broad Belfast accent. Jack stands next to his wife and clasps her hand.

'Yes, I see what you mean, dear. It's not like the pictures in the brochure, is it? That was just restaurants and the nice woman on the stage and all that stuff, like.'

'Oh Jack, do you think we should get off?'

Jack considers the question and answers hopelessly.

'No, no I don't dear. There's a lot of water round here because we're on an island, so we do. I'm sure there'll be a lot less of it when we get to the hot places.'

'Why do you think that, Jack?'

'Because that's why it's hotter. I think. It will probably have evaporated a lot more down there. That's why it's hot, you see.' Jane wilfully accepts this explanation and they embrace in an endearing way.

Two decks above, Mr & Mrs Bitters are appalled at their room. This is not unusual. Everything appals Mr & Mrs Bitters. They have written over a dozen letters of complaint about everything from their noisy neighbours to the colour of the seats on the local buses in their home town of Chorley – since last Thursday. The letters have delivered remarkable results, and most weeks they receive compensation for something or other.

'Look at this room – look at that terrible view!'

'You're right – that's not what we've paid for.' Without even unpacking, the Bitters study the ship plan in preparation for an indignant march to the Reception Desk – the starting point for the lodging of their objections.

Newlyweds Douglas and Susan have been led to their suite. They're pleasantly delighted as their steward, Casper, takes them through the various facilities in the cabin.

'And here's the minibar which we will keep stocked up at your request. And here is a bottle of champagne with the compliments of the Line for your special occasion.' As Casper continues, Susan beams with delight. It's a dream come true. She looks at Douglas and knows she has married wisely. Douglas dents the moment slightly with a stupid question.

'Casper, will you actually be staying in the room with us.' Not knowing if this is a joke, Casper shakes his head cautiously. 'Where will you be staying then?'

'Er, in my own cabin sir. I would not wish to intrude...' he tails off, staring uncertainly at Douglas.

'But what happens if Susan – my wife here – needs something at night?'

Many images flash through Casper's mind, and momentarily recalls an incident where one of his colleagues was offered cash to 'service' an elderly single lady's needs at sea. He goes as white as a ghost. Casper decides to hedge his bets.

'I can provide food and drinks and such like – even your laundry. The rest you will be best advised to do for yourself, Sir.' There is an awkward moment as Douglas digests the inference. Then he bursts out laughing, and slaps Casper on the arm.'

'Oh I see what you mean! Yes, yes, don't you worry about that! Marvellous! Yes, well done!' Susan is blushing as Casper makes his awkward excuses and leaves. He knows this couple will, above all else, only be interested in room service.

It was the travel deal of the century but as Dave and Trev stare down at their double bed on the inside cabin, it suddenly doesn't seem like such good value after all. The plastic beakers of lager drip spots of amber nectar onto the carpet. Dave's annoyance is partly fuelled by the fact he's already had four cans of strong beer prior to embarkation. He isn't sure if the room layout is 'normal' or not, and decides to play it safe by sounding laddy.

'Well done, Trev. Deal of the century, eh? You never said nothing about a double bed. Now everyone will think we're puffs.'

'No they won't. Course they won't. Anyway, who's going to see it?'

'Well the geezer who does our room will for a start. He'll tell everyone about the 'bum bandits' in A116. And, anyway, how are we going to pull birds if you and me have to share a bed?'

Trevor privately regrets not researching the travel offer more fully. He too is slightly inebriated, but it tends to make him conciliatory. Anyway, he managed to relieve his nerves during their improvised two man Conga on the deck.

'Come on Dave, let's make the most of it, mate, eh. It's only a couple of weeks, and anyway, you can always go back to their place if you pull. Eh? Eh?'

'THEIR place?! It's not bloody Peckham. It's not like they're going to have a little flat of their own somewhere on the deck. There'll be with their mum and dad probably. And their older brother. I mean, it's crap, this. You said we'd be having a bargain fortnight of sun, sea and shags. That sounded great.

'It is great Dave.'

'Not if it's all going to be in here with you, Trev.'

Trevor is briefly at a loss to make the best of the situation. Then he hits upon a brilliant idea. He opens his suitcase, which contains two pairs of jeans, a couple of T-shirts and unfeasibly garish Bermuda shirt - and 24 cans of Fosters lager.

'Here, let's start with these.' They sit on the bed and contemplate their situation in silence. Trev burps.

'Give it a rest, Trev.'

'I'm nervous. It just came out, mate.'

'Yeah, and it's dangerous, an' all.'

'How can a burp be dangerous!' Dave looks at the walls.

'Well, the cabin could burst, or something.'

'Burst? How the hell could the cabin burst, mate?' Dave points all around at the air.

'Air pressure. And no windows, see? Where's it going to go?' Trev processes the challenge and realises Dave has made a fair point.

'Sorry mate.'

'What's that noise?' Monty looks furtively round the room, as Mrs Major unpacks their clothes. 'I can hear a mechanical device. Do you think they're recording what we're saying?' Mrs Major says nothing. 'I think they're recording us. It's disgusting.'

'Monty, why would they be recording us?'

'I don't know, it's probably a European Union directive to find the terrorists. Or something like that.'

'Oh come on Monty, who do you think would come up with a paranoid thing like that?' she doesn't stop hanging up the clothes.

'Because it's a sign of the times. There are a lot of suspects, dear.'

'Like whom?'

'Well, the French. And the Germans. Or the French AND the Germans.'

'Why would the French and the Germans want to get together to listen to you?'

'Well, let's face it, they've collaborated before.' Monty takes on a more conspiratorial tone. 'And let's remember that those who forget the lessons of history are doomed to relive them.'

Mrs Major thinks to herself that most women are far luckier than her, but Monty is a good hearted man and in fairness the most unreliable car he ever owned was a Citroen. And they were once delayed in Frankfurt airport for a long time – so she understands why he feels he does have something of a point.

'Have a look in that corner, dear,' she offers, recalling the last time they were on a cruise. Monty opens the cupboard.

'Darling, it's a fridge!' The mystery buzzing is no longer a mystery. 'Who on earth put that there?' Mrs Major considers his question.

'The Germans?' Monty inspects the unit.

'You're right! It's a Blaupunkt.' Monty removes the bottle of wine from the refrigerator. 'And this is French!' He looks suspiciously around the room. 'Whoever put these here is a bloody good operator.'

'In what way, dear?'

'Well, how could they have known we'd be in this room?'

'Perhaps they've got an insider in Bletchley Park – where they cracked all those Nazi codes in World War II.'

Monty grunts knowingly, glances round the cabin and makes a mental note to be on top alert to spy out shifty men with the lilt of a Bavarian or Gallic tone. Seeking clues, he picks up the little card which welcomes then to their stateroom and announces: 'your cabin steward is Fritz le Breton.'

Chapter 3 :
Sinking feeling

M r and Mrs Bitters are finally at the reception desk in the ship's cavernous atrium. In front of them is the receptionist. Her hair is perfectly styled in a ponytail, which flows elegantly over the back of her pressed uniform.

'Can I help you sir,' she says with an automatic but genuine smile. Her poise and grace are in stark contrast to Mr Bitters, who is wearing a damaged cardigan, which he himself found in a shop and purchased it in order to secure a reduction on its price. Bitters clears his throat. Just from the way he does it, the receptionist recognises that this man is not here to offer praise.

'Yes, I DO believe you can help us, young lady. We -' Mr Bitters pauses to bombastically point to himself and his wife, 'are Bitters. Mr and Mrs Bitters. And we must complain. And it is a serious complaint of significant importance.' The receptionist maintains her practiced smile, but privately she already knows that the gentleman in front of her can only be consoled by the offer of compensation, which she has not got the slightest intention of even hinting at.

They specialize in creating and sustaining misery – for themselves, whether feigned or authentic, and for others. They feed off imperfection, and make a career of proving that the world is a disappointment. As complainers, Mr and Mrs Bitters are at the top of their game. These half-empty individuals inhabit the domain of feedback forms, formal procedures and arbitration. Their existence is dedicated to knowing the price of everything, and getting it for less. If it's ripped, stained, incomplete or boring, they're in business. In an environment where reasonableness is essential for the orderly functioning of society, Mr and Mrs Bitters exploit other people's good will and extract very real sums of money out of service providers, who pay out simply to contain the problem such folk present to the running of communities such as an ocean going cruise liner.

While it would be tempting to place them at the bottom of the priority list, this is not the most effective strategy. Instead, they are handled with courtesy and respect. Sooner or later, whingers betray their complaining disposition to other passengers. By and large, cruise passengers take a positive view of ships, staff, entertainment and the seaborne life. They absorb minor inconveniences and even more major ones, for cruising is not to seek perfection, but rather, to find peace in a pastime as unpredictable as the oceans themselves. To reveal a complaining nature to seasoned cruise passengers is considered poor etiquette, comparable to shouting in a library. Then, and only then, will the staff be in a superior position to stymie the negativity.

The elegant receptionist is brought back from her private thoughts by the rasping drone of Mr Bitters. 'When we, that it my wife and I, booked our balcony room we were promised a sea view. I have it in this email. See here, it says we will definitely have a sea view. Well, no sooner do we go into the room than we discover we have nothing of the sort.' The receptionist takes the paper and reads it carefully. She nods as Mr Bitters expresses the disappointment which he and his wife are suffering. Mrs Bitters contorts her face in an effort to display sadness and anger. To the receptionist, she looks like she is gurning, a quaint activity designed to amuse audiences in places like the South West of England and Yorkshire. It is rather out of place on board a ship. The receptionist realises that Bitters has concluded.

'I fully appreciate the importance of a sea view, Mr Bitters. You do have a sea view.'

'NO WE DO NOT,' shrieks Mrs Bitters, her timing intended to add emphasis to her husband's monologue.

'If you will allow, you do have a sea view but you will not be able to view it just yet.' This incenses Mrs Bitters even more.

'Why not? It's OUR view – we paid for it and YOU, or to be precise, your company of which you are the current representative here and now, you have not delivered the service for which we have paid in advance and in full.'

'I fully understand your enthusiasm to see the sea, Mrs Bitters.'

'DO YOU?' she exclaims so loudly that everyone in the foyer stops their own conversations momentarily, causing Bitters to involuntarily blush. 'Do you?'

'Yes, madam. I do. In fact, I share your passion for the sea. You will not be able to see it yet because we are in port and your side of the ship is facing the land. When we set sail, in under an hour, your view of Southampton will become a view of the sea.' Mr Bitters pauses, then finds his momentum again.

'How do you know? You haven't seen our room.' The receptionist maintains a sincerity which would exceeds the patience of most ordinary mortals.

'Mr and Mrs Bitters, I can assure you that this is a fact. However, if you are still unable to see the sea by 9pm tonight please do come back and I promise we will resolve this issue for you.' Mr Bitters glances at his wife who shrugs doubtfully.

'Well, you'd better be right. I very much doubt you'd have sorted this problem out if we hadn't brought it to your attention.'

'Yes, Mr Bitters, thank you for bringing this matter up. And yes, we will sort this out for you as soon as we set sail.'

As Mr and Mrs Bitters depart he mutters to his wife.

'If we hadn't come down here, we'd be looking at that horrible little town for the next three weeks, no doubt.' Mrs Bitters concurs.

'Yes. I don't think they CAN sort it out. After all, how do they expect to move an entire city and replace it with water in under three hours? It's ridiculous.'

Down in the Red Curtain Theatre, Monty and Mrs Major are impatient for the safety drill to begin. They're standing next to Jack and Jane Jitters.

'I wish they'd bloody well get on with it,' snaps Monty, causing Jack to jump nervously. Mrs Jitters says something to Monty in a Northern Ireland accent so broad that to him it sounds like 'av ye comb on tha cruz aften?'

'Pardon? Do you speak English?' This confuses Mrs Jitters.

'Aye.'

'Well please do so then.' Mrs Jitters repeats herself more slowly.

'Have you come on the cruises often?'

'Cruised? Many times, madame. In fact, I'd be willing to bet I've had more days at sea than the captain. Oh yes, I've seen a thing or two. I've seen things that would make your eyes pop out of your head, if you know what I mean.' Jane is suddenly intrigued.

'What kind of things?' asks Mr Jitters. Monty savours the moment.

'Oh, all kinds of things. Island peoples who have never made it to proper civilisation – I mean true barbarism where they do not even have such basic essentials as electricity, or gin. Waves the size of this very liner. Storms so fierce that life boats were ripped off their moorings and swept away in icy seas.' Monty takes on a more conciliatory tone. 'But you needn't worry. There are enough of us on board who know the ropes, so to speak. Should anything untoward happen, we shall be able to direct the crew to take the necessary actions.' Jack is feeling much more apprehensive now.

'What's the worst that can happen, like?' Monty ponders the question.

'Well, the worst would be to sink in a mighty storm into sub-zero waters. That's not survivable really.' Jack and Jane wait for reassurance but none comes.

'Oh dear,' squeaks Jane. 'Should we maybe keep our life jackets on after this? You know, better safe than sorry if ye know what I mean?' Monty isn't listening and nods – inadvertently causing the Jitters many days of discomfort.

The safety demonstration covers the various meanings of ship's siren, as well as where to go if there's an emergency. At the point where they are told NOT to put their life vests on, inevitably a proportion of passengers put them on anyway.

After the safety demonstration, Trev and Dave decide to explore the ship. Their primary aim is to 'check out the female talent.' Two false starts cause them to circumnavigate the ship on different accommodation decks without making any real progress at all. They eventually find a staircase on the inside of the ship and climb towards the light. Minutes later they're up on deck, basking in the glorious drizzle which Southampton has served up. Trev laughs out loud.

'This is brilliant mate!' Dave looks around, bemused.

'What's brilliant? The rain?'

'Na, we're here. We're really here. You know, living the dream!'

'Which dream would that be? Getting wet or spending two weeks in the same bed as you?' Trev is undeterred.

'Come on, mate. This is what you make it. We've got the whole world ahead of us – and just think of all the totty that's got to be on board a ship this size. It's brilliant!' Dave considers the situation. He's in an inside cabin where the only changing scenery is Trev. They've got 22 cans of Fosters left, which won't last more than two days. And so far, they've got a double bed and have just been to a safety demonstration telling them what to do if the ship sinks. It's not a dream Dave particularly wants to live.

'Oi, oi!' says Trev, and suddenly the whole situation is turned on its head. Three stunning young ladies in white are purposefully walking across the deck towards the stern of the ship. Without needing to be told, Dave follows Trev in pursuit. The pursuit is far shorter than they had expected, as they end up standing in very close proximity to the three angels at the entrance to the health spa. The tallest of the three smiles sweetly at Trevor.

'Hello, sir, can we help you?' Trev winks at Dave like the cat that's got the cream – in a 'watch this' kind of way.

'I think so ladies – my mate Dave and I were wondering if you'd like to spend some time with us.' Dave looks down at the lady's badge. 'So, er, may I call you Dorothy, what do you and your friends say?' 10 minutes later, having been taken through the full set of options in the health spa, Dave and Trevor have both signed up to various massage and health treatments, totalling over £200. As they leave, Dave is in an even more morose state than before.

'What did you have to sign up for all that stuff for?'

'It's a way in mate. I mean, it's worth it, eh. That Dorothy is the key to it.' Dave says nothing. He's not sure booking them in for all that stuff was good value for money. 'Anyway, what's not to like? It'll be great!' Dave continues to say nothing. Then, after a few moments, he raises another concern.

'Why did you have to tell them we're sharing a room, Trev?'

'I had to! They have to book us in. That's how it works. With the room number and all that.'

'It's embarrassing.' Trev stops walking and looks at Dave.

'Actually, you're right. It was embarrassing. But it was only embarrassing because you had to tell them 'we're not gay.' Now they think we ARE gay.'

'What did you expect me to say?'

'Nothing at all would have been better.' Trev and Dave wander towards the back to join the Sailaway Party, where Jane and Jack have already arrived. They are the only two guests still wearing their life jackets. They're drinking orange juice and preparing themselves for the departure of the ship, which they presume will be rocky and fraught with danger. DJ Christian – an effervescent member of the entertainments team – introduces himself.

'What's with the life jackets, folks?' Jane fiddles with the whistle nervously.

'Better safe then sorry, as they say.' Jack nods vigorously. Despite DJ Christian's best efforts, he fails to convince them that the moment of departure is unlikely to be catastrophic. He compounds the problem with a pointless quip the edgy couple have heard many times before: 'Jitters by name, jitters by nature,' for which he immediately apologises, while Mrs Jitters bites her lip. 'We're not going to sink, woman!' he explains awkwardly.

'How do you know? Why do we have to do the drills?'

'In case we sink, but we're not going to sink.' Mrs Jitters wells up in tears, causing Mr Jitters to put her arm round her.

Monty, who is within earshot of the exchange between DJ Christian and the Jitters, decides to assist. 'Don't worry, dear, everything's going to be fine. In fact, a few years ago, we were on a ship that did nearly sink - ' Mrs Major turns to Monty. 'No dear. Not now.' He gives it one more go. She raises her finger to his lips. 'Shh.' Mrs Major wins the day.

And then, bang on schedule, the great Spirit of Dogger V slips its moorings and with a great series of blasts from the ship's horn which makes everyone jump, they have commenced their circumnavigation of the earth. And not one soul on board the gracious liner has the slightest inkling of the implausible events which will make this a cruise to remember.

Up on the bridge, Bladder is studying the news from the Met Office. There are warnings of gales in the infamous Bay of Biscay. It tickles Captain Bladder; because Bladder's got a personal obsession – with storms.

Chapter 4 :
The Bay

There's a little ritual, shared by those hardy voyagers who make ocean life a part of their regular recreation. The custom goes like this. One sea-faring traveller will say 'We'll be going through Biscay in December.' The rest then breathe in through their teeth and nod knowingly: for the Bay of Biscay is regarded by one and all as a cruising 'rite of passage' – a great caldron of storms. It's an expanse of water which seemingly has the capacity to convert a mere breath of air into mountainous seas, the likes of which would adorn any children's comic book to the awestruck wonderment of a youth.

And it's true. Biscay's underwater terrain is verily a minefield of lumps and cliffs, forcing the waters above to seethe and boil in a most distinctive fashion. On occasion, the relatively flat bottomed hulls of modern cruise ships struggle to maintain a moderate keel at the hands of the awesome shifting force of the ocean. At the height of such a tumult, it can seem as if giant, watery fists bang the hull with thundering blows. Each juddering smash shakes the courage of quivering guests, who surrender their appetite to those remorseless, raging punches.

It is also said there is an alchemy of colour in the wildest tempests so that the whitest of crests makes the greenest of guests. At times like that, bountiful larders lie undisturbed. Empty bars resonate to the echo of waves pounding the vessel's long suffering sides. And staff stand idle, administering their culinary services to the few brave souls who insist on dinner regardless of the raging storm – because, at the end of the day, it's only water.

As the Spirit of Dogger V inches out of Southampton's cosy port, edging carefully past the Isle of Wight's crafty sand bars, Captain Bladder has been looking at the weather charts. He has a great respect for these waters, straits which he has navigated his whole life. However, on this particular occasion, he also sees an opportunity for sport.

Far to the West of Plymouth Sound, out there in the untamed firmament, a depression has begun to make mischief. It's a deep one – 976 millibars, a real stinker of a cyclone - and it's travelling East with the determination of a locomotive. Captain Bladder has been talking to the Met Office. The weather boffins have concluded that there is little possibility the depression will be near Biscay at the same time as the Dogger. But Bladder is a seafaring man to his core and sees it differently. The very same traits which cause him to resent his human cargo draw him addictively toward wild seas. His greatest infatuation is a love of storms. Only by riding King Neptune's ferocious rollercoaster does this salty sea dog feel at peace with nature. Bladder has looked at the charts. He intuitively concludes that the Met Office computer is taking a naively benign view of the immediate future. He knows the microchips have called it wrong. This depression won't stop at 976 millibars. It is his judgement that it will descend to 952 millibars, or thereabouts. The lower the number, the greater the storm.

'We're going to need to baton everything down,' he tells First officer Ward.' Ward shakes his head.

'It doesn't look so bad, Captain. A force 8 or 9. The sea state will be rough but no worse than that.' This is a moment the Captain savours. He looks sagely at the First Officer.

'Do as I say.' Everyone hears his instruction, and the mood on the bridge changes with the speed of a shiver. A chill flashes through the minds of all on the Bridge. Bladder has little time for heroics, but as a younger man he saved a ship from catastrophe when, as a First Officer himself, his superiors panicked and with a badly judged change of course, brought their vessel into a precarious alignment with the cruel seas. They were within a few degrees of capsizing. It was only the immediate and virtually insubordinate actions of one maverick First Officer Bladder in a force 12 storm which prevented that cargo ship from sinking - in a situation where all hands could well have been lost, together with 35,000 tonnes of vessel. This incident, which entered the history of maritime seafaring with the status of a legend, confirmed upon Bladder – who is arguably the greatest curmudgeon in the cruise ship world – the unchallenged reputation as a grandmaster of his oceanic craft.

Bladder tells the Met Office that they are underestimating the storm. His implicit warning carries such weight that six ships alter their plans, two darting for the safety of Cadiz and another couple scurrying North for the protection of Le Havre. The remaining two reduce their rate of progress, to wait and see what transpires. Only the Spirit of Dogger V sails on, at 19.9 knots, due south, as planned. If Bladder is correct, for anyone else this would be a voyage for madmen. For Captain Bladder it's an opportunity to commune with raw nature – an antidote to the untroubled waters he is regularly encouraged to sail for the comfort of his customers.

Dave and Trevor are getting ready for dinner. Their preparations are very simple: three cans of Fosters - each.

'So, where do we eat?' Dave studies a bit of paper.

'It says here we're on table 64 in the Medusa restaurant.'

'Where the hell's that?' says Dave, without a hint of irony, but with more than a hint of Fosters.

'Well, it's got to be on the ship.' Dave looks up. Trevor bursts out laughing and for the first time since they got on board the two likely lads share a moment of mirth. Then, somewhat unexpectedly, Dave lets out a simper, causing Trev to sit there, momentarily paralysed with confusion. Trev tries to form a constructive sentence.

'What was that about mate?' Dave fiddles with his can of Fosters and after along period of preparation, he musters the courage to respond.

'I'm allergic to fish.' This catches Trev by surprise.

'So what?'

'Well, I can't eat fish.'

'Don't then. Eat something else.'

'That's all they're going to have, isn't it? Just fish. I mean, maybe other seafood too.' Trev stares at Dave in disbelief.

'Why do you think they're just going to have fish, mate?'

'Because, mate, you can't fit cows on a ship can you? Did you see the size of the door we came in on? And fish are smaller, apart from whales, I mean the fish not the country, obviously. But they probably wouldn't have whales anyway.' Trev tries to figure out whether the better option here is reassurance or ridicule – and whether it's even worth tidying up the true status of whales.

'Don't be a prat mate. For a start, Whales aren't fish, they're dolphins -' Dave starts crying again so Trev adds apologetically, 'look, never mind that, even if they've mainly got fish they've probably got small animals like, um, toads – which is fish as well I suppose – but like rabbits and rats and deers.'

'Deers are pretty big too. They wouldn't fit.'

'Well, OK, not deers but rabbits and rats anyway.'

'What if they don't, Trev? What do I do then?'

'Come on Dave, mate, you can still eat the vegetables. They'll fit veg on a ship, no probs.'

Monty has dressed for dinner. The evening dress code is casual, but not for Monty. He has standards, and he's proud to celebrate them. Anything less than a bow tie disrespects The Empire. Mrs Major is proud of Monty's high standards. Monty turns to her.

'Mrs Major, you look ravishing. Come on dear. Let's make this first night very special.'

As they proceed along the corridor on Deck 11, hints of a lateral swell guide them to the left and right as they march towards the forward lift shaft. Jack and Jane are standing there already, waiting for the lift. They're wearing their life-jackets. Monty nods approvingly.

'Very prudent for first timers. Once you've been at sea a little longer, you can take them off.' Jack looks at Monty for encouragement.

'Really? How long do you think we should wear them for?' Monty looks up as if to make a calculation.

'Well, until you're fairly sure you're not going to fall in, what ho!' He laughs effusively, causing Jack and Jane to chuckle unconvincingly. As it turns out all four of them are heading to the Medusa restaurant. The waiter is taken aback by the arrival of two people in life jackets but has done the job long enough to know that saying nothing is the most diplomatic course of action.

'Would you like to sit in a group or alone?' Before Jack and Jane can answer, Monty intervenes.

'Together, together of course! The more the merrier!' They're seated on a table for 10. They aren't the first to arrive. Two miserable looking people are already seated at the table. Mr & Mrs

Bitters had arrived early in the hope of being able secure a table for two. However, they were directed to table 64 instead, much to the annoyance of Mr Bitters in particular. Monty offers greetings which are only weakly reciprocated by the dour duet.

'Why are you wearing your life jacket,' asks Mrs Bitters of Jane.

'It's our first time, you see. We're just finding our sea legs.' Mr Bitters intervenes.

'How does wearing that stupid thing help you find your sea legs?' In the ensuing silence Mrs Major seeks to pour oil on troubled waters.

'Well, we all find our sea legs in different ways. Maybe that's how these two are going to find theirs.' Mrs Bitters is in a literal mood this evening.

'You know, they don't give you actual new legs or anything. You just have the legs you always have, and I don't see how wearing a buoyancy aid is going to change that.' Mr Bitters chips in.

'Yes, donning a piece of foam is not going to give you extra powers. To think that is a bit ridiculous. Frankly.' Again, Mrs Major interjects.

'So what do you do?' Mr Bitters responds with pride.

'Mainly, we complain. You could say we're sort of guardians of the consumer, just making sure that bad service is rewarded with compensation. For example, we didn't have a sea view when we got on and we complained and now we have one.' Jane is surprised by this.

'Oh, did they move you into a different cabin?' Mrs Bitters explains.

'No, they moved Southampton and put sea there. And I'm sure they wouldn't have done that if we hadn't complained.'

Dave and Trev finally arrive at Table 64. They sit uncomfortably together, as the conversation dies.

'Greetings, boys,' announces Monty, offering his hand to Trev, who takes it uncertainly. 'I'm Monty, this is Mrs Major, these two in the life jackets are scared people and – I've just realised I don't know your names, but they speak a very odd form of English. And I've only just met these two.

'Mr and Mrs Bitters.' Monty nods appreciatively.

'Mr and Mrs Butters. And you are?' Trev goes first.

'I'm Trev.'

'And I'm Dave. But we're not gay or anything, we're just sharing a bed by accident because Trev sorted it out that way.' For a few moments everyone considers Trev and Dave's sexual orientation, till Mrs Major seeks to relax the moment of tension.

'I'm fine with the gays. I mean, I just don't mind gays at all.' Monty scowls at Mrs Major. Next up is Mr Bitters.

'I don't like the gays, actually. I think it's wrong, disgusting really. I mean, if they were meant to do that kind of thing then they'd be, well, born a woman, or at least have women's things in some way.' Mrs Bitters nods to her husband in silent agreement and swings round disparagingly to engage Dave and Trev, causing Dave to look at the napkin and Trev to gasp in exasperation. Presently, everyone apart from Mrs Bitters turns their attention to Jack and Jane. Jane speaks up.

'Um, well I don't mind it really and if you want to share a bed, that's up to you.' Mrs Major and Jack nod. Monty continues to stare at his wife angrily and Mr & Mrs Bitters turn to look at Trev and Dave and shake their heads. Dave feels a need to defend himself.

'Look, I don't want to share a bed with Trev, I just have to!' Mrs Major turns to Trevor.

'You shouldn't force him do that kind of thing. I mean, that is NOT right.' Trev responds angrily and with the volume of four cans of Fosters.

'We're not gay!' This causes a lull in conversation as a number of tables around them look over, and then return to their conversations, which are now evidently about Trev and Dave. Monty speaks.

'We had some batty boys in the army. But it wasn't official. I believe they were afraid that the gays would be too busy kissing and touching eachother up to do any proper fighting.'

'Can I take your order sir?' The waiter's unexpected intervention ends the discussion about Trev and Dave's sexuality, at least for now.

Conversation drifts on to matters relating to the Bay of Biscay, views of the sea and Germans. The two remaining places on the table remain unoccupied throughout the meal. When it comes to Dave's order, he sees his opportunity to clarify what seems important to a slightly drunk man with no experience of cruising.

'The steak, um, is it from, well, is it from a cow or from a smaller animal?' The waiter is confused.

'What kind of smaller animal? A small cow, for instance?'

'A rabbit… or a rat?'

'Ah, I believe not so sir… it's a steak from a cow.'

'How do you get them on board?' Mr Bitters rolls his eyes in unreconstructed dismay.

'Typical homo.'

And so the eight eat together, leaving two empty spaces at the end of the table. The newlyweds haven't made it for dinner.

Up in the Bridge, Captain Bladder has a short conversation with everyone on duty.

'It's going to be rough. In fact, technically, the swell will be phenomenal. Force 11 for most of the night and 12 plus in the morning. So, treat this as a training exercise. Watch and learn – and tell the team downstairs to store away all the glass.'

Chapter 5 :
Storm Force

After dinner, Trev and Dave go in search of a pub. Dinner didn't go particularly well. In the end, only three conversations prevailed: Monty's views of what's wrong with the army, Mr and Mrs Bitters' views on what's wrong with the dinner and everybody's implied views on what's wrong with Trev forcing 'people like Dave' to 'do those things.' Somewhere between dessert and coffee the ship had begun to move around a little more, causing Monty to tell some chilling stories of storms past.

Dave is both drunk and angry. He fears the next weeks are going to be a festival of humiliation, with the people on their table insistently oscillating between 'tolerating' the fact that Trev and Dave are 'sleeping together,' and condemning them as the sexually deviant spawn of Satan. Mr Bitters took offensiveness to new levels by offering everyone his belief that since same sex couples can't have kids, eventually they're bound to simply 'become extinct.'

Dave and Trev eventually stumble into the pub – Winners – on Deck 7. There, they find a welcome sight – Fosters on tap. Predictably enough, after a couple of pints, they begin to feel decidedly worse. The room appears to be swaying – because it is. Curtains are swinging to and fro - and people drift in synchronisation as they struggle to negotiate the moving floor.

'What's going on Dave? Is it 'it' or is it us?'

'Dunno. Funny though, isn't it, whatever 'it' is?' Trev pulls a confused face which momentarily makes him look very stupid, and then says:

'Sorry, you've lost me there, Dave,' and they return to their tactless pastime of watching unsteady people trying to walk through the bar.

In this same instant, others are converting the growing energy of the ocean into internal storms of a more gastronomic nature. Mr and Mrs Bitters are decidedly unwell now, their grim determination to eat all five courses at dinner combining with the ship's increasingly pronounced movement to generate a, literally, explosive combination. The Bitters couple are a testament to the saying: 'the greater the swell, the less swell I feel.' As far as vomiting is concerned, the Bitters couple are now unstoppably on the final countdown – evidence, were it needed, that the ocean metes out a kind of visceral justice towards intentionally miserable people. It is a warning they will pay for tonight and subsequently ignore again to their much greater cost.

Where are Monty and Mrs Major at this moment? Veterans of cruising, they're weathering the beginnings of the storm with stoical British resolve. In fact, they're not wasting the evening with anything as petty as sea sickness. Instead, they're at the 'Syndicate Quiz' – which requires guests to form teams of up to six and collaborate to answer 20 pretty difficult general knowledge questions. Having convinced a lady and gentleman who 'are well dressed enough to probably have been privately educated' to team up, this gang of four is doing well. They're on question seven. So far, they've only missed one correct answer, guessing – incorrectly – that between Prague, Budapest, Warsaw and Cracow, the last of these is the most easterly. Still, they have a good chance of winning tonight. As others glance restlessly out the windows at wisps of spray, weeping down these windows 60 feet above sea level, Monty remains engrossed in the game – trying to recall the definition of 'palindrome.'

Elsewhere, Mr and Mrs Jitters are sitting by the window on Deck 6 staring at the walls of water repeatedly striking their bedroom window, drowning out the moonlight every 30 seconds. Neither says anything until Jane breaks the silence.

'I think we were safer in Belfast,' she says about the birthplace of the Titanic.

And the newlyweds? They have yet to leave their room.

On the Bridge, the Captain is studying the weather charts. He's in good spirits. These seas are what he had expected - with more to come. First Officer Ward is standing next to him. He hasn't seen 'The Bladder' in such good form for months.

'11 to 12 I'd say, Ward.'

'What? Wind force?'

'No, no, boy, that will certainly be Force 12 gusting to 80 knots. By '11 to 12' I refer of course to wave height – in metres. It's phenomenal. That'll put hairs on the back of your chest.'

Although to the uninitiated, 'phenomenal' may sound merely like dramatic use of language, Captain Bladder is right, both in terms of his forecast and also in his use of terminology. That's because there are technical definitions for 'wave heights.' These are used every day for the Shipping Forecast by the British Met Office. They are a timeless pillar of the country's obsession with meteorological matters, built into the very consciousness of an island nation which has, more than once, been saved from invasion by the fortress of the ocean.

Let's recall these definitions. One might imagine 'Rough' to indicate heavy seas. Nothing could be further from the truth. 'Rough' refers to waves less than 4 metres in height. While a wave which can engulf a bungalow may seem intimidating to a small yacht, to a large ocean cruise ship such as the Spirit of Dogger V it's a mere blip, causing little more than the occasional distant shudder for its occupants. On the other hand, waves undramatically referred to as 'high' span a range of 6 to 9 metres. These will make a serious impact to comfort on board, and the tally is measured in sickness and broken glasses. But the largest of all, those above 14 metres – or 45 feet – in height, are given a very special name: 'phenomenal.' Such waves represent the height of a London bus on top of a London bus on top of another London bus – and then some. For 'phenomenal' waves, that's the minimum.

The highest waves ever recorded in a storm are more than twice that height – around 48 metres or 150 feet from trough to crest. This is a ferocious quantity of kinetic energy. When such monster waves make contact with a seaborne structure, such as a ship. The moving water weighs many thousands of tonnes: vessels depend for their safety in such testing encounters upon the quality of the vessel's design, seafaring prowess and the Grace of God. There have certainly been larger waves than the highest ever reported, and in all probability mankind has encountered them. Perhaps the greatest waves upon our seas were not survived by those who witnessed them. The relationship between man and sea is thus an ever-changing one, dependent on wind and currents and seabed and tides - where the only constant is that the oceans possess fantastic power. Humans do well to respectfully respond to the mercurial moods of the seven seas.

We return to the bridge of Spirit of Dogger V, where Ward finally plucks up the courage to challenge Bladder's decision to enter the storm head on.

'Is this altogether wise sir?'

'Wise? WISE? Is it wise to pack an ocean going vessel with a hoard of land lubbers who fall apart at the first sign of a swell? Is it wise to allow people stuffed with rich food and strong liquor to enter the oceanic fray in the sure knowledge that they can only be saved from any given catastrophe by our crew's brute force and quick wit? Come on, man. If we are to be guided by wisdom, the act of cruising would have been doomed from the start.' A great wash of brine strikes the bridge windows, 105 feet above the theoretical 'sea level,' causing the windscreen wipers to work overtime. The Captain continues. 'No, Ward, our job is to educate these people in the lore of the sea. By signing up for a world cruise – a WORLDIE Ward – they haven't just got the right to experience heavy seas – they have got an obligation! And, as it happens, dear old King Neptune – the great Monarch of the Seas - happens to be obliging us this very evening on both counts.'

There's a certain logic to Captain Bladder's argument. However, Ward is quite sure a large proportion of guests won't see it that way. But short of a mutiny, there's nothing he can do about it. Besides, by the looks of the charts, they're far too close to the storm system to escape it now. If the waves really are to become phenomenal, they'll have to face them head on for reasons of comfort and safety. It must also be said that cruise ships don't like to fall behind with itineraries. A lost day creates monumental administrative problems, as the entire schedule must be rebalanced to accommodate the slippage. This is also the one thing which riles normally placid guests. Once, a cruise ship was forced to miss a Pacific island due to mechanical problems. The guests put together a petition calling for the resignation of various staff, and a mutiny was only narrowly avoided. Sailing through storms may rock the boat, but in the long run it solves more problems than it causes.

The main force of the cyclone hits at around 1am. The result is virtually instant, due to certain topographical factors on the sea bed. The waves grow from around 5 metres in height to 9 metres within minutes. The Spirit of Dogger V begins to respond to the onslaught by swaying from side to side and pitching lengthways. Papers slide off the tables in the Bridge, and the ship oscillates energetically in the grip of this livid sea.

'I'll take it from, here,' says the Captain, and he commences a manual handling of the great vessel, pointing the bow into the livid boiling ocean. The untimely rolling settles to a more sedate rhythm, the greatest part of the movement transferring to the length of the ship. The Captain alters the speed until, suddenly, the Dogger calms to an almost hypnotic pitching, as if cradled by a giant and caring hand. This is out of keeping with the deep howl of the wind, now reaching 60 knots and gusting to 80.

For hours Bladder says nothing, save to ask two questions: the depth of the ocean beneath, and the air pressure. And all the time he makes small adjustments, in deference to the size and wavelength of the giant swell. It's a dance between a man and nature which few can perform with such aplomb.

The passengers fall into two categories: the sleeping and the petrified. Those asleep are no more vulnerable than those who are not. All depend on the wisdom and experience of the Captain for their safe passage. The only difference is the extent to which they think it. Mr and Mrs Bitters are arguing over turns in the toilet bowl. Monty and his wife are resting peacefully, their many years at sea a valuable lesson in perspective. Jack and Jane sit silently hand in hand, awaiting the end of their days.

'I've always loved you, Jack.'

'And I you.' These are their only words in the sleepless hours of their night.

And Dave and Trev? After making a mountain out of a staircase, they finally find their quarters and collapse exhausted on the mattress, drifting into a deep and dreamless sleep, even as the ship creaks all around them, rolling gently together and apart as Dave squashes the less circular Trev every 60 seconds.

By dawn, there is no abatement in the storm. The wind has sustained its intensity. But the waves have grown. They're as big as anything the crew has ever seen – 14 metres or more. Now, they're officially phenomenal. Spray drenches the bow, washing the windows of the Sailor's Nest bar above the Bridge with salty water. As the light improves, passengers gaze agog at the sea, its peaceful demeanour now replaced with a terrain of raging titans, each wave hitting the vessel with the force of a hillside. The metal judders and the greatest of the waves give the impression of momentarily stalling the Dogger's progress, its momentum apparently matched by the colossal mass of seething water.

Mostly, the ship is deserted now. Passengers stay in their cabins. They're afraid. Each shudder of the hull persuades them of the fragility of their lives and of the fallibility of human inventions. A very few endeavour to attend breakfast. These people end up holding the cutlery and their plates on the table, their tea cups half full to compensate for the incessant pitching of the ship.

At 0900 precisely, Captain Bladder makes an announcement.

'Ladies and Gentlemen, this is your Captain speaking. Well, I hope you all had a pleasant night and a peaceful sleep. As you may have noticed, we've encountered some slightly inclement conditions, and this has caused the vessel to move around a little during the wee small hours. However, I can inform you that we've just passed through the centre of the storm and from now the conditions will ease. Please enjoy your breakfast and, whatever you decide to do today, I trust our entertainments team will keep you well occupied.' The Captain concludes his announcement. Ward looks at him dubiously.

'That was all rather understated, Sir.'

'Ward, the Captain's job is to provide reassurance. They will accept what they're given. And mark my words, they won't complain about anything else we go through.' Ward is sceptical – and to an extent angry – about the Captain's ghoulish decision to ride the storm. It seems to him irresponsible. They'll assess the damage once the seas are calmer. For now, he stares out at sheets of rain combined with spray and reckons they'll have hundreds of complaints once they emerge from this onslaught to mayhem and motion.

Dave and Trev awake at roughly the same time, mainly because Dave's telephone alarm is set to its loudest level. It's 09.30. Trev rubs his eyes.

'What just happened?'

'I dunno, I remember us being in the bar place and then all this movement.'

'Yeah. How cool was that!'

'I don't think I can face breakfast.' Dave is still full from last night. He remembers the conversation. 'Everyone thinks we're puffs.'

'Well don't go on about us sharing a bed all the time, you idiot.' Dave says nothing and Trev has a brainwave. 'Hey Dave mate, fancy a lager?' Dave cracks open a couple of cans and within a few moments the rocking of the sea is a rosy tonic.

'Do you think we're going to die, Jack?' Jack looks at his watch. It's 09.15.

'No, I don't think so, darling. Not now.'

'Can we go to sleep then, please?'

Jack and Jane finally go to bed, still wearing their life jackets. They're too tired to care.

Mr and Mrs Bitters have completely emptied the contents of their stomachs into the toilet. In keeping with their general behaviour, they've also blocked up the loo by the use of enormous amounts of non-proprietary tissues, and now the vomit sits like a pond on top of the papier mache blockage. This only serves to make them more ill. Between bouts of wretching, Mr Bitters lashes out for someone to blame.

'Whoever blocked this toilet will pay for this,' he splutters. 'I'll get them for everything they've got.' Even Mrs Bitters sees the flaw in his argument.

'Then you'll have to sue yourself' she says, and returns to her gut-wrenching activities. She inadvertently vomits over her husband's hand.

'Look what you've done!' he exclaims with the indignation of a man who's never taken responsibility for anything in his life.

'Sue me,' she says and returns to the job in hand.

By mid morning the storm has subsided enough to enable the ship to return to something like normal service. Guests begin to emerge from their cabins with a bemused air. Staff begin to tidy up the rooms vacated by the passengers, finding a rich variety of broken glasses, illness related detritus and toiletries on the floor in room after room.

The First Officer decides to go on a walk about before knocking off for his down time. What he discovers is amazing. People keep stopping him and asking him to convey their thanks to the Captain for his expert handling of 'The Gale', 'Te Hurricane' and 'The Tornado'. The Officer is at a loss to blame Bladder for sailing them into it in the first place and merely announces he'll 'pass it on'.

Up on the Bridge Bladder takes a look at the anemometer to gauge wind strength. It's down from 60 knots to nearer 40.

'You can take it from here' he tells his junior. This boy wouldn't have dreamt of ever having such responsibility in a force 8 gale. But now it doesn't seem such a big deal. 'I'm going to get some rest but if it gets worse again, then wake me immediately.'

'Aye, aye sir.' The Captain stops at the door.

'By the way, what was the lowest pressure?'

'It was... 952 millibars, Sir.' The Captain nods.

'Tell the Met Office. And tell them to warn the others it's going to be worse in Biscay for another day.' He's about to leave when one of the junior staff hails him.

'Captain?'

'Ah, yes?'

'I hope you don't mind me saying so, Sir, but you're a ledge.'

'Pah. I'm nothing of the sort. I merely know my trade. And the word you're looking for is legend.' Bladder leaves with a hint of a smile and a mountain of vindication.

Chapter 6 :
Syndicate Quiz

It's 22.30, ship time, and all is not well in the Billabong Room. This is the location for the Syndicate Quiz, an angst-ridden ritual which involves teams of up to six people, each of them hearing questions and submitting 20 verdicts to the entertainment crew member seated at the apex of the L shaped room.

Nobody enters this quiz for fun. It is, in reality, a final vestige of the ancient tradition of jousting, in which there can be only one winner, with all other contenders left wounded or psychologically scarred at the hands of the victorious party. The quiz master is in full flow, but about to pose a question which will lead to violence.

'Greenland is the biggest island in the world. But what was the biggest island in the world BEFORE Greenland was discovered?'

The muttering suggests a great outpouring of geography on every table. Eyes dart suspiciously from one table to another, in the hope of a lip-read slip or a raised whisper to the elimination of possibilities.

Tensions rise as the captain of one team ostentatiously submits his kabal's answer on a piece of paper speedily, to the suspicion of all the other groups. Presently, the Quiz-mistress counts down to close the question.

'Three...two...one...' and representatives from all 32 teams scurry forward to submit their guesses. 'And the question is...' table 13 makes a last moment submission, 'thank you, the question is now closed. So, Greenland is the biggest island in the world, but what was the biggest island in the world before Greenland was discovered? Well, we have a lot of different answers. Australia – that's a continent, by the way - Madagascar, Iceland, Ireland – really? – Japan, Great Britain – very loyal there – Spain - an unusual choice considering it's not even an island, but there you go - and Baffin. Only one team got it right – the biggest island in the world before Greenland was discovered was, of course – and you'll kick yourselves - Greenland.'

Team 24 cheers as howls of protest erupt across the room. The quiz-mistress watches the commotion smugly. 'You needed to listen to the question, ladies and gentlemen. Greenland was still there, even before it was discovered.' Accusations of 'cheat' and 'fix' fill the air. As the symphony of abuse reaches a crescendo, Mr Bitters marches up to the quiz-mistress. The room quietens.

'I came on this cruise to get away from all the suffering I have and enjoy myself,' she states with a surly grimace. 'I did NOT come here to be made a fool of by people like you or to expand my mind.' There is a smattering of applause, some of which is clearly ironic, and then the room cools back into curious silence. 'Either you replace that ridiculous question with a proper one or I will have no option other than to report you.' The quiz-mistress assesses Mr Bitter carefully, and immediately recognises all the hallmarks of a complainer. She scans the room. Those present are evidently attentive for two reasons: curiosity at the gall of a woman who has failed to grasp the absolute power of the quiz-mistress. And secondly, anticipation that this little vignette is worth watching in the same way one may slow to observe a road traffic accident on a motorway.

'Sir, the fact that one team in fact got it right suggests to me that the question was a fair one.' Table 25 cheer theatrically, their mirth quickly dampened by Mr Bitters' continuing and obstinate presence at the front of the room. Nothing is said for an awkwardly long moment, causing the atmosphere to alchemically mutate from golden jocularity to leaden tautness. 'Sir, can I suggest that we just leave it this time – after all if you look at your team's current number of points, you'll see you're not going to win or lose based on the points for this question.' Mr Bitters breathes in.

'Officer, it's a matter of principle. I will not allow this quiz to proceed unless you retract the question.' At this Jerry from Table 25 – the one team to have correctly answered – erupts with rage. He marches up to Bitters and stands within inches of his face.

'Listen buddy, I used to work in Greenland, and I think I've got the right to suggest you're being a bloody prat. Now, are you going to sit down and let the lady move on to question 18 or am I going to have to make you?' Mr Bitters breathes in deliberately.

'And how do you think you would do that?'

'Like this.' Jerry punches Mr Bitters in the face so hard he collapses to the floor, as the room gasps in surprise. Mrs Bitters rushes to her husband's side as the staff call for assistance. Suddenly, Jerry is the villain. He stands there, awaiting arrest as Mr Bitters smiles weakly at his wife and mutters:

'This should pay for the cruise.'

The quiz resumes without further incident. Table 25 are joint first with table 13, but lose on the tie-breaker question: 'who was America's tallest President?'

Chapter 7 :
Lunch

Lunch on a ship is an opportunity to meet other people. In the buffet one serves oneself and chooses where to sit. It's informal - and somewhat random. Downstairs, the seating is posher but also somewhat informal in regard to the seating plan. As people turn up to dine in the Medusa Restauruant's exquisitely elegant environs, they are allocated to spaces available in a very orderly – but chronologically logical - way. So, for example, if two couples and a group of four walk in at once, they will likely be invited to share a table for eight – thereby maximising the efficiency of space usage, and marginally reducing the workload for the staff. This also generates a notable side effect: lunch is a socially unpredictable occasion where the passengers are brought together by the wizard of timing rather than the rigour of compatibility.

So it is that newlyweds Douglas and Susan enter the Medusa restaurant with wide eyed excitement, unaware that the fickle finger of fortune alone will point them to. The waiters are experts at directing arrivals to places. They form a line of human signposts 30 feet apart, ushering the diners towards vacant spaces in ones, twos, threes or fours.

The room is already humming with the conversations of 200 guests, as Douglas and Susan wend their way to table 105 to join six others already placed at a table for eight. They smile at the others and sit down. Those already seated absently acknowledge their arrival, recognising their presence with the weakest of nods. Susan and Douglas take their places for what will turn out to be a rather strange and self-effacing comparison of cultures. At this stage, the talk is about what they know of the toilet blockage drama on deck 11. It is also an unstated object lesson in the reality of a culture in which the language of common choice is English, regardless of the difficulties this causes those not fortunate enough to hail from Blighty.

'I heard from someone in the launderette that a passenger has tried to flush away something unspeakable,' sighs the Dutchman.

'What was it?' enquires the German. The Dutchman, hesitates, and considers revealing the unspeakable thing... before leaning back in his chare, shaking his head somberly.

'I cannot speak about it. It is unspeakable.' This is how rumours start on ships.

'We had an experience of a most surprising kind,' nods the German in response. 'It was in the Pacific, two years ago. I can hardly even go into it.' The German is re-living a traumatic event, as he lowers his eyes, commemorating some terrible disaster. His wife clasps his arm considerately and adds, 'I remember it well.' The table sits quietly, sharing the couple's apparent sorrow in ignorance of the facts.

This is the beginning of a familiar behaviour on ships: recounting the dramatic, heart-stopping incidents which, perhaps for reasons of confinement, seem multiplied in their seriousness when on the high seas. Few people would recall a blocked toilet in a house many years after the event. You just call a plumber. But on a ship, it's different. The stories become magnified over time, until it sounds as if the performance of the very engines themselves were in some way dependent upon the unblocking of toilets, or some such task. There is also a certain amount of one-upmanship with these tales of woe, as each seasoned traveller seeks to embellish the conversation with their own private moment of seaborne 'truth.'

All eyes are still on the German, who continues to shake his head in melancholy and shocked nostalgia...

When it become as apparent that the German is not going to reveal more of his ordeal, the Spanish lady speaks out.

'I remember, back about 10 years ago, we were in the Mediterranean. The weather was like one of those sudden storms, you see? It was calm than then - woof! – everything was flying about. A grand piano went out of the window, all the way. I am not kidding.' She looks at her new found fellow diners others for confirmation and, in keeping with the etiquette, people nod dubiously. 'Yes, and everything was flying about. It was such a frightening thing. I thought we were having the end of our days.'

The German nods sympathetically. 'Yes, I have had a worse experience, even than that. There was a hole in the bottom of the ship and we were sinking.'

'Heavens above! How on earth did that happen?' inquires Douglas aghast. 'Did you hit something?'

'No, it was just a hole, it happened, in a surprising way. It was surprising. But we lived to tell the tale.'

There is a second silence, but again the German is in a quiet place in the past.

The Dutchman pipes up. 'On a ship we travelled on, everyone had food poisoning. It was a terrible virus. Many were very ill.' This isn't quite enough to elicit a response. 'Even the Captain was ill... ' he adds uncertainly. The others on the table look at each other doubtfully. It's too much and the Dutchman knows it, '...but he got better. The Captain got better. Very fast.'

There's a pause, the Dutchman having evidently over-played his hand. This stalls the game. Inevitably, attention turns to the only couple unable to share stories of horror from a previous cruise – the newly-weds. The Spanish lady initiates a new focus upon them.

'It appears we are next to a couple having a lot of fun, says the Spanish lady saucily. I do believe you call it by the name of 'hanky panky.' The entire table laughs, apart from Douglas and Susan, who are too embarrassed to respond. Their bashfulness is taken as an admission of responsibility. 'Of course, there is nothing wrong with this. It is, natural for a lady and a ladyman of your ages.'

The next comment - from the Dutchman - is intended to be conciliatory. 'And I am a man of Holland – well actually of the Netherlands, to be exact. We are liberal minded. You do as you please, Sir. We are happy for you and your beautiful lady in your conceptual activities.'

'Er, thankyou,' mutters Douglas, in an effort not to sound awkward. He sounds very awkward indeed.

'We in Germany have every respect of young love. It is what makes the world go round and is MAKING the world go round, yours and mine. My wife and I, we have had some times. Some very good times indeed.' He looks at his wife, who averts her gaze in a coy fashion, glances at Susan and winks. Her husband leans forward to Douglas, conspiratorially. 'But one warning. On board, NEVER put condoms into the toilet basins.' This causes everyone else on the table to suddenly breathe in with shock and nod their agreement emphatically. Douglas looks back and mouths something which doesn't come out loudly, but sounds like 'I see.'

The Dutchman notices the embarrassment of Douglas, and abruptly changes the subject. 'What do we all think about the global warming situation? We ourselves, coming from Holland, are a bit worried about it. We already live below sea level. I always fear we will go home to a waterworld.'

'That would be terrible,' says the Spaniard. 'I will feel sad if that occurs – even to Hollanders.'

The Dutchman smiles. 'Do not be sad for. If it happens in that way, the ships in future will come to our door. That saves us cash from trains and taxis.'

The German looks amused. 'I hold myself responsible, for always having driven a large petrol engine car. But you will be glad to know I now drive an electric vehicle. And if you were to ask me if I like it that way, I would have to raise my eyes to the sky like this... and say that 'we do our duty.'

How fast does it go,' asks Douglas.

'The electric vehicle will achieve 280 kilometres per hour – where permitted. Which is nowhere, these days.' The rest of the table nods sympathetically, in line with the continuing etiquette in such situations. In the ensuing moment of calm, the Spaniard takes the initiative to change the subject, again, and rather catches Douglas off guard.

'Senor, I have a question about the language of English. I am wondering if you could please explain the meaning of the phrase 'bum's rush?"

Douglas looks around, to realise the entire table is staring at him. He's got no idea what the Spaniard is asking him.

'I'm afraid I'm not sure what, er, you... mean.' Everyone continues to look at Douglas. 'Could you put it another way?'

'Not really, Senor. After it is the bum's rush phrase which I am seeking to understand. Is it to do with fast bottom sex of a sort?'

Silence returns. Douglas himself has heard this phrase but has never really understood it himself. Yet, with some sense of loyalty to what he fears could be a core British term of reference, he feels obliged not to admit his ignorance.

'I think it might be that. Yes.' He looks at his bride, who shrugs and widens her eyes.'

The Spaniard ponders the response. 'And is this something which would be done by you on your honeymoon?'

Everyone is looking at Douglas.

'Er, sometimes.'

The Spaniard continues, apparently with no sense of awkwardness. 'And will you at some point in this cruise, be taking your new wife and giving her the bum's rush?'

Douglas looks at Susan, who is shaking her head. Susan speaks again.

'I have always been very keen on the work of Margaret Thatcher when she was the British Prime Minister.' The other six look at each other, stand up and leave. Susan looks at the departing crowd. 'What was that all about?'

Chapter 8 :
Outbreak

By afternoon, the mighty Vessel has all but escaped the heavy seas. She sways reflectively in a moderate swell, and steams ahead with majestic purpose, towards an island destination – The Canaries. Captain Bladder is once again a little restless. Plain sailing has never been his thing. But there aren't any storms for 500 miles and he stoically accepts his steady fate, grateful for at least having had the pleasure of the boat that rocked only hours ago.

There's been an entirely unexpected – and ironic - outcome from yesterday's storm: passengers are overwhelmingly grateful to the Captain for sailing them safely through the raging firmament, unaware that they were only in it because of Bladder's obsession with high numbers on the Beaufort Scale and his passion for the formidable turmoil of phenomenal waves. Nevertheless, today he is the man of the moment and no guest has a bad word to say about him.

This is not the case in the Galley. The Deputy Restaurant Manager - a Frenchman known formally as Monsieur Ricard Tumé – is morose about all the broken crockery bequeathed by the monster storm. He's also fretting about bacteria.

Somewhat unfairly, Ricard's health and safety record aren't purported to be good. He was once held responsible for a ship-wide outbreak of E. Coli – occasionally referred to by medically unqualified travellers as 'the squits' - after he purchased a large consignment of what an Englishman in a tatty white van on a Tilbury quayside enthusiastically referred as to 'top class unpasteurised French cheese with all the milk in it and everyfink.' Ricard ought to have been suspicious: after all, it cost him a dangerously small sum of money, and the receipt was almost illegible, apparently referring to the goods as 'top class various cheases from Franc.' Furthermore, few Englishmen Ricard had met had struck him as capable of discerning the difference between exceptional French dairy products and out-of-date milk. His procuring moment of madness was thus fuelled primarily out of curiosity, and he knew he was breaking many regulations. But he also prided himself on giving his passengers that little bit extra. Unfortunately, on that particular occasion, the 'little bit extra' had turned out to be explosive diarrhoea on an industrial scale.

After the on-board malaise, the vessel's whispering machine pinned all the blame on Tumé, which was a little bit excessive, given that he had purchased the dodgy dairy delivery in good faith. All the same, his dalliance with White Van Man and his mouldy cheese earned M. Ricard Tumé the nick name 'Dickie Tumé - a label he loathes but has been unable to shake off across the years.

The upside of that little misfortune is Ricard's hawk-like observance of procedure. He can sense tummy trouble from 40 paces and is on extra special alert this evening. He's heard verbal reports from bar staff of a potential case of the stomach churning, dreaded Norovirus on Deck 8. Apparently, a gentleman was seen to convulse violently up in the Sailor's Nest cocktail bar this morning. It's most likely to be alcohol related, or sea-sickness, but he can't risk an outbreak and has decided to play it safe by keeping a close eye on the gentleman in question – whom he has cautiously elected to reposition on a single table away from the centre of the restaurant for tonight's dinner. He also decides to greet all the guests himself this evening, in order to evaluate each of the arriving diners, his true intentions concealed by a beaming smile and a Parisian lilt.

As 18.30 arrives, the 'First Sitting' guests shuffle in. It's a casual dress code this evening, and it never ceases to amaze Ricard how wide the latitude of interpretation appears to be. His clientele have concluded that 'casual' is everything from black tie to what he would consider barely acceptable in a bedroom. He is a trifle unprepared for the couple who come in wearing shell suits. Naturally, it's Mr and Mrs Bitters. He is uncertain whether to challenge them or not. He steps forward.

'Bonsoir Monsieur, bonsoir Madame. Can I help you?'

'No.'

There's nowhere to go with the conversation, but he tries anyway.

'M'excuse, are you planning to dine avec nous ce soir?'

'If you're trying to ask if we're here to eat, the answer's yes.'

'Um, m'escuse, but are you perhaps aware of our dress codes, non?'

'No.'

The Deputy Restaurant Manager tries to tackle the issue gently.

'It would be conventional to wear, well, how you say, the daytime clothings, when dining in Le Restaurant.' This does not please Mr Bitters.

'We paid good money to be in this restaurant. We can wear what we want.'

The Deputy Restaurant Manager backs off.

'Ah, of course not. Bon appetite.' This is the sort of thing which drives Ricard wild with rage inside, but he's duty bound to maintain a courteous air. Despite the temptation to mete silent revenge in the kitchen, Ricard has long enforced a culture of respect towards even the most irksome passengers.

'What's up Ricard?' asks his boss – Al Garr - an enthusiastic and practical man of many years experience in the trade.

'Regardez! Look at those two - no ordinary restaurateur en Paris would put up avec your English habit of shell suits like that. Pah! It is not clothes, it is an insult to our profession. Just because they're on a ship they think they can, how you say, do what le bloody hell they like, as you say in England.'

'That's because they – well, they can, Rick. Try throwing out a couple of guests for wearing shell suits at dinner and see how far you get with head office when the papers accuse A&G of being clothes facists.' Before the conversation proceeds further, the boss nudges his Deputy. 'Aye, aye, he's the one. You know, the honker from Sailor's Nest.' They watch as the man in his late 50s staggers down the steps and towards a table somewhere near the centre of the room. 'Does he look ill to you?'

'Je ne sais pas – but the last thing we need is an outbreak on the third day of a World Cruise.' Al and Ricard gaze on silently as the man sways towards his table, as if reliving last night's storm with every uncertain step. Ricard nods at one of the waiters who swings into action and whisks the drunken diner 90 degrees to the left and off to a table on his own in the port side far corner. Almost as if unaware of his altered table, the man collapse into the seat like an unsupported balloon filled with mud, and seems to partially dissolve into a heap of confusion, apparently summoning all his effort to hold a menu somewhere near his face.

Across the room, Table 64 is already inhabited by Monty and Mrs Major, Mr and Mrs Bitters, Trev and Dave and the O'Neill duo. Monty is explaining the rationale behind a 'military pincer movement,' using knives and forks to represent the advancing troops, and the salt and pepper to represent a platoon of beleaguered Germans. A young man and woman gingerly approach the table. The conversation stops.

'Excuse me, is this Table 64?' asks the well dressed young man.

'Roger that!' chirps Monty on behalf of the table. 'Can we help you?'

'Ah, I think we're supposed to be eating here,' says the girl. Monty shakes his head.

'I very much doubt it Miss – this table, indeed the whole restaurant, is only for passengers, not crew.' There is a confused moment of silence, as the two newly weds glance at each other uncertainly.

'But we were directed here,' protests the lady very gingerly. Monty sniggers knowingly, and responds swiftly and firmly.

'I very much doubt it at YOUR age, Miss,' he explains. There's an awkward moment as the man checks a small card.

'Yes, this is definitely our table.' He hands the card to Monty, who inspects it as a jeweller might inspect the diamond in a suspected forgery.

'Good heavens! It DOES seem to suggest you're being allowed to join us. How peculiar. This must be a change in policy. Not sure I like it but this is not the time to challenge it.' Monty stands up, and offers his hand in formal greeting. 'In that case welcome.' Once the two have settled into their seats, Monty progresses to introductions. 'I'm Monty and this is Mrs Major. Those two are the Bitters, and next to them are Mr and Mrs P. O'Neill. And the chaps next to you are Trev and Dave – and this is their first cruise together.' The young lady speaks again.

'I'm Susan and this is Douglas and this is our first cruise too. And we've just got married!' Monty is stunned.

'Heavens above! You're PASSENGERS! You can't be a day over 20!'

Mrs Bitters pipes up, her shell suit rustling as she shifts in her seat.

'So when's it due then?'

'Pardon?'

'When's it due? I mean you got married, didn't you?' The girl scours Mrs Bitters' face for any hint of irony, and finds none.

'I'm not pregnant. We're in love.' There's an awkward silence. Mr Bitters starts shaking her head unsympathetically.

'I'm sure the tax benefits of marriage haven't escaped you.' M rs P. O'Neill speaks next.

'Oh how wonderful, two young couples on the same table. How rare!' Dave interjects.

'We're NOT a couple – we're only sharing a bed, that's all,' causing everyone to look across at the likely lads with a mixture of disapproval and smirking, prompting Trev to whisper something angrily to Dave. Mrs Major leans towards the newlyweds.

'That explains why you missed dinner last night then. Oh the passion of young love!' Douglas considers explaining that the actual reason they missed dinner last night was because they were scared. They've never seen so many elderly people in one place before, and they found the whole experience briefly overwhelming. 'How far are you going... so to speak!'

'To Havana,' says Douglas. 'So a couple of weeks. We're doing something else after that.'

'I BET YOU ARE!' gaffaws Monty so loudly that other tables cast stares in is general direction. 'Oh yes, indeed!'

'We didn't really know what to expect to be honest,' says the girl. 'I must say it's a lot grander than we expected.'

'Grand?' challenges Mr Bitters. Pesonally, I think it's all rather disappointing. Look at the décor. And these knives are a boring.' Everyone looks at Mr Bitters' as she waves knife around like, and tries to consider how a knife might be considered boring. It is not an easy concept to grasp. Bitters absent-mindedly points the knife towards the windows. 'And we didn't even have a sea view until we left Southampton.'

By pudding the dining room has settled into its traditional conversational hum, with intense discussions about food punctuated by overly loud laughter as people chuckle irresistibly at their own jokes in order to force the rest of their company to follow suite. Teas and coffees compete for space between the wine glasses and presently the tableware is cleared in an effort to encourage the revellers to move out and onto the various entertainments, which will occur in the many venues throughout the Dogger V. And then it happens. The man sitting in the far corner stands up, throws up in a spectacular and projectile fashion, covering the hapless victims on the neighbouring table with vomit, before collapsing with such force that he destroys a dessert trolley in the fall. A collective gasp is followed by silence. Al Garr looks at Ricard for a second opinion regarding action, but the Frenchman has apparently already darted towards the supine torso. Al turns to the staff closest to the door.

'OK, seal the room.' He's taking no chances. If this is an outbreak it's going to be contained here in the Medusa Restaurant. The staff close and lock the doors around the hall. 'Tell the Bridge. I'm going to find out what's going on here.' As the staff seek to settle those shocked by events, Al scurries around the tables to Ground Zero, where RIcard is cursing in French at the corpulent torso of the man, covered in cake and spew. The man appears to be breathing, but he stinks of booze – and most of what he's thrown up appears to smell of Pernod. 'That's a relief, a false alarm,' he mutters to himself. A passenger leans forward.

'Is he alright?'

'I think so, ma'am,' says Al reassuringly. 'I think his condition may have rather more to do with what he drank than what he ate.' Al looks for help from the other staff – who have taken defensive positions at each of the doors. He signals for assistance, and two male waiters march across to help with the messy and odorous task of removing the comatose individual from the restaurant. Al stands up. 'It's alright everybody, he's just had a bit of a turn, that's all.'

'Is he dead?' asks the same woman.

Al leans down reassuringly to the body at his feet and smiles, 'I'm sure he's not going to die tonight.' With that they haul up the spew covered gentleman and carry him out the main exit towards the medical centre, as Ricard applies himself to clearing up the mess as undramatically as possible.

'Did you hear that!' exclaims the lady on the table next to where the drama has occurred.

'What did the chef say?'

'He was sure the man's going to die tonight!' Shocked concern ripples out from the scene of the crime. A gentleman grimaces a few tables away.

'Well, it seems the Manager is sure we're going to die tonight.'

'It must be that deadly virus. The food one. Oh, how terrible. And LOOK! They've locked us in. They've left us to perish like animals in a prisons of our own bacteria.' Anger rises in the room. Others are speaking in angst ridden terms. Some improvise masks using napkins. Others shout at waiters, demanding to be allowed out. A few have taken out their mobile telephones and are calling home:

'Darling, it's mama. Apparently, we're all going to die. A deadly food virus has already killed one person in just seconds. Yes I saw it all - right here in the dining room. Please tell the others what's happened. I love you. Goodbye.'

Down in the sick room, the drunk man fails to show signs of consciousness. The doctor looks up at Al, who's hurried into the sick room with barely disguised panic.

'Is he dead, Doc?'

'Dead? He's absolutely crapulous, Al.' Al awaits further clarification from the Doc, who stares back silently, apparently satisfied that 'crapulous' is all the explanation that's required.

'Crapulous?'

'Crapulous Al. Totally and utterly crapulous. In fact, more crapulous than any case I've seen in years.' The Doc shakes his head disdainfully as he looks at the wreck of humanity on the bed.

'Does that mean he's dead? Or is it food poisoning? Or are you just using a poncy word to say he's crapped himself?'

'I didn't know,' said Al.

'I didn't either, until I overheard it when I happened to be passing the Syndicate Quiz. It was one of the questions.'

'I didn't know you listened in on the quizzes.'

'I don't normally, but I was getting so many people coming down here for sea sick pills last night I did a quick round to hand them out to anyone who needed them.'

'Shouldn't you let them come here for them?'

'Usually, yes. But the storm was such a monster that if I'd let them all come down here, I'd have been up to my neck in spew. So, Mohammed went to the mountain, so to speak.'

'How sick were they?'

'Put it this way, Al, if I had a pound for every passenger who looked likely to throw up I'd have, oooh, probably about 50 pounds.' Al thinks about that.

'That's not very much.' The Doctor nods in agreement.

'Mmm, saying it out loud like that, you're right, it doesn't. I'm not really very creative like that, really.' The Doc returns to his casual examination of the patient. 'Anyway, this one here, whatever else is wrong with him, at the moment this fellow is just plain plastered. He'll be alright in a while, but I'd better keep him here for a bit to make sure he doesn't choke on his own stupidity or anything. He does smell strongly of Pernod - it makes me fancy one myself.'

'You're disgusting Doc.' The Doctor bows his head as if receiving a compliment.

Upstairs in the Medusa Restaurant, the guests are revolting. Al returns to be stopped outside the door. He can see through the stain glass that they are beginning to congregate at the exits, and it's clear that imminently the anger and panic will spill over into direct action and a forcible escape from the room which they have come to see as their lethally infected coffin.

'I wouldn't go in there Sir,' says the waiter on the outside. 'They have become like mad people – I fear they are going to do a bad turn.' Al, unaware of the prolific work of the rumour mill, can't understand the reaction to a simple case of a man who drank himself into a stupor. He demands to be let in. His arrival causes a brief lull in the riot.

'Ladies and gentlemen, please calm down. There is absolutely no cause for alarm. Everything is under control.' This seems to settle people. 'I have informed the captain we are having an incident.' This is the absolutely wrong thing to say, as people exclaim the last work to each other, apparently confirming their morbid fears. The guests seem to be forming into vigilante groups ready to break out of the room. He appeals for calm again, but this time to no avail, so he picks up two metal trays and bangs them together. Unfortunately, this is taken as a signal to advance by some of the gentlemen who immediately begin an assault on the main door with an improvised battering ram comprised of a table leg wrapped in a table cloth. With a few hard bangs, the door gives way and flies open, causing a stampede which almost empties the room in moments. In the ensuing calm Al takes stock of the group madness he has just seen and tries to plan his report to the Captain in his head. Ricard is standing aghast in the doorway having observed the escalating panic from the first moments. The two officers look at each other with angst.

'Excuse me,' says a shaky female voice from behind Al. He turns to see an elderly couple at a table for two. 'Would it be possible to have a word?'

'What about?'

'Well, we both thought the steak a little tough. It is so disappointing when everything else about the meal was so nice.' Then she turns to her husband and adds 'let's skip the theatre tonight – we can't compete with those young ones who just left!' Her husband nods. 'Though judging by their enthusiasm to get there this evening it's going to be quite a show!'

Chapter 9 :
A matter of life and death

'Tell me all that again,' says the Captain to Al Carr, the Restaurant Manager.

'Well, it really is as simple as that, Sir. It boils down to this. The drunken man threw up and collapsed, we took him to the sick bay, and when I got back the other guests battered the door in and stampeded back to their rooms. Apparently, they thought the boozer had copped it, thanks to some kind of super virus.'

The Captain is shaking his head.

'Is this anything to do with your Deputy – the mouldy cheese chap – Dickie Tummy?'

'Ah, no Captain. Nothing to do with him at all. But the guests really do think this fellow died in the restaurant.'

'How on earth can they have thought that? I mean, it's ridiculous. You know this story is making headlines around the world now?' Al says nothing. 'Do you know what they're calling us? The 'Plague Ship of Death.' And 'HMS Bacteria.' And 'Sailing into the DEADiterranean.' And this one hurts the most: 'Bladder's final voyage goes viral.' This is not how I intended to end my career – sailing a ship with the reputation of a floating leper colony.' He turns to Al. 'How could you let this happen?'

Al is at a loss to calm the anger of his superior. He looks at the others on the bridge, all of whom pretend to be focussed on their duties but every one of whom is listening in with varying degrees of amusement.

'What does the Doc think?'

'Well, he doesn't' think the man is dead either sir.'

'How has the Doc assessed the man's condition?'

'Crapulous.'

'What?'

'Crapulous. That's the word he used. Apparently it means steaming drunk sir.' One of the other Bridge officers bursts out laughing, immediately apologising to the Captain who sees nothing amusing about the situation.

'Sort it out Garr.'

'I'll get onto it now, Sir... I'll,er, make an announcement and then go and talk to the guests personally.' The Captain stares at the Restaurant Manager, and, after a long silence, expels something halfway between a sigh and a grunt. Garr shuffles out awkwardly, as the Bridge officers studiously stare down at their various duties, doing their utmost not to reveal their mirth at the situation. The Captain writes a short note requiring a check on the state of the French cheese, signing it 'A.B,C.' – short for 'Alfred Bladder, Captain.'

There is no respite for Garr, who is beginning to become slightly irritated that one man's alcoholic excesses appear to have caused Garr to feel like the victim of a manslaughter charge. As he arrives on the Promenade Deck, he can tell that the atmosphere is charged with rumours. As soon as Garr is spotted, he's surrounded by dozens of guests.

'We demand a vaccine for the virus.' Al shakes his head but makes no progress.

'Why did you let that man die?'

'He's not dead.'

'Yes he is,' shouts a man at the back.' There's general agreement from the others.

'Sir, he is NOT dead.'

'Yes he is – you said he was dead last night – I heard you.' More agreement from the group. 'And you said we're all going to die too.'

'He's NOT dead.'

'Where is he then?'

'He's resting... down below.'

'Liar.' The group takes on the character of an angry mob as one lady claims to have seen the man's dead body being tipped over the side into the ocean. Al tries to calm the group.

'Ladies and gentlemen, what evidence do ANY of you have that this man is dead?' An elderly lady steps forward.

'Sir, I heard it in the launderette. From Violet Cryer.' There is silence. Al's blood goes cold. He has been on ships long enough to know that laundry gossip is roughly the equivalent of hearing the 'news' on the BBC. Furthermore, he's come across Violet Cryer before. She is a cruise ship veteran of 30 years standing – and the unchallenged Queen of the Launderette gossip machine. Faced with the truth versus gossip from Violet Cryer, most truth hasn't got a chance. He has only one option now.

'Ladies and gentlemen, I'll get the Captain.' He leaves the ashen faced group and returns to the Bridge, knowing the only solution will be an audience in the theatre with Bladder himself.

As the minutes go by, ship gossip grows to new levels of angst ridden worry. The key topic of conversation amongst the unsettled majority is the grizzly death of the man in the restaurant. By now, he didn't just fall over. It was far worse than that. Dave and Trev are sitting up in the Tea Tree cafeteria on Deck 12. It's strangely quiet.

'Where is everybody,' asks Dave, poking absentmindedly at his bacon and eggs.

'Dunno, maybe they all had a heavy night.' A lady stops and looks down at Dave's breakfast. 'Why are you looking at my breakfast like that?'

'You're brave.'

'Why?'

'Well, with the death bug and everything. Most people would rather take their chances with starvation.'

'What death bug?'

'Haven't you heard? Last night. A man in the Medusa Restaurant ate something and within seconds his stomach exploded and he died. Apparently, we're all going to get it now – it's just a matter of time. That's why we're still at sea – no country will let us dock because it could cause a global epidemic.' Dave and Trev look at each other with surprise. Trev tests the logic.

'So where did this virus come from, then?' The lady leans down conspiratorially.

'Apparently, it came down from Space. My neighbour used to be in the army and he says he knows the military have known about this virus for years. They've kept it quiet till now. But it's happened before you know. That's what the Bermuda Triangle is all about. It's all very hush, hush. There's no cure.' Trev looks at Dave with shock.

'Dave, how do you feel, mate?'

'Er, a bit peaky, mate, I suppose, but I thought that was just all that lager and that.'

The lady interrupts.

'That's the first sign. You poor boys – you're so young.' She puts her hand sadly on their shoulders. 'So young. At least you'll be together, when the end comes.' She shuffles off to join what she expects will be her last game of bridge. Trev looks at Dave, who shouts after her 'we're not gay!' Trev is pondering the sobering information they've just received.

'Na, I can't buy it. That's just bollocks. Death virus my arse.' Dave looks uncertainly at his bacon and eggs.

'Fancy a pint, just in case?' Trev and Dave abandon the cafeteria in favour of a last drink instead. They've also got their appointment in the health spa with Dorothy and her friends, and even if it's all true, they don't want to die before they've given dishy Dot a go.

It's noon now. To the second the ship's bell is rung – only this time, instead of making the customary announcement on the tannoy, Bladder has resentfully left the comfort of the Bridge for the overfilled and tense surroundings of the Red Curtain Theatre. It's packed to the rafters – three quarters of all the 1,850 guests have squeezed themselves into the seats, aisles and steps of the hall. The Captain looks out from behind the curtains. This is his worst nightmare. 1,400 misinformed and riled passengers, all waiting for his statement. Violet Cryer is sitting right there in the centre of the front row with her arms crossed.

'What do they expect me to say?' he mutters partly to Al, but mainly to himself. 'What CAN I give them? The last rites? It's going to take a miracle to fix this.' He rolls his eyes up at the loaded circle and around at every corner of the theatre, swallows hard, and steps out.

The theatre goes silent. The captain clears his throat. 'Ladies and Gentlemen, it has been brought to my attention that various stories have been circulated relating to an incident in the Medusa Restaurant last night.' Violet Cryer shouts out.

'We all know he's dead!' Others mutter in agreement.

'Ladies and gentlemen – if you will allow me –'

'We're all going to die too!' adds Cryer. More agreement. The Captain knows he has only seconds before he loses control, and even now the murmurs grow into chatter which risks drowning him out.

'LADIES AND GENTLEMEN – if you will allow me, let me put things right.' With this he signals to the staff on the left side of the stage. They wheel a trolley with a body upon it; the drunk man is still too ill to walk onto the stage. The trolley is parked in front of the captain. There is a hushed silence in the theatre now. The Captain clears his throat, which inadvertently sounds almost theatrical, as a magician might attempt to increase the sense of drama.

'Mr Morgan – will you sit up.' Mr Morgan doesn't stir. The Captain shakes Mr Morgan with his hands. There is a tense moment as nothing. 'Mr Morgan, I'm asking you to sit up - to show them you are NOT dead.' Slowly Mr Morgan stirs, and sits slowly up shakily on his arms. A huge collective intake of breathe can be heard in the theatre, with various expressions of amazement from all sides. The Captain continues. 'Are you dead or alive, Mr Morgan?' Mr Morgan is still groggy from two days of drinking. He runs his hand across his face.

'Er, I'm alive.' The Captain turns smugly to the audience.

'Yes, they thought you were dead but by some miracle you are indeed alive.'

A man stands up in the audience and points at the stage.

'It's a miracle! The Captain has brought him back to life!' There is applause the like of which has never before been heard in the theatre. It escalates into a standing ovation. Bemused, the Captain looks at Al off stage, who can only shrug his shoulders in bemusement. The Captain's measured words of explanation are drowned out by the rapturous adulation in the room. People are nodding and, wide eyed, comparing with each other the remarkable restoration of life which they just saw, right there before them. The Captain's pleas for calm are washed away by the awestruck passengers.

Only Violet Cryer remains stubbornly in her seat, temporarily at a loss to regain the initiative from the Captain.

'So you see, you will live,' Bladder shouts over the applause. 'You will all live, just like Mr Morgan. Now, please relax and let's hear no more nonsense about all this. Have a good afternoon ladies and gentlemen.' As he walks off, the tumult cheer and shout, as two crew wheel a very confused and uncomprehending Mr Morgan off stage.

As people stream out, their mood is a combination of relief and awe. Many agree that today they observed some kind of spiritual phenomenon, the like of which hasn't been reported since the writing of the New Testament. Behind stage, the Captain wipes his brow with a handkerchief.

'Well, that went well, I think,' he says to Al, who tries to find an appropriate reply.

'Yes, Sir. It did. I think they believe you... er... brought Mr Morgan back to life.'

'Nonsense. I explained everything.'

'I don't think they heard that bit, Sir. I think they believe you performed some kind of miracle.'

'Oh come off it. Nobody's that stupid. Go and check the Medusa Restaurant is all fixed up for lunch.' And with that the Captain marches out for the comfort and safety of the Bridge.

Trev and Dave have arrived at the health spa.

'Hello Dorothy.' She looks up and momentarily stares at the two lads blankly. Then she looks back down at the list.

'Oh, of course. You are Trev and, um Dave, yes?'

'Yes we are Miss, and we're here for our treatments with you.'

'Well, that is fine and you are on time too.' Dorothy chats, mainly with Trev, as Dave makes idle small talk with one of her comrades. 'Alright, we are ready now, please come with me.' She leads them to a couple of rooms at the back, provides them with white robes and invites them to undress and get into the robes. As she leaves, Trev bangs the wall.

'Wey hey hey! We're in here mate. And remember I saw her first!'

'Good call, Trev mate,' shouts Dave through the wall. Moments later, Dorothy returns to Trev's room. Only that it's not Dorothy. It's Yuri the Russian massage expert dedicated to straightening out back muscles, regardless of the short term pain for that long term gain. Next door, Dave has just met Andrei, Yuri's cousin from Kazakhstan.

This is the moment both lads regret being completely naked, and also purchasing 90 minutes of treatment. Dave yells out in pain first, and the next 88 minutes continue in the same vein.

As they emerge from the treatment rooms they stare at each other in numbed silence. They walk past Dorothy, who says;

'See you soon again I hope boys.'

'Yes, er, we'll be back.'

Trev and Dave shuffle back to the poolside bar on Deck 12. They hold their pints of lager and consider their experience.

'What was all that about, Dave mate?' Dave has another sip of lager.

'I'd say that was an error of judgement, Trev, mate.'

'Having said that, we've broken the ice.'

'And our backs. Though, saying that, I do feel pretty straightened out. Just wish I hadn't been naked.'

It's lunch time. Al is back in the Medusa Restaurant. He is repeatedly stopped by guests asking if they could meet the Captain. A group of individuals with various mobility issues surrounds him, each pleading for a few moments with Bladder. Al is evasive.

'I'm afraid the Captain needs to attend to certain navigational duties madam. Can I pass on a message for you?'

'Yes, could you ask him if he can cure my angina? It holds me back something terrible. And Geoffrey here, he's my husband you see, well he hasn't been able to use his left hand properly for years.' The requests begin to merge into a muted wail of pleas for redemption from their physical ailments.

Such is the peculiar world of cruising. Within three days Bladder has risen to the status of a storm cheating mariner with the capacity to bringing guests back from the dead. Al's sense of astonishment is matched only the sense that, despite his decades serving aboard cruise ships on the Seven Seas, he can still find himself inspired by the passengers' collective ability to believe in the phenomenon of miracles.

Chapter 10 :
The Rock

Monty and Mrs Major are up on deck. She is seated in the sun with a copy of Catch 22. Meanwhile, Monty is at the railings, straining to identify the coastline past which they are sailing. He is next to a man with a walking frame who seems to be attempting to get away. Monty grabs his arm.

'Yes! These are most definitely the shores of historic Morocco,' he says to the elderly stranger. 'I spent some time here you know, on active duty.' Monty leans over to the man conspiratorially and whispers. 'Very hush-hush, can't say more about it. But I think it's fair to say I made quite a difference. Cracked a code. Shortened the war. On the QT now, keep it under your hat.'

The man adjusts something in his pocket which causes his hearing aid to emit a high-pitched sound.

'What?'

Monty raises his voice.

'I'm saying, IT WAS TOP SECRET, Sir. HUSH HUSH. Shortened the war. Can you hear me?'

'What was?'

'I WAS. I SHORTENED THE WAR. OFF THE RECORD,' bellows Monty.

The elderly man appears to be calculating something.

'That would make you much older than I am.'

Faced with this chronological complication, Monty stutters for a moment.

'Not THAT war. Not World War II.'

'Which one was it then?'

'An...other one. Involving Morocco, which is why I know every inlet, every beach on that war-torn shore.'

Without looking at the coastline the elderly man continues his suspicious stare at Monty.

'That's not even Morocco. I hope you weren't in charge of

navigation in this war of yours, and with that he shuffles off along the deck, muttering 'liar' as he departs.

Unable to further detain his audience, Monty resorts to his hardy perennial, Mrs Major. Noticing his approach, she studiously lifts the book to act as a kind of paper barrier between them. He stands in wait. Eventually, with an irritated sighs she rops the book on her lap. 'What is it Mr Major?'

'I told that man some PRETTY sensitive information, and all he could do was call ME a liar! I don't know why I bother sharing these hush-hush confidentialities, if people don't appreciate it. I'm trying to educate them and all I get rewarded with are insults.'

'Well then just keep it hush-hush Monty. Besides, it's not very hush-hush if you shout it so loudly even the dolphins can hear. Didn't you once tell some people at an aquarium that we must be wary of dolphins because the Russians taught them to spy for communism?'

'That wasn't in the Bay of Biscay. Most sailors here speak English or Spanish.'

'Why would that be a problem for the dolphins, Monty?'

'Because they spy in Russian.'

'Oh for goodness sake.' He ignores her admonition and, narrowing his eyes towards the coast, proceeds to give his commentary to an audience of one.

'Oh yes, Morocco The place was full of foreigners. Little fellows they were, millions of them. Like ants.' In an effort to find an audience, he spies Mr and Mrs Bitters, standing a short distance away on deck. 'Good morning to you. That's Morocco, you know.' Mr Bitters shakes his head.

'So what?'

'What do you mean so what? What's the point of being at sea if it is not to broaden the mind and expand our understanding of the world around us?'

'That's not why we're here,' mutters Mr Bitters.

'Why ARE you here?'

'We're here because our house is being renovated after water damage. A pipe burst and we are claiming compensation.'

'Really,' asks Monty, genuinely interested. 'How much damage?'

'We lost everything. Nothing left at all."

That's a bit squiffy. How long did you have the leak?'

'Two years. We didn't notice you see. It was one of those things.' Monty struggles to understand how anyone could not notice a house-destroying leak for two years, but being a military man accepts the explanation at face value.

'Are you going all the way?' Mrs Bitters is offended.

'That's a bit of a personal question!'

'No, no, are you doing the whole world cruise?'

'Yes,' sighs Bitters unconvincingly. 'It's going to take that long for them to fix it. It's going to take a very long time in fact. And we were able to claim this trip on insurance.' Monty looks oddly at Mr and Mrs Bitters.

'So, the cruise, what do you think of it so far?' Mrs Bitters sighs again.

'Rubbish. Firstly we didn't have a sea view - till we complained. Then there was that terrible storm, which made us both very ill, so the toilet was blocked. And now it turns out we're going to go to places which aren't even English. And then there was the dead man,' Monty interjects;

'But the Captain brought him back to life, didn't he?'

'Yes, but he shouldn't have been allowed to die in the first place. And what if the Captain hadn't been able to do that? Then we'd all have died of the virus. And think of the compensation for that. So, all in all, the cruise has been very disappointing actually. We're certainly not looking forward to the other 100 days.' Monty thinks of something encouraging to say, and can only come up with, 'Cheerio then – see you for dinner,' causing Mrs Bitters to reply laconically,

'I suppose so, but only if nobody else dies.'

Trev and Dave are getting excited. They've had a few pints each and feel vaguely assured to learn that the dead man wasn't dead in the end.

'Do you think he really was dead, Trev?'

'Um, nope. I mean, come on, mate. He was hammered. That's all. He's like us. In fact, we ought to go on the razzle with him – sounds like a geezer.' Dave concurs.

'So, are we going to get off in this place we're going to, Trev? Where is it – Gibralter?'

'Yup – let's see if there's a pub – and some birds.' Dave smiles. He looks out the window. The sun looks warm and the seas are blue. Perhaps this really is the holiday of the century.

As the Dogger approaches the harbour, the decks are crammed with guests. Mr and Mrs O'Neill have abandoned their lifejackets in the room, on the basis that if the first storm didn't kill them, nothing will. Mr and Mrs Bitters are now in their cabin, deliberately sitting on the balcony facing away from the port – in order to be able to lodge a further complaint. Monty and Mrs Major are on Deck 7, watching intently as Monty describes the docking procedure to everyone within earshot.

Thousands of people are lining the quayside. They are cheering and making a lot of noise. As the vessel approaches the dock, it becomes apparent that this is not a welcoming party. It's a demonstration. Placards are being held high in the air saying 'Plague Ship Go Home' and 'No Death Bug Here.' Evidently, word of the incident has spread to shore and the local population has turned out in force to prevent the infection of this little community with what has been reported in the global press as 'a space-born virus which mysteriously landed on the Spirit of Dogger V during a strange storm in the middle of the Bay of Biscay.'

The Captain hasn't planned for this. He's got to sort it out, as far as the bad press is concerned. The story goes away after Gibraltar. But he also needs The Rock here and now. This is where the fuel is tolerably priced. He paces up and down the Bridge thinking of a solution.

'Ward, what do these people on the rock care about?'

'I don't know sir – the usual things, money, families, work, homes.'

'Have we got anything they need or want?'

'they've also got small baboons.'

'What on earth has that got to do with it!'

'Er, nothing Captain. I was just trying to find points of difference. I mean, let's face it, Gibraltar is really just Northampton with sunshine. They've even got a WH Smith and a Marks & Spencer.'

'So how the hell do we get them, that lot with the placards, to calm down and let us dock?' Ward hesitates to make a suggestion, but then decides that necessity is indeed the mother of invention.

'What about if you get Mr Morgan – you know, the dead man - to go ashore to prove he's alive, with some of the people who thought he was dead?'

'What good would that do?'

'Well, Sir, they might find that reassuring – though there's also the risk they'll all want to worship you afterwards.'

'OK, do it.' The Captain doesn't take the warning seriously, but can see the logic of the proposal.

Presently, a small delegation is allowed down the gangway, led by Mr Morgan, who confirms he's been 'cured' and that if we ever were dead, he isn't now. Passengers support his story, adding helpfully that they saw Bladder bring Mr Morgan back to life in a large theatre, even though his stomach had exploded, killing many members of staff in the process. Mr Morgan agrees, because he has no recollection of the incident whatsoever.

The discussions take 30 minutes, and after a check up by a Gibraltar doctor – who pronounces Mr Morgan to be alive – the demonstration relaxes its opposition. However, there is one condition – that Bladder comes ashore personally to 'administer' to those who are sick and infirm. When informed of this condition, the captain laughs out loud, but for the sake of expedience agrees.

As Bladder steps off the ship, he is immediately surrounded by locals, who tug at the hem of his jacket and plead with him to lay his hands upon them. This he does, gracelessly and with the patience of a man who is concerned about missing a bus. After about 10 minutes he calls a halt to it and, despite the pleas of the local citizens, scurries back up the gangway to his sanctuary on board. The guests, who have watched these proceedings from the deck, are further in awe of the Great Captain Bladder. What further proof do they need that the ship is being captained by a great prophet, who must surely have found his inspiration from a Higher Power.

Dave and Trev are looking for a lower power. They're on shore and find a bar. And there they drink. The pretty barmaid flirts with them to ensure they don't wonder off to sample the delights of any rival hostelries. Around them, guests amble around the humble and very British environs of the square. They watch naively as others apply themselves to this first opportunity to carry duty free back to their cabins. And the usual contingent of excursion seekers travel up the treacherous roads of The Rock in a typically dented tour bus to marvel at the caves within the mountain, and laugh politely as monkeys playfully scratch their arms and try to steel their cameras.

Bladder fills the tanks of the Spirit of Dogger V with marine diesel and muses silently at the ignorance of people who seem to believe that a man of healing abilities and spiritual importance might find himself trapped in the Captaincy of a ship like the Dogger. And all the while, Ward looks on, trying to make sense of events – asking himself whether he is destined to play second fiddle to this accidental hero for the next 100 days. And, in an emotionally ironice way, he knows that if this is to be his fate, he'll be unabashedly proud of it.

Chapter 11 :
Star signs

A few hundred feet above the Spirit of Dogger V, in the azure skies which bless this sun soaked region of Europe, Celebrity Speaker Doctor Lucas Starwalker is looking nonchalantly out of the starboard window as they fly past and to the left of the ship he'll shortly join. Doctor Starwalker doesn't mind flying. In fact, he likes it. He loves being closer to the stars at any opportunity. As a scientist with a fine reputation in the field of astronomy, he knows a fear of it is irrational – and that, statistically, you're more likely to die on the way to the airport than on the flight itself. This is fact, as much as there can be any certainty in life.

By contrast, the lady sitting next to him appears terrified. This is Mystic Maria, who reads palms, studies horoscopes and looks deep inside the minds of people in order to reveal their innermost thoughts. She's not very good at what she does. She is looking out the window.

'I don't like flying and I really don't like this landing part at all,' she says to no-one in particular.

'Why not?' inquires Dr Starwalker. 'It's perfectly safe. And anyway, a flight would be tremendously unproductive if it never landed – leaving aside the logistical challenges of a never-ENDING flight.'

'Well, I'm Virgo you see, and Virgo people aren't good in the air.' Lucas turns his whole body to her.

'I'm Lucas.' She does not espond. 'I don't see what some notional star sign has to do with flying… I'm an astronomer you see.' Mystic Maria shrieks with delight.

'What a coincidence! I'm an astrologer too! I'm getting on a ship to talk about it. How long have you been practicing the art?' This is the one thing which always annoys the doctor.

'I'm an astronomer, not astrologer.'

Same thing!'

'No, no NO. The first one is to do with the scientific study of the universe – the second one is pointless mumbo jumbo believed by gullible people who are scared of the future. Frankly, astrology is about as practical as a cardboard potty.' He wonders why he chose to use this particular analogy and frowns - just as the pitch of the engines happens to increase. He inadvertently makes eye contact with the stewardess who misreads his expression. She smiles patronisingly at Dr Starwalker and mouths the words 'don't worry, it's fine.' The doctor mouths back 'yes, I'm not worried thank you' and looks out the window again. He returns to his sporadic conversation: 'So, if you're so scared of flying why didn't you just get on the ship in Southampton?'

'I had to conduct a séance yesterday for some people who believe they are living in a haunted house in Shropshire. They hear banging noises.'

'Banging noises – all the time?' asks the Doctor. Mystic Maria shakes her head.

'No, apparently only when it's windy. The wind seems to provoke the spirits.'

'Oh for goodness sake,' mutters Starwalker.

The twin-engined Airbus aircraft is now fixed in the last few hundred feet of its final approach. The pilot is making final adjustments to the flight path and prepares to set the wheels down at Gibraltar International Airport – regarded by some as the world's fifth most dangerous commercial runway.

'30 feet Captain,' offers the co-pilot. The pilot doesn't respond. His silence causes the co-pilot to look up and immediately follow the pilot's startled gaze ahead and towards the ground.

'What the hell's that!' The co-pilot sees it too. A dusty and dented pick up truck packed with oranges is parked on the centreline of the runway with its bonnet open. A man has his head buried under the hood. 'We have to go round! Full power!' snaps the pilot. With engines screaming at 110%, the Airbus rises up from the runway, missing the pick up truck by a few feet, sending hundreds of oranges across the centreline and causing the vehicle's startled owner to throw himself to the ground. Everyone at the airport stops what they're doing and watches the spectacle of the giant silver bird climb dramatically back up into the skies. A few shake their heads disapprovingly. They know exactly what's happened - again.

Gibraltar International Airport has one of the strangest traffic arrangements on earth. For reasons related to the lie of the land, the runway is crammed into a flat bit of territory between 'The Rock' on the right, Spain on the left and ocean at both ends. But that's not the oddest thing. There's a road across the runway – for cars and people and horses… and anything else that people want to take in and out of the diminutive British territory. The traffic is supposed to stop every time a plane takes off or lands. Pedro Gonzalez didn't. He'd stopped to talk to a friend of his - an airport worker - and ended up on the wrong side of the barriers. Then, effecting his escape, he floored the accelerator, flooded the engine and broke down in the middle of the runway. The Air Traffic Controller was focussed on the approaching plane rather than on Pedro's decrepit truck, and the rest was an accident waiting to happen.

As the plane climbs from the airport, a brief moment of panic ripples through the passengers on board. Dr Starwalker feels a tremendous sense of irritation. By contrast, Mystic Maria looks back at the high points of her life, and ahead to the things she'll never do. He scowls at the stewardess and mouths: 'must try harder.' She looks back wide eyed and shrugs helplessly.

'Would you mind letting go of my arm,' says Dr Starwalker. She releases her vice-like grip on the Doctor's jacket.

'Sorry. It was, er,'

'Yes I know. It was the go round. There'll have been something on the runway. There's a road across it you know.' Mystic Maria gasps at the Doctor's claim.

'How is that supposed to work?' she exclaims to herself.

'Well, as you can see, it doesn't really. It's a stupid arrangement. Have you seen the monkeys?'

'Monkeys? Um, I really don't know what you mean.'

'Monkeys. They've got monkeys on The Rock. Some people think they're cute but I'd have them put down.'

'Do you think we're going to die? Asks Mystic Maria, still traumatised by the screaming pitch of the engines.

'You're the psychic – you tell me. Speaking of which, if you can see into the future, why didn't you see that coming?' She tries to formulate an answer, without success. 'Well, you'll be glad to know we haven't landed in the sea.'

'Oh what a relief – thank you, thank you.' Skywalker turns on the lady.

'So, have you predicted the end of the world? You know, the way people do, causing rituals and a lot of tourism to ridiculous places.' The doctor returns to his window vigil as the plane swings round for a second go at landing.

'No – but I do believe it's supposed to be happening next December. It's to do with a South American prophesy and there's a U.F.O. in a mountain in France. It's going to save some people.'

'Is it really,' muses the Doctor. 'Do you have to speak French to be saved, or can anyone go along?' Mystic Maria considers the question.

'I honestly don't know, but I suppose anyone can go along. The aliens have probably thought of that.'

'I'm sure they think of little else.' He turns to take another look at the lady who briefly strangled his arm at the moment of crisis on the aircraft. Her mousy long brown hair and pale complexion are a pleasing combination, giving an almost disarming charm which sits comfortably with the innocence of her youth. He smiles. 'Would you like to hear a prediction?' She indicates assent. 'I predict we will land safely.'

'Oh I do hope so. But you just never know, do you?' The Doctor wonders how successful Mystic Maria has been as a fortune teller.

As they disembark the doc stops in front of the stewardess. 'My compliments to the pilot.' She smiles formally.

'Have a nice stay. Sir.' The moment passes and she hopes he doesn't.

As they exit the luggage arrival hall, there are two names on the taxi driver's greetings board. One is 'Senor Skywaller,' which he presumes is a Spanish approximation of his name. The other name is 'Senorita Wildy.'

'Be you Mista Skywaller and be you Mease Wildy?' asks the affable driver.

'No, Mystic Wilder,' she corrects – before the doctor interrupts.

'Yes, yes, she's Mease Wildy, can we go now, porfabor senor?' With nods and a piece of paper showing the quay they want to get to, they head off to a battered old Volvo 144 in search of the Spirit of Dogger V. As they cross the runway the driver points at squashed oranges on the tarmac.

'Car breaked here, big problem for plane, going round.'

'Ah, that's what it was. See what I mean – we're crossing the runway right now.' Mystic Maria is amazed.

'I'm amazed,' she says predictably. I thought you were joking.

'I wasn't joking about the monkeys either.'

'What do you mean by that?' asks Maria. The Doctor points up to The Rock.

'They've got a monkey colony up there on the top of The Rock and for some reason tourists think it's essential to be photographed with them. Meanwhile, the aggressive little wretches are busy whooping and nicking jewellery and stuff from people's pockets. Brits go up there with hopes of a quaint picture, and come back down with no wallet, a monkey bite and rabies. How long are you on the ship?'

'Till Havana.'

'Same here. I never cease to be amazed some people can last out for three months on a world cruise. Just think - spending 15 weeks with hangover induced heatstroke. And how much food is that? Does anyone ever actually explode on board?' Mystic Maria recalls a news item he saw.

'I read that there's an outbreak of some killer space bug on board.' Starwalker shakes his head.

'You really think so? I'll very much doubt it. I expect someone collapsed in public from too much booze; then someone else who craves a little gossip claimed he 'died before our very eyes.' After that, it's retold by a High Priestess worshipping at the alter of the tumble drier in the Church of Launderette and, bingo, there's your story. Personally, I expect the ship hasn't suffered so much as a cold.' The Doctor's enough of a seasoned cruise line speaker to know how it works.

'Oh good. So we'r enot going to die then.'

'Well, yes, you will die – eventually. But probably not yet.'

The Cruise Director is at the bottom of the gangway, ready to greet the two guest entertainers. 'Welcome to Spirit of Dogger V!' chirps the Cruise Director. 'You must be Miss Wilde, our resident astrologer.' Mystic Maria then does an odd thing. She extends her hand, but a little too high for him to shake it. He tries to do so all the same, but she raises it even higher until it hovers in front of his mouth. He suddenly realises she expects him to kiss it, which he does awkwardly, and to the amusement of his Deputy. Doctor Starwalker extends his arm.

'For me, just a normal handshake will do thanks.' The Cruise Director looks at the two of them.

'Well, I guess you pair have had a lot to talk about – being in the same trade and so on.'

'Astronomer and astrology are totally different.'

'Astronomy, astrology, whatever, either way it's all about star signs, isn't it.' Maria titters.

'Actually, we've mainly been talking about monkeys and rabies and we nearly died in the plane.' Her joyous demeanour leaves the Cruise Director at a loss on whether to sympathise or celebrate her comment.

'Oh, right – well, anyway, let's get you checked in.'

The arrival of Starwalker and Wilde creates excitement amongst those guests who have not disembarked for a look around Gibraltar. Word spreads of the 'Celebrity Speakers.' Nobody knows who they are, but rumours abound. Speculation points to comedian Tommy Cooper, singer Bobby Darrin and politician William Gladstone; even though all of them are dead and, indeed, one of them passed away over a century ago. Apparently, this has done nothing to tame the appetite of the rumour mill, which is now more than ready to accept that anyone is possible, even if it's necessary for them to be brought back to life through the Messianic talents of Captain Bladder.

At 17.15 Captain Bladder takes a deep breathe holds it for a moment… and then sighs a great, sad sigh.

'I hate doing this.' He breathes in again and prepares to make his customary announcement. 'Well, ladies and gentlemen, welcome back on board the Spirit of Dogger V. I do hope you had a very pleasant time in Gibraltar. As we make our final preparations before departing, the engineer is checking we have the right number of winds on the elastic band, and that everything is working properly, which it is. So, can I suggest as we sail away on this beautiful evening you go up on deck to joint the entertainments team at the Great British Sailaway Party and get yourself a gin and tonic, and why not make it a large one. Whatever you choose to do on board tonight, I hope you have a wonderful evening.' Bladder takes his finger off the button and shakes his head slightly. 'Alright, Ward, let's get going.'

As the vessel slips its moorings and Dogger V drifts gently away from the quayside, the roar of 'Hope and Glory' is heard from deck 12, followed by 'Rule Britannia' and a series of songs requiring everyone to dance in silly ways.

Doctor Starwalker is up on deck, watching the spectacle uncertainly. Monty spots him.

'Are you who I think you are?' Starwalker considers the question and its ridiculous content.

'That's an unanswerable question.'

'I thought it was you! Do you remember me? From the Aurora? We – my wife and I - came to your talk about astrology.'

'I'm NOT an astrologer. I'm an astronomer. There's a tremendous difference.'

'So, it IS you! How splendid. Are you on holiday or doing some talks again?'

'Talks.'

'I'll be there – my wife is quite partial to the predictions in the papers – she's Virgo I think.'

'Monty, I'm Libra.' The Doctor sighs.

'I don't actually read star signs – but I understand the other speaker who joined the ship today is very much into all that sort of thing. Mystic Maria – that's her over there.' Mystic Maria is standing dressed in a kaftan next to the railings with her back turned, performing some kind of ritual apparently dedicated to the setting sun. 'Yes, for all things astrological, she's your woman...' though he adds thoughtfully, 'though I'd tend to stay away from predictions, if I were you.'

'Are you here for the whole cruise?' inquires Monty.

'All 104 days? Er, un-fortunately not, just two weeks.'

'Can I ask you a question – do you think the world's going to end on the 14th, like that Zulu prophesy says?' The doctor is tired of trying to allay fears of doom. He considers the inquiry and the gin and tonic he's consumed causes a flash of mischief.

'Yes.' Monty and Mrs Major are silent. 'At midday. On the stroke of noon – ship time.' Mrs Major puts her hand to her mouth and lets out a distressed whimper. Monty tries to recover the situation.

'Surely not Doctor! We're rational, British men. You don't believe all that prophesy business do you?' Starwalker has just noticed that Wilde has finished her rituals.

'Well, actually, I'll just go and check.' He stops and turns round. 'Oh, and in fact the end of the world is exactly what my talk is about tomorrow. Do come along and, well, hopefully see you there. Now you'll have to excuse me.' He ambles off in Mystic Maria's direction. They watch as he strikes up a conversation with her. Mrs Major and Monty watch carefully.

'Well, look at that,' says Mrs Major. 'They're obviously taking it seriously; otherwise those two wouldn't be on board, would they? Oh Monty, if he's right we've only got four days to live.'

'No, that can't be correct darling. If it were true, the Captain would have told us. Surely? However, I do think we'd better go to his talk – just to find out what's what and what's not.'

'If the world ends, do we still have to carry on paying all the standing orders or will they be cancelled automatically? After all, we won't be here to cancel them.'

'No, I think they'll be cancelled automatically. I'm more concerned about who's behind all this. Have you noticed there aren't many Germans or Frenchmen on board, not even as servants. What do they know? I suspect there's more to this than meets the eye. And if it is the Bosch, we've stopped them before and we can do it again. Perhaps I ought to have a word with the Captain.'

'Did you hear about the flying saucer in the French mountain?' Monty shakes his head.

'No, but it sounds like the start of a rather weak joke.'

Trev and Dave are also on deck, vaguely following the dance moves being shown by the Ents team from the raised stage. So far, the boys' search for girls has been unproductive.

'Trev, how about that one there?'

'Dave, she's about 13 years old!'

'What about that one?'

'She's over 70.'

'Trev, there's no-one! There wasn't anyone in Gibraltar either. I mean getting the beers in is fine, and all that, but you said this would be the holiday of the century.'

'Don't worry mate, we'll go on a major totty search tomorrow, alright mate?'

'Great, mate! Where are we tomorrow?'

'Er... ', Trev looks at the itinerary. 'We're at sea.'

'What about the next day. Mate?'

'Er, at sea. And then the next day we're at sea, but the day after that we're... um at sea again.'

'Trev, mate, that's just catastrophic. We're prisoners on this sexual desert – I mean the only totty under 100 years old are Dorothy and the other birds in that massage place – and jailbait kids with their parents who probably think of us as their worst nightmare.' Dave looks out at the disappearing elevations of Europe on the North and Africa on the South. 'I mean, I don't even know where we are.' Trev considers their situation.

'We're all at sea at sea, Dave mate. We're all at sea.'

Chapter 12 :
End of the world

The guests aboard the Spirit of Dogger V wake early. Word has spread from bow to stern that on this day they will be informed of the timing and nature of how the world will end. It's all there in the Daily Programme – a newsletter printed with remarkable reliability every single day for the benefit of those on board. Doctor Starwalker's talk is advertised on the front page. There are two typographical errors in the entry for the doctor's talk, causing it to read like this:

'The end of the world is Nigh

11.15am Red Curtain Theatre

Internationally acclaimed astrologer Doctor Lucas Skywalker returns on board to share the results of his research into the likely date of the end of the world and what will cause it. If you want to know when you're going to die, this presentation is a must! There will also be a book signing after the presentation.'

Dr Starwalker isn't happy with the errors, but he saw the Daily Programme at the same time as everyone else, and by then it was too late to do anything about it. Furthermore, his general policy has been to reassure the public, rather than to stir up concern. He also knows there's one great compensation in the situation –he's going to be a guaranteed a full house – in his experience, the three primary topics of conversation on a cruise are the food, the weather and death.

Starwalker enters the theatre to a full house. Almost every seat is taken, and a number of the crew are also standing at the back. As he enters, there is something of a hush in the room. This can mean only one thing. There has been discussion of the matter in the launderette, and therefore rumours will have confirmed the worst fears of those on board. He doesn't know what those rumours are, but he knows he'll find out soon enough.

As he prepares to begin his talk, he hears a 'psst' sound from behind the curtains. When it happens again, he turns to investigate. It's the Cruise Director.

'Yes?'

'Doctor, I'll introduce you in a moment. But I've got to tell you, there's a lot of fear on board now. Somebody died the other day and the Captain brought him back to life.'

'What!'

'Well, obviously, he didn't actually die, but the guests thought he had – and then they thought he was resuscitated by Bladder.'

'What's the truth?'

'The chap was just crapulous. That means drunk.'

'So why didn't you just say drunk?'

'I don't know. It was a quiz question, I mean the word, not the drunk. Anyway, the passengers we've got this time seem to believe anything and always the worst version of it. So can I just ask you don't scare them too much, because it's just going to make the next 98 days impossible?' The doctor isn't going to be bullied by the Cruise Director.

'I'm afraid my talk is my talk. They're not going to find it reassuring.' It's 11.16 and a restlessness is emanating from the audience. 'Can we start?' Without further ado the Cruise Director introduces Starwalker, who enters from stage left without the customary applause. Starwalker looks at the faces in the audience and clears his throat.

'Ladies and gentlemen, I am going to take you on a very strange journey: a journey which takes us from the beginning of the world to its end. Many of you will have heard rumours and claims that the earth will end as a result of certain prophesies. Well, let me say from the start the one thing you all want to know: is the end of the world nigh?' Starwalker savours the moment. You could hear a pin drop, as every face awaits his next pronouncement. 'Ladies and gentlemen, the answer is… yes.' There is unified gasp from the 950 people in the theatre. A voice near the front shouts out.

'What's the earliest this can happen?' The doctor pauses for effect, satisfied that he has the full attention of the room.

'The earliest that it can happen is… now.'

The theatre erupts in wailing and panic. People get up to leave, others are consoling each other as still others take out their mobile phones to send final texts to their loved ones. The Doctor's efforts to tame the throng are futile. He hadn't figured on this. Starwalker's naïve assumption was that people would listen to the rationale for the answer. Instead his words are drowned out by the hullabaloo which has now erupted in the theatre. The theatre starts to drain and despite the doctor's protestations, he is eventually left with a tiny contingent of 15 people still engaged in his talk, four of whom are crying and four of whom are asleep. The other seven are Monty and Mrs Major, Mr and Mrs Jitters and Trev and Dave – and Mystic Maria. Dave raises his hand.

'Excuse me, are there any girls in the afterlife?' The Doctor is taken aback by the question.

'Um, I'm not really sure. But really, that's not what my talk is about. Can we leave questions till the end?' Mrs Major is weeping.

'But it IS the end!'

'No, no, as I said, the earliest the end of the world could be is now, but it's much more likely to be later.' Monty interjects.

'Next Wednesday?'

'NO. It's probably going to happen in about five thousand million years.' There's silence in the room. Monty is angry now.

'So why the hell didn't you say that at the start?'

'I did say it – it's their fault for not listening.' Monty stands up – he's on a roll.

'Look what you've done. The whole ship's preparing for Armageddon because of you. And all you can say is it's their fault. Are you German?' the Doctor shakes his head. 'French?'

'No, I'm British.'

'Well you're acting like a bloody Kraut. You owe this entire ship an apology, frightening people like that.' Mrs Jitters raises her hand.

'You don't really have to raise your hand like that.'

'Excuse me, Mr Skywalker, when are you doing the palm readings?'

As the Doctor drifts out of the auditorium with Maria, she breaks the silence.

'That was quite a show, Lucas. Not bad for a rational man! Wow.' Starwalker sighs.

'The problem is, people always want life to be sensational. Exceptionally good or bad but not anything in between. I was just trying to liven it up.'

'In that case I'd say your talk was 100% successful.'

Up in the Bridge, the Captain shakes his head solemnly as the Cruise Director reports on the incident in the Red Curtain Theatre. When he's finished Bladder considers the options.

'We've had this chap on before, haven't we? He wasn't any trouble then.'

'No Sir, but it seems that we've got a particularly, er, jumpy compliment of passengers this time. I don't know what it is – it's as if they're paranoid or something. Everything gets exaggerated. I can't explain it. All I know is we've now got about 1,800 people who think the world's going to end. Apparently Mrs Cryer has been spreading it in the launderette. And you know how people are about what they hear in there – especially from her.'

The Captain nods sadly. He recalls in fond terms the time that his 'passengers' would quietly lie in cold storage for the long voyage from New Zealand to the United Kingdom.

'I'll have to talk to them. Make the announcement for noon.'

At noon, the theatre is once again crammed with guests, many of whom are now wearing their life jackets – since rumour has circulated in the last 30 minutes that the Skipper will be announcing that a giant tidal wave is circling the earth. Bladder steps onto the stage followed by Doctor Starwalker, who has been briefed to keep his comments simple and direct. The midday bell is tolled and the Captain begins.

'Ladies and gentlemen, er, good afternoon. I have, er good news. Many of you attended Doctor Starwalker's talk this morning, and concluded that the world might be about to end. I have been working with the Doctor since that time, and he has an announcement for you all. Doctor?' The Captain steps aside and Starwalker shuffles forward. Violet Cryer is in her usual place in the middle of the front row, with her arms crossed and her eyes shut pompously.

'Ladies and gentlemen, I'm happy to announce that the world will not end now.' A ripple of applause rises and falls. A voice from the audience shouts 'why not?' The Doctor continues: 'well, I have been working with the Captain and that's why I'm making this statement now.'

'Is the Captain responsible for it?'

'Yes, I'm making this statement because of the Captain. I'm telling you this thanks to him.' There's a murmur in the room, and someone shouts out 'Captain Bladder has saved us.' There is spontaneous applause and as the clapping grows into a tumultuous wall of noise, people stand to their feet. In the face of the standing ovation, Bladder steps forward to try and clarify that he made the statement possible, but it's too late. These same people who have already seen Bladder bring the dead to life are now convinced he has also prevented the end of the world through the same Messianic quality which resuscitated the corpse. Unable to abate the adulation of the crowd, he nods at the Doctor and they leave the stage. Only Mrs Cryer maintains a stony coldness, resenting her second media failure of the week.

Off stage, the doctor is first to speak.

'That seemed to go well, Captain.' Bladder rolls his eyes.

'It depends on your point of view. This lot already think I can raise the dead. Now they think I can save the world my life will be insufferable. Do me a favour Skywalker, for your next talk, just stick to star signs.'

Back on the Bridge, the Captain has resisted going for his customary walkabout today, as he just can't bear the requests for life changing miracles. Instead, he has requested the Cruise Director keep him posted on ship morale.

'Apparently, they're all convinced the world isn't going to end now. Well done, Sir. Somehow you turned it round - again.' The Cruise Director hesitates. 'Er, you may be interested to know that the press have picked up on it. Look at this one.' He hands the Captain a printed copy of the front page of a British tabloid paper: 'Saint Bladder Saves Ship from deadly Tsunami.' The Cruise Director continues. 'Apparently, all the guests were convinced some kind of tidal wave was going to wash us all away. Don't ask me why. You know how it is on board.' Bladder puts down the print out and shakes his head in disbelief.

'What is wrong with these people? How can they make so much out of bugger all?'

'Well, Captain, this lot truly are a strange bunch. It's as if someone's put something in the water. Still, at least we've got the answer to one question.

'What question would that be, Ward?'

'What you should do when you retire at the end of this cruise.'

'Which is?'

'Start a church.'

Chapter 13 :
All at sea

We're on the way to St Lucia, a five night sail from Gibraltar. This Caribbean paradise is scheduled to be the next sun soaked next port of call in this epic world cruise. They're over half way across the vastness of the North Atlantic Ocean, on a 'great circle' track which will take them across over 2,000 miles of landless sailing in unpredictable and deep, dark waters.

Trev and Dave are still in bed. They have nothing to get up for. Trev is thinking of making another appointment in the health spa – but apart from Dorothy and her friends, there's no other reason to do that, and he's not sure he'd survive another massage with Yuri. So they sleep on in a room which already smells like a cross between a men's changing room and a beer soaked carpet. They're both snoring and have no intention of getting up out of the windowless darkness of their inside cabin. There's no way to tell the time of day in here – so it doesn't feel ridiculous to be in bed at midday. Dave is snoring, as he usually does when he's been drinking. Trev just dribbles. Trev belches so hard it wakes both of them up momentarily. Dave looks at Trev's dribbling, unshaven face and says 'I could never love you' and they both drop off into a dreamless stupor once again.

Monty returns from his 'constitutional' walk from the deck and enters the silence of the library. Six people are reading quietly, and two ladies are asleep, both coincidentally with opened copies of the same book on their respective laps, a saucy block buster called: '50 shades of grey'. Monty's cheeks are red with the exertion and his spirits are high.

'Darling!' he announces loudly enough to cause others to jump and the two sleeping ladies to wake with a start. Mrs Major admonishes him.

'Shhhh! People are reading.' Monty immediately tempers his tone, reducing his volume to a remarkably loud whisper.

'Sorry darling. Guess what? I've just seen dolphins. Loads of them! Come and look,' and without giving her the chance to even return the book to the shelf, he tows her out. As they depart one a gentleman in one of the comfy chairs raises his hand towards Monty and mouths 'thank you for leaving.'

Mr and Mrs Jitters are sitting up on the sun deck, also reading. Mrs Jitters is reading the Daily Programme. Mr Jitters is reading the safety literature, which he has almost memorised. They are no longer wearing their life vests, but have them to hand just in case the ship suddenly sinks for no reason. Mr and Mrs Jitters also have the great misfortune of sitting next to Mr and Mrs Bitters. Mr Bitters has been eyeing up Jack's interest in the safety literature.

'Won't do you any good you know.' Mr Jitters looks up.

'Pardon?'

'That safety stuff. It won't do you any good. It's deliberately designed to make us do the wrong thing. When the ship sinks, the last thing they want is for us to survive.' Mr and Mrs Jitters look at Mr Bitters quizzically.

'Why would they ever want us to drown?' stammers Jane uncertainly.

'Compensation,' replies Mrs Bitters. 'They don't want to make the payments and dead people don't make the claims. Mark my words, they'll have us going down with the ship faster than you can say Titanic.' Jack and Jane pause. Jack feels compelled to pursue the debate.

'Er, how exactly would they do that?'

'By trapping us. That's why all the muster stations are down below.' Mrs Bitters leans forward conspiratorially, looking over her shoulder should the ship's Propoganda Police be listening in.

'Yes, down below so they can lock us in!' She waves at the two lifejackets. 'You shouldn't have done that – they'll put you down as trouble makers. You'll see.' The four of them look about nervously for signs of a crew mob preparing to take them away. Spotting the behaviour of the four, a waiter scurries towards them and addresses Mr Bitters.

'Can I help you, sir?' Mr Bitters swallows hard and points at Mr Jitters.

'It's not us, it's him. They're the ones you need to watch,' leaving the waiter utterly confused and Jack and Jane feeling utterly betrayed.

Casper is standing outside the newlyweds' cabin once again. He listens carefully for signs of hanky panky and then enters quietly, just in case. The newlyweds aren't there, but they've left a message for Casper. 'Dear Casper, we would be very grateful if you could tell us of any young married couples on board. Many thanks, Susan and Douglas.' Casper shakes his head sympathetically. At some point this kind couple are going to have to come to a difficult realisation: they're it.

Trev has finally bothered to get up. Out of boredom, he opens the door in his underpants to retrieve the Daily Programme from outside the door. In his grogginess he drops it and as it flutters towards the corridor floor he swings to catch it with both hands. Trev retrieves the document at exactly the same time the door shuts behind him.

'Oh bollocks.' Trev stands in the corridor in his underpants knocking on the door. 'Dave. Dave! Open the door. To his horror he hears the shower turned on – and doubts Dave can hear his banging over the sound of the high pressure water. He raises his voice: 'Dave! DAVE!' This causes the elderly well dressed lady from the room opposite to open her door, flooding the corridor and Trev's underpants in her balcony's blinding sunlight. Trev is momentarily disorientated, then in panic begins to hammer at the door. 'DAVE!' The lady titters endearingly.

'Oh you two!' Trev turns towards her.

'No, it's not what you think.' At this point Dave opens the door behind him. Having just come out of the shower, he's dripping and stark naked. The lady surveys the duo.

'Oh, that's better, isn't it. Have a nice afternoon,' and with a saucy wink she shuts the door. In unison Dave and Trev share a sentiment.

'Oh bollocks.'

Up on the bridge, Bladder is at peace with his world. Nothing serious has gone wrong for a couple of days – and the early paranoia of the guests appears to have been burnt off by the increasingly Caribbean sun. First Officer Ward looks at the Captain's positive humour.

'We'll be there exactly on time, Captain.' Bladder nods approvingly.

'Trev – look at this!' Dave almost jumps up from his bar stool at the open air Surfer's Bar near the pool. He's hit the jackpot for their holiday of the century. He taps the Daily Programme and sticks it under Trev's nose. 'Listen to this. 2.15pm, Friends of Dorothy, Sailor's Nest, Deck 13. We've got to go to her event. They'll all be there – Dorothy and her friends.' Trev looks at his watch.

'Oi, oi! It's already started.' They jump up only to stop a few feet from the bar, turn and in unison empty their lagers, before rushing off for the event they've all been waiting for.

Mr and Mrs Bitters are continuing with their diatribe to Jack and Jane.

'And then there's the question of the meals on board. I mean, we ought to be getting compensation for that night of the storm. A full refund for dinner.' Jack interjects with impatience.

'If you didn't eat dinner that night, well, it's hardly the fault of the crew is it?' Mrs Bitters grabs the moment.

'Ah, that's the thing, you see. We DID eat the meal, but it all came up during the night. So, in effect, the ship took back what was rightfully ours. It would be like buying a car and then finding someone repossessed it while you were in bed.' Jack isn't convinced.

'Well, it's not really the same is it? It's not like they stole the food from you.' Bittes is tediously persistent.

'Alright, who do YOU blame for the meal we in effect never had? And since a meal was included in the price, we deserve some of that price back.' Jane turns to Jack.

'We need to go now darling. We've got an event to go to.' Jack furrows his brow.

'Which event?'

'Anything, dear – or perhaps we should go and wait in the muster station for when the ship sinks. That way, our friends here will be able to keep more of the compensation.'

'There's no need to be like that!' whinges Mrs Bitters.

'No there isn't,' responds Jane, 'but I thank you for giving me a confidence in 72 years I didn't realise I had. Enjoy the rest of the cruise, though I imagine that will be impossible. Come on dear.' Mr and Mrs Bitters watch Jack and Jane depart from the deck. Mr Bitters shakes his head.

'What a couple. I don't know what's wrong with people like that.' Mrs Bitters agrees.

'So rude.'

Trev and Dave arrive at the Sailor's Nest. They look for the beauties they've come to meet. There's nobody they recognise. Trev asks the steward.

'We're here to meet up with the friends of Dorothy.' The Steward signals towards the far corner, where a crowd of people are sitting and talking. 'Thanks mate.' The wander over, where the crowd become quiet. 'Are you the friends of Dorothy?'

'Yes, welcome. I'm Geoff.' We're the Friends of Dorothy. We're glad to meet you.' Dave and Trev get the feeling that they've misunderstood the situation. Trev stands there looking at Geoff. Dave steps forward.

'Come on Trev, mate, at least they're not 100 years old. Anyone fancy a pint lads?'

Back on the bridge Bladder and Ward are talking about the next day's arrangements – the last day at sea prior to landfall on the first of the islands – St Lucia. Bladder's looking at the weather charts.

'Ward, the ocean has been amenable. Let's make sure the crew drills all go smoothly and with a minimum of fuss. I've also decided to postpone them by a day. I'm leaving tomorrow drill free for the guests to relax without all the sirens and so on. It'll put the complaints back by 24 hours.'

And so Spirit of Dogger V sails on towards an archipelago to fulfil the best of the passengers' dreams – as the glistening triangles of sun on the water dance like a crystal highway taking them towards paradise.

Chapter 14 :
Desperately seeking Susan

Douglas and Susan 'have been pondering a note from Casper which gently explains that, while there are some other young guests, they're the only young man and wife. He suggests they simply introduce themselves to people they like the look of, regardless of age.

'Douglas darling husband, I've had an idea for what we can do today.'

'What's that my dear wife?' Susan sits up and turns enthusiastically towards her sleepy spouse.

'If we can't hang out with other young couples, then let's find out about what the old people do. How they think, something about their culture?'

'Their culture? You make them sound like a tribe or something.'

'I know Douglas, but travel is meant to broaden the mind, and we need to improve our understanding of others. I want to seek knowledge and many of these people are three or four times older than us. Some of them might even be five times older!' Douglas makes a calculation.

'I doubt anyone on board is 130 years old, even if they look like it. Anyway, how do you propose to conduct this research?' Susan goes through the Daily Programme – she suggests that the two of them visit various events during the day which are likely to attract old people. Although Douglas doesn't like the idea, their relationship is still at that early stage where they're willing to be flexible with each other.

Their first visit is to the 'individual quiz' in Pretender's Bar. About 40 people are there, in teams ranging from one to six people. To the newlyweds, the questions – on the theme of classical music – seem impossible. In the musical round, the quizmaster –himself an accomplished pianist – plays individual notes from which the teams are supposed to guess the name of entire symphonies and their composers. Everyone else seem to be writing down answers.

Douglas whispers to Susan;

'How on earth can anyone guess these from a single note?'

'Well, these tunes were probably in the charts when they were young, so they probably recognise them from the old days.'

Next, the newlyweds attend a line dancing practice up on deck. Over 100 people are pariticpating.

'There are just so many of them!' exclaims Douglas. They watch in awe as these seasoned line dancers perform to unchallenging ditties in perfect formation.

After that, they go to lunch and deliberately choose to sit with the oldest looking people in the restaurant. Susan opens up a conversation with a man who, to her, looks absolutely ancient.

'Excuse me, Sir, I'm Susan and this is my husband Douglas.' The man looks up.

'What?' She says it again, much louder.

'You're married? Why on earth have you done that? Are you pregnant?' Susan shakes her head bashfully. 'When I was your age I was busy having sex with a lot of girls. We had plenty of fun especially in Asia. In some countries we even paid for it. How old are you?'

'We're both 26.'

'26 are you? Well, if you live as long as me, then you'll have to satisfy each others' sexual needs for the next 78 years. Unless you have an affair or something. My wife and I didn't get together till we were in our 40s. Even then there were times when we got bored with each other.' Susan and Douglas desperately seek an appropriate comment. Douglas goes first.

'Well, when I met Susan I just knew she was the one for me.' The old man shakes his head.

'How the hell could you know that at your age? That's just naivety young man. Have you ever been with a Chinese woman? Or an Indian? Or a Colombian? No? Well, how do you know you wouldn't enjoy you life with one of those instead of your English rose here? Thos oriental could teach you some tricks, I can tell you – and unfortunately, they can give you the clap faster than you can say Hong Kong Dollar.' Douglas glances uncomfortably at the old man's partner, who is busy eating some bread.

'How long have you been with your wife?'

'35 years – in my view 10 years too long.' Douglas feels a need to display a modicum of chivalry.

'I'm not sure you should be saying that.'

'Why not – it's bloody true.' Douglas and Susan are even more surprised when the old lady begins to nod in agreement.

'So why are you still together then?' The old man raises his eyebrows.

'This isn't my wife – she's my mistress. I know what you're thinking – a miserable old git like me couldn't possible have a mistress. Think again – I can do things you wouldn't even have dreamed of. Isn't that right?' She looks up from her bread roll, tilts her head and widens her eyes. 'Oh, yes, there's no substitute for experience young man. Which is something you can't get now you're married. You'll just have to fumble about and work it out through trial and error and porn. Douglas looks at the old man's mistress.

'Er, does your wife mind about your – er - mistress?'

'I don't imagine so. She's dead. Waiter, can I have the soup followed by the lamb. And I don't want any of that mint sauce because it makes me fart.'

After lunch Susan and Douglas attend the ice sculpting demonstration on deck. Many elderly people are watching on, listening to the commentary from the Deputy Cruise Director. Presently, the sculpture is finished – an angel with great transparent wings, glistening in the afternoon sun. The venerable crowd moves forward. Each person reverently touches the ice and then rubs their wet fingers together, as if testing to see if the water is in some way real.

'Why are they doing that?' asks Douglas.

'I don't know but we should do it too.' Susan joins the shuffling audience and eventually she, too, touches the sculpture. Its cold, wet quality is inexplicably soothing and she leans forward to touch it again.

'You've already had your go,' snaps an old lady behind her, causing Susan to scurry back to Douglas.'

'Well, darling, do you feel better for that,' he says sarcastically.

'Actually I do. You should try it.'

'I'll put it on my list.' Susan feels a hint of annoyance at Douglas' lack of initiative.

Next, they call through a meeting of the Friends of Dorothy, believing this to be a reunion with an old lady who lives onboard the vessel. The men look up with slight surprise at the arrival of Susan and Douglas.

'Hi, welcome to the, er, Friends of Dorothy?' Douglas shakes hands and introduces himself and Susan.

'Are we early?'

'No not at all.'

'Is she on her way?' The man realises exactly what's happened.

'Not exactly, Douglas. This is a meeting of gay and lesbian guests.' Douglas and Susan feel a sudden flush of embarrassment. 'Please join us – it's a pleasant change to have people with your comparatively odd sexual orientation!' Before Susan and Douglas can respond, the others laugh and start introducing themselves. Douglas and Susan recognise two men at the back.

'Trev? Dave?' The lads feel intensely uncomfortable at being 'outed' as members of the group. Dave tries to explain.

'It's not what you think!' Douglas and Susan shrug as if to say it's not a problem. 'No, honestly, they're our mates - I mean as in drinking pals.' The smirking amongst others in the group becomes a mild titter. Douglas and Susan sit down, and conversation continues in the group in a most agreeable manner.

Their final stop is at the Sailor's Nest get together for those 'travelling alone.' As they approach, the two dozen people stop chatting and stare at Douglas and Susan, who are holding hands. A man in his 60s raises his eyebrows.

'Can I help you TWO?' he says emphatically. Susan smiles.

'No thanks, we were just hoping to, well, listen in.'

'What for? You do realise this is a single travellers' event.' Susan looks uncertainly at the man and then at Douglas. Well, we just thought that, you know, we just wanted to see what happens here.' The single travellers look at each other in shock.

'You-just-wanted-to-see-what-happens-here, did you? Madam, this is not some kind of freak show for your entertainment. We're not sitting here thinking 'I do hope someone comes to gawp at the single travellers.' Douglas steps forward.

'Now listen here, this is a public space and we have every right to go where we like.'

A murmur spins round the group. The leader continues.

'Oh so now you're making up the rules as well. And where will that end? How about if I drive on the right hand side of the road because I feel like it? Or shoot your dog because it's barking? Or declare war on Africa because I don't like the black people?' The others are muttering their agreement. 'Young man, your way is the highway to anarchy. So, unless you have come to announce that you and your child bride have decided to get a divorce, can I suggest that you choose to spend your afternoon imbibing in any of the many excellent hostelries on board this fine ship – other than this one.' Susan is visibly upset by all this. Douglas prepares to defend her honour. The man stands up. 'Only joking, pull up a seat. I'm Marcus, and welcome to the singles club. In fact, perhaps you and your fine lady would be so kind as to give us some pointers! Would you both like a drink?'

As the sun goes down, Douglas turns to Susan.

'So, what did you learn today, my wife?'

'Well, I learned that old people are very much like real people just… older. They talk about sex and have mistresses and a sense of humour. Probably the one thing I didn't like was when the man at the singles club washed his teeth in his whiskey and then drank it.'

'Yes, that was a bit shocking.'

'And I also think that the Friends of Dorothy isn't about an old lady who lives on the ship. Nice to see Trev and Dave making friends with like minded people.'

'I don't know why they get so embarrassed.'

'Me neither. Douglas, I think we should go along to the Syndicate Quiz tomorrow.'

At dinner, all 10 seats are filled. Monty is in an excited state and speaks of his plans to participate in all the quiz events on the next day. Trev and Dave seem a bit subdued, and look at their food more than anything else. Mr and Mrs Jitters look like they're a little more nervous than usual, but say nothing. When Monty finishes explaining his quiz plans, Susan makes an announcement.

'My dear husband and I have been investigate old people today.

They're really nice!'

'Nice?' booms Monty. 'Of course we're nice. We've had a lifetime's exprience learning how to not be horrible.'

'Well, yes, Monty, ' continues Susan. 'But you know what it's like to be young. We've never been old.' Monty violently disagrees.

'Young? I was born old. I didn't like children even when I was one. Couldn't wait to get to 50. But you, my dear youths, the advantage you have is something altogether more delightful. You've got love on your side! And that will take you very far.' Mr Bitters is provoked into making a comment.

'There's no such thing as love. It's a biological thing which makes us want children. A trick of nature.' Everyone looks at Mr and Mrs Bitters. Susan questions their claim.

'But you're married aren't you.'

'Yes, but with the benefit of hindsight it was an error. I don't really like her and if I could afford it I would rather live on my own.' Mrs Bitters concurs.

'My husband is a very dull man. At the time marriage the tax advantages were quite favourable, but those have changed since then. It seems unfair that they didn't change the rules relating to marriage at the same time.' Susan looks at Douglas who winces at the candid misery which the Bitters couple seem to inhabit. The table continues with their pudding in silence. Jack Jitters speaks now.

'Actually, on that point, my wife and I are on board because we've decided to renew our marriage vows the day after tomorrow. We would be very honoured to invite you to come along.' Everyone apart from Mr and Mrs Bitters offers heartfelt congratulations to a couple evidently still in love after all these years. Mrs Bitters can't help herself.

'Frankly, your decision to do that is disrespectful to everything my husband and I have just told you. Personally, I feel quite insulted.' Jack and Jane are at a loss to respond, but Trev comes to the rescue.

'Oh come on you miserable old tosser. Can't you give it a break for just one time?' Mr Bitters retaliates.

'We're not going to take lessons from a couple of arse bandits.' Dave is on the verge of standing up when Monty intervenes.

'Now let's not ruin dinner shall we. Those who wish to come

along to Jack and Jane's happy day should do so and others are entitled to give the occasion a wide birth.' There's a moment where the conversation could go either way, but the day is saved by Douglas who returns to their day.

'As a matter of fact, we went to the Friends of Dorothy get together today, which we thought was about an old lady who lives on the ship. In fact, it's a get together for the gay people. It was really excellent – lovely people.' Susan agrees.

'What did you think of it Trev and Dave?' The lads stare at Susan like rabbits in headlights. Trev feels obliged to respond.

'It's good – they're good fun. Great drinking buddies.' Susan continues.

'Can the gays renew their marriage vows on board too?' Dave raises he glass.

'Here's to Jack and Jane.' Everyone apart form Mr and Mrs Bitters toasts the happy couple.

After dinner, Douglas and Susan spend a while on the Promenade deck, savouring the warm summer darkness and the quiet swish of calm waters brushing past the hull.

Douglas has been mulling over something all afternoon.

'Maybe. Susan dear, do you think we're too young to get married – you know, like that man said today?'

'Yes.'

'Really?'

'Well, the old man - at lunch? – yes, I do believe he had a point.'

'Oh dear. So what should we do?'

'Nothing. It's too late. We're married. And anyway there's one other thing - I love you Douglas. And that's not rational either, is it? Let's worry about the future in 30 years, shall we? At least what we really learned to day is that there's life after youth.'

'Yes, we did learn that today – and also that And that the on board gay contingent is rather agreeable.'

'Douglas, do you think Trev and Dave are gay?' Douglas pauses as the sun sinks down behind the oceanic horizon. He turns to his adorable, beautiful and big hearted bride.

'Frankly, my dear, I don't give a damn.'

Chapter 15 :
Never mind the Buzzcocks

'Monty you're hurting me.'
'I'm afraid I can't pull it out, darling. It's too far in!'

'Put the light on.'

In the flickering neon light, Monty looks dolefully at his hand, wedged firmly in the crack between the two mattresses, his considerable bulk serving to squash the left part of his wife.

'I just can't seem to get it out.'

'What did you put it in there for in the first place?'

'To see if there was any money.'

Monty's wife, as ever, seeks the lesson in the situation.

'And did you find any?'

'No,' replied Monty gruffly, still struggling to remove his fingers from the confined space. 'But I can't sleep, I'm too excited.'

His wife nods understandingly.

'I know you are, darling. We both are.'

It's a big day for Monty and Mrs Major. Shortly they will rise from their bed to prepare for one of the great rituals in their cruising calendar: the Syndicate Quiz. Ordinarily, Monty is quite competitive. But, by special permission of his wife, he is allowed – on one day only – to devote himself to the pursuit of excellent and triumph in every quiz of the day. This is that special day.

Monty observes certain rituals in keeping with his quiz adventure. Firstly, he and Mrs Major attend breakfast for his customary Quiz day breakfast.

'And for you sir?'

'Kippers, my man. Just kippers and a pot of Earl Grey tea.' He hands the waiter the menu. 'Oh Mrs Major, this is the life, eh. Sunshine, wonderful service, exotic destinations and the honour of my company. You're a very lucky lady!' Mrs Major smiles gratefully. Monty spots two familiar faces entering the restaurant. 'It's the newlyweds dear. Douglas! Over here.' Monty waves at Douglas who looks like he's dressed for tennis, and Susan, who's wearing a sexy mini-dress and high heels, his pre-quiz excitement spilling over into a hyperactive waving action. Susan sees Monty first and directs her reluctant husband towards Monty and his wife. 'Good morning tomorrow people! And look at you Susan - you're a bit of a minx aren't you? But what possesses youths of your diminutive years to turn up for breakfast at this unearthly hour? Shouldn't you still be in bed having sex?

'Monty!' berates Mrs Major. 'Please.' But his childlike verse propels him to pursue the subject further. 'I remember when I was about your age - how old are you, fiftee, sixteen?'

'Darling,' intervenes his wife again – 'if they were fifteen they couldn't really married could they?'

'It depends on their culture – if they're from Holland it's a different matter. Anyway, when I was roughly your age I was unstoppable, like a freight train through the night! Oh yes, a marvellous time when you didn't have to worry about the clap or getting people pregnant. Oh yes, it was a simpler time. The sexual revolution they called it, and boy did we army boys revolve! And not many gays either as I recall. Even the long haired menhad intercourse with women of the opposite sex. And then along came all the new disease from those monkeys and the contraception and everyone got scarred. I suppose our generation spoilt it for yours, really. It's such a shame.' Douglas looks at Mrs Major.

'I'm sorry about Monty – it's just that he's a bit over-excited because it's his special quiz day.'

'It is indeed! And a very important day it is too.' Monty explains his game plan – which starts with an hour in the library to get into the mood. His kippers arrive. 'And, this, my friends is my starting point – kippers. It's brain food you see – gives you extra IQ points as soon as you start digesting it. In the event of a tie breaker, these kippers could make the difference between success and failure. Do you like quizzes, or has the art of knowledge passed the next generation by?'

'Actually, we do go along to the local pub on quiz nights sometimes. Douglas is very clever, he' s a historian. And I'm not bad at popular culture.'

'Excellent! Why not come along to the syndicate quiz tonight? You never know, this could be a winning team!'

Mr and Mrs Bitters have arrived in the self service restaurant on Deck 12. They overload their trays with food and sit on an empty table for 10. Presently, two other guests come to the table.

'Mind if we join you?' they ask.

'Yes, but we can't stop you, can we.' They sit down, realising only a moment later that Mr Bitters isn't joking. As if to emphasise the point, Mr Bitters adds; 'why can't you sit over there with those people instead?' The pleasant couple look at each other, and he decides to stand his ground.

'Well, we're here now.' Mr and Mrs Bitter sigh purposefully. They sit in silence for the next 15 excruciatingly uncomfortable minutes. Such is the oppressive misery which the Bitters exude that these unfortunate guests feel unable even to speak to each other. As they finish, he thinks of something to say to the Bitters couple, but Mr Bitters goes first.

'Please don't sit with us again.' After they've gone Mrs Bitters shakes her head.

'What makes people like that so rude? Couldn't they see they're weren't welcome?' Mr Bitters sighs.

'Some people will never have any manners. It makes you wonder why they even bother coming on the ship.' The Bitters couple go onto plan their day: sunbathe till lunchtime and then tour the ship looking for exposed nails and wet floors which could offer potential compensation claims.

'What's that noise?' Jack and Jane Jitters hear it at the same time. It's a kind of knocking sound. It's coming from the other side of the curtains – the balcony window. 'What is it, Jack? Could it be a sea monster, do you think?'

'Possibly. But would a sea monster be that polite? Wouldn't it just smash the glass and eat us?'

'Oh Jack, what have we done to deserve this?' Jane becomes tearful. Jack tries to reassure her, but there is no escape from the need to be brave. He gets his white bathrobe and ties it decisively round his waist. He walks towards the curtain. 'Be careful Jack.' Jack puts his hand on the edge of the curtain, counts to three and whips the curtain back. Behind the curtain a living being is indeed attempting to get into the cabin.

It's a man. He's wearing dirty underpants and he's knocking at the glass. Jack slides open the door. The two meet stand before each other. Morgan burps.

'I'm sorry.'

'Who are you?'

'Morgan. Captain Morgan. I didn't mean to be here.' Jack looks at Jane and then back to Morgan.

'Captain Morgan?'

'I used to be on a trawler from Swansea.'

'How did you get onto our balcony?'

'I fell here.'

'Where from? Swansea?'

'Deck 11. I was sitting on the railings. Sorry.'

'Are you alright?'

Captain Morgan comes in. Jack gives him the other bath robe.

'I'm alright thank you sir. Sorry.' He leaves for the deck above. Jack looks at Jane who says:

'I never thought cruising would be so exciting.'

Monty and Mrs Major arrive for the 11am specialist subject quiz. It's all about ancient monuments. It's a tough set of questions. He isn't in the first three – or even the top five. Their score – 10 out of 20 – is not particularly successful but isn't a humiliation either. As the contestants drain away, Monty conducts an autopsy.

'Never been a strong suite for us darling. Old buildings – who cares. Military history, science, history, all fine. But bricks – not my thing thank you very much.

'Never mind dear. We'll do better at the individual quiz, I'm sure.'

Captain Morgan has another problem. Since he fell off the balcony, he doesn't have his key card. Morgan goes down to the reception desk to get someone to let him in. In front of him is Mr Bitters who looks round at Morgan.

'You stink of whiskey and I find your apparel offensive.' Morgan looks at Bitters in the way one might observe a bird dropping on a windscreen.

'What?'

'You smell.' Bitters turns away and marches to the desk to complain about the hum which the air conditioning makes in his room. Morgan is next.

'I locked myself out.'

'Certainly sir. What's your room number?'

'A202.' The receptionist looks up.

'Mr Morgan?'

'Yes. Captain Morgan. I fell off the balcony.' The receptionist knows exactly who Morgan is. She organises for a steward to enable him to re-enter the cabin and once he's gone she phones an officer.

'Hi there. Just to let you know that Morgan's just been here. Locked himself out. Says he fell. Yes, that's what he said.'

Shortly afterwards the officer has a chat with the Deputy Cruise Director.'

'Could it be that he was trying to kill himself by jumping off the ship? I mean to 'fall off the balcony strikes me as unlikely. The thing is, it's not all that easy to kill yourself from Deck 11. As Morgan found out, you don't end up in the sea. You end up on Deck 10.' Nikky is thoughtful.

'Let's keep an eye on him. We know he's a bit of a handful, but suicidal? I doubt it. On the other hand, is anyone really so stupid as to sit on the railing?' Morgan's future actions will answer that question in spades.

The Individual quiz starts on time. Monty and Mrs Major have teamed up with Trev and Dave in the Winners bar to play. Dave and Trev and don't take it seriously.

'OK, question 12: apart from a search engine on the computer, what is a google?' Trev leans forward and whispers to Monty and Dave:

'A porn site.' This causes Dave to laugh out loud.

'Shh, take this seriously. Does anyone know?' Dave leans forward:

'I know. It's what posh people do when they stare at breasts.' Trev finds this hilarious.

'Come on, we're doing well – please take this a little more seriously.' Dave tries to look serious, but bursts into laughter again. Monty turns to his wife. 'Any ideas?'

'It's a 1 with 100 noughts after it.' The three of them freeze.

'How the devil do you know that?'

'It was an answer on Who Wants to be a Millionnaire.' Monty looks at her again to see if there is any flicker of doubt, and writes the answer.

'Nine teams got this one right. We've got the following answers: a pair of binoculars; an electric car; a type of beetle; a galaxy. Well, six teams got this right. The answer is, the number 1 followed by one hundred zeroes.' Dave jumps up and punches the air in victory, causing indignance from Monty.

'I don't see what you're crowing about – you thought it was about posh boobs.' He turns to his spouse. 'Well done darling and remind me never to team up with queers again.' Dave says, just a little too loudly;

'We're not gay.'

'Well you're acting like one. Grow up.' Trev and Dave go into a sulk as the quiz progresses.

The quizmaster has reached the final question.

'OK, number 20: Neil Armstrong and Buzz Aldrin were the first two men to walk on the moon. Who was the third astronaut on the Apollo 11 mission in July 1969?' The whispering and debate springs up around the room. Monty shakes his head.

'Any ideas?' Dave crosses his arms.

'I know it.'

'You do? Spit it out man.'

'No.'

'For goodness sake, we've got a chance of winning.'

'Nope. Not until you apologise for calling me childish.' Monty's eyes bulge.

'But you're being childish again now! Come on man – this is meant to be a team effort.' Dave looks out the window with his arms crossed. Monty looks at Trev who simply shrugs, then back at Dave. 'Alright, look, I regret calling you childish. Now will be please be an adult and tell me the answer.' Dave breathes in, as if pondering whether to accept the apology. Then, he turns to Monty and says quietly, 'Jim Lovell.'

'Thank you David.' Monty writes it down and leans back.'

'Alright, swap your papers, and let's go through the answers.' By the 20th question, Monty's team have a creditable 15 points.

'We're in with a real chance here,' he says excitedly. Even Trev and Dave have started showing an interest.

'So question 20, the third man in the Apollo 11 mission. We have five answers: John Glenn, Jim Lovell, Michael Collins, Yuri Gagarin – he was Russian by the way – and John Carpenter. The right answer was… Michael Collins.' Monty looks up at Dave, who goes decidedly red.

'You said you knew. How dare you.' Dave feels sheepish and mouths the word sorry to Monty. They come second by a point. 'We'd have gone the tie breaker if it wasn't for you. And you are childish, and I'm not retracting that. Monty breaks the pencil in two, tosses them towards Dave and storms out. Mrs Major looks at the boys.

'You shouldn't have guessed,' she says quietly and scuttles off to calm her husband.

Trev stares at Dave.

'What?'

'You shouldn't have guessed, mate. Now dinner's going to be crap tonight, with him and the bitter couple going on at us. And you were being childish.'

'Look, er, just shut up and leave me alone.'

Dinner is indeed tense this evening. Monty and Mrs Major eat in silence. Mr and Mrs Bitters are notably miserable, even by their standards, with Bitters complaining about the remorseless sunshine. The newlyweds are engrossed in each other and Mr and Mrs Jitters are nervous about the prospect of another balcony invasion by Captain Morgan. Dave eventually speaks.

'I'm sorry about the quiz, Monty. I didn't do it on purpose.' Monty doesn't look up.

'You have no idea how much I've been looking forward to today, Sir. Was it too much to ask for a team effort? I think not. I'm sorry you didn't appreciate the gravity of the situation.' Susan sits up.

'You do the quiz? That's great, can we play?' Monty eyes her cautiously.

'How much do you know, young lady?'

'Well, Douglas knows a lot about history and I know quite a bit about popular culture.' Monty proceeds to test their knowledge about various issues. After this he passes judgement.

'Alright, we'll be participating in the Syndicate Quiz in the

Billabong Room at 10.30. See you there -' he shifts his gaze to Dave, 'but not you.'

'Can we come as well?' asks Jane Jitters. Monty nods energetically.

'Naturally. A little maturity in the team is most welcome.

It's 11.15pm. Monty's team has tied with team 22 at 16 points each. They're on to the tie breaker. Monty turns to the team.

'It's the penalty shoot out – so to speak. Now listen closely. I don't want any grandstanding and no guesswork. Only answer if you know. Good luck.' The quizmaster looks up.

'Alright, here's the tie breaker: give the surnames of ALL of the Spice Girls.' Monty's jaw drops.

'What kind of question is that? It's popular nonsense.' He rants about the question as if the Quizmaster has just committed an act of treason against the Royal Family. When he's finished, Susan speaks.

'Haliwell, Bunton, Beckham, Brown, Chisholm.' Monty is stunned. He looks at her for some kind of confirmation. She nods.

'Are you absolutely sure?' She nods again. He hands the paper to her, and she writes them down. Monty insists on taking the paper up himself. 'Well, it's all or nothing.' Tense moments follow.

'We have a winner. The correct answer is: 'Haliwell, Bunton, Beckham, Brown, Chisholm. Congratulations to table 12!' Monty jumps up and punches the air.

'We did it, we did it!' Now the whole team is delighted. A voice rings out.

'They cheated.' In the ensuing stillness Monty looks round for the cause of the criticism. 'They cheated.' It's Mrs Bitters in team 22. Monty is outraged.

'Why, Mrs Bitters, do you believe we cheated?'

'Well, you've got the young people on the team and that's not allowed in the rules.' Others nod for no better reason than the fact that Mrs Bitters sounds like she knows what she's talking about. 'And I know for a fact that these youths have used their phones to access the answers through the internet.

'Rubbish!' shouts Monty. 'This lovely couple is as honest as the day is long! You have been nothing but misery since you set foot on this ship!' In the ensuing war of words the Ents Officer steps forward to adjudicate.

'Gentlemen please. There's no rule about the minimum age of team members, only a rule than not more than six people can be on the team. It also seems unlikely that there was use of the internet.'

'How can you be so sure?' interjects Mr Bitters.

'Because currently we are out of range. Thus, I think we can say that table 12 won it fair and square.' Mrs Bitters looks at the Ents Officer.

'You haven't heard the last of this.' Then turning to Monty she adds – we shall not be dining with you again tomorrow night – or ever.' Mr and Mrs Bitters walk out in the silence. Once they're gone the room erupts into frenzied gossip. Monty turns round to his team.

'Well done. And may I say, Susan, when it comes to irrelevant and salacious tittle tattle, you are a veritable genius.'

'Thank you, Monty,' beams Susan. 'Er, what does veritable mean?'

'It's a good thing, my dear. A very good thing indeed.' The victorious team proudly depart with their A&G bottle of white wine.

Up in the Sailor's Nest the pianist is playing a crooning refrain. They sit in the softly lit bar with their wine glasses in hand and consider their achievement. Monty stands up.

'My friends, it was an honour to compete in the same team as yourselves in tonight's Syndicate Quiz. And once again, Susan, I can only thank you for your fortuitous contribution this evening. Let us raise a glass to our triumph.' They clink their drinks and settle into a moment of satisfaction. Sitting down again, Monty breathes out. Susan is next to talk.

'I'm just glad I watch a programme called Never Mind the Buzzcocks. It's a pop quiz. Douglas kisses his wife. 'Well done my wife. It's just such a pity Mr and Mrs Bitters put a damper on proceedings.' Douglas thinks about the actions of the Bitters couple. 'Why are they so mean-spirited?'

'As a military man, I'd say it's a lack of discipline in younger life. This has, in turn caused them to become what we in the army used to refer to as miserable buggers.

I'd be willing to wager they have gone down to reception to complain that the internet service is not working! If the Bermuda Triangle means anything at all, perhaps it might cause those two to disappear. Anyway, they are not going ot ruin our celebrations so well done one and all for a spiffing performance. Hip hip -'

'Hurray!' they say together three times.

It is a night to remember.

The doctor enters the Captain's room pensively.

'I've got some more bad news, Captain.' If looks could sigh, Bladder's face would be making a despairing sound right now.

'Go on Doctor,' says Bladder, bracing himself for the next crisis in what's turning out to be an eventful cruise. 'What's happened now? Are you going to tell me there's been an outbreak of leprosy on B Deck? Or a touch of scurvy amongst the crew? Or perhaps it's something else completely, like another virus from the cosmos which is turning our guests into placid, pleasant and gracious fellow travellers?' What Captain Bladder would most like is an outbreak of some kind of illness which converts the entire compliment of passengers into frozen lamb.

'Well, the thing is, we've got a proper outbreak. Not like before, not just a drunk falling over. This one's real.'

'Where?' says Bladder, with a tone that resembles something between a resignation and anger. The doctor measures his words, as if answering a quiz question.

'Well, that's the thing, Captain. It's not a normal pattern. It's not on one deck, or related to one restaurant. And the only people who seem immune are wheelchair users. And there's another thing –and this is really weird, Sir. All the patients have high cabin numbers. Which isn't logical, I know. But it's what's happening.'

'So you're telling me we've got numerate bugs, are you?'

'I know this sounds insane, but the patients are all coming in from Cabins 260 and upwards.' There's silence in the room, as if Bladder is expecting clarity to suddenly arise from the tranquility. It doesn't. He scowls.

'Well, Doctor, that is impressive, but perhaps no less than we might expect from a ship on which people are preparing for Armageddeon and where the Captain can raise people from the dead. So the virus can count, can it? I know passengers who can't count to 260. And here we have a disease that's chugging along in the hundreds. Perhaps we should employ it in the Purser's Office. What do you think?' The

Doctor shrugs nervously, and wonders whether Bladder is taking this at all seriously. 'So, tell me, Doctor, what are the symptoms? A fear of electronic calculators? Or do they just vomit and get the runs like a good old normal affliction.' The doctor realizes Bladder is being sardonic, but he's pondering the facts.

'The usual, Sir. It's not norovirus though. More like a hygiene related disorder – the kind of thing that's transmitted through contact with animal faeces. I don't know what to make of it – but there has to be a pattern of some sort. I mean, it's just not plausible that the high numbers are a coincidence.'

'We've got an astrologer on board, haven't we, Doctor? Perhaps you should employ her services. Perhaps all the sick people are Pisces.' The Doctor stares at the Captain neutrally. He can tell that Bladder has little sympathy for this most recent adversity. By and large, Bladder tends to believe that passengers become ill because they don't wash properly – a perspective reinforced by an unfortunate incident five years ago. Here's what happened.

A couple from East Croydon had taken it upon themselves to keep using a toilet they themselves had blocked by attempting to flush away the remains of an infected, dead mongoose they'd bought in a market in Honolulu as some sort of perverse souvenir. Unable to find any means of cooking the hapless beast, they forced the stinking, decomposing body of the oversized rodent into the vacuum toilet system, instantly blocking it.

Even at this stage the situation might have been recoverable. However, not satisfied with the reckless flushing felony which they'd already committed, the dopey duo then proceeded to carry on using the toilet until it overflowed with enthusiasm onto the bathroom floor. Unwilling to report the blockage, they proceeded to step in the effluent and spread its virulent contents all over the ship. This led directly to an outbreak of what might euphemistically be called 'explosive diorrihea,' incapacitating dozens of innocent fellow travellers with physical symptoms which wouldn't be out of place in a Ridley Scott science fiction movie like Alien or Prometheus.

Incredibly, this same couple managed to repeat the offence later on during the cruise - when the man found a colourful dead fish on a shoreline and smuggled it on board in his pants. The only ultimate victims were the couple themselves, who had to be medi-vaced back to England with a suspected case of food poisoning. It is due to this, and other related incidents, that Bladder long ago concluded the most pernicious contagions on board are invariably the passengers themselves.

'Sort it out, Doctor, and you have my permission to quarantine anybody who, in your professional view, smells of shit.'

'Pardon, Captain?' inquired the doctor, unaware of the irksome memories his report to Bladder has evoked.

'You heard me. And follow up on the numbers. I'd be willing to bet there will be other anomalies here. Put them together and you'll have your answer. I'll give you some staff to observe what's going on. Use them to watch the corridors where the illness is peaking.' Bladder knows that, usually, there will be clues to how a disease is transmitted – as long as one takes the time to spot them. And with that the doctor leaves to embark on his investigation.

Mrs Bitters is looking morosely out at the passing ocean. It's almost as smooth as glass – with a gentle breeze caressing the railings and chairs which adorn their balcony. She has come to a decision.

'I need to be sick. And probably have a crap too.' Mr Bitters looks at her uncertainly.

'Are you sure? If you're sure, I'll get the camera.'

'What for!' she exclaims, momentarily forgetting the compensation creed which has made their existence a well paid misery for over 15 years.

'It's evidence, isn't it,' snaps Mr Bitters, his tone admonishing his wife for neglecting the ethos which lies at the heart of their social ostracism. 'Are you going to do it now or do I have time for a pee first?' But it's too late. Mrs Bitters is already vomiting onto the bed, and unfortunately for Mr Bitters, all over the camera he'd got as far as removing from one of the drawers. Not wasting a second, he swings into action. 'Try and keep some of it in, because it's better if I can take a shot of you actually vomiting. Otherwise they might claim we just made ourselves sick on the bed.' Mrs Bitters embarks on a fight against the odds to hold it in, as her husband picks the camera dourly out of the pool of regurgitated lunch and inspects the device. He smiles. 'I think it's alright – so no harm done.' He lifts the camera, fiddles with the controls, and nods to his wife. 'Alright, do it now,' he says assertively. To his great surprise, she expels a jet of spew which once again makes contact with the camera, as well as spattering Mr Bitters himself. She gasps for air. Mr Bitters is motionless. He looks at the camera, still dripping with his wife's contribution. Then he looks at her. 'Yes, that's perfect, in fact it's quite artisitic. Look.' He turns the camera to his wife. She clears her throat and coughs.

'I think a number 2's just come out as well.' Mr Bitters considers this news.

'It's no good. Even with a photo it would be hard to prove that it's your bottom.'

Monty is reading on their balcony. The sun is glorious and caresses his skin with the touch of a playful elf. He feels almost tickled by its attentions, and oddly fears this guilty secret is a form of vague infidelity to his wife. She seems not to have noticed as she sits in the room, arranging a pile of laundry which must be taken for cleaning.

'Great Scott!' exclaims Monty in such energetic tones that even his wife, who has heard all his tones before, looks up.

'What is it, Monty,' she inquires, genuinely curious. She sees he's gazing out to sea, but can spy nothing in his line of sight. But it's obvious he's looking at something. 'Monty, what can you use?'

'See? Look!' He points out at the featureless ocean, and she follows his line of sight fruitlessly across the sun frosted ripples, cautiously shaking her head. 'Look, dear, there – out there – look at all of it!' Now she shakes her head more certainly.

'No, I can't see anything, I'm afraid.' Monty looks at here emphatically.

'Of course you can – it's right there – our world! It's a water world! Water – everywhere! As far as the eye can see. This is it!' Mrs Major wonders if Monty is having a bit of a turn.

'Are you having a bit of a turn, dear?'

'Yes I am! A turn of discovery. An awakening! A passage from darkness to enlightenment. Communing with the great thinkers and pioneers of our species! Aristotle, Caesar, Boudicca, Henry VIII,

Cook, Darwin, Churchill, Bradman, Bannister, Coward, Cooper –'

'The boxer?

'No, the comedian, Tommy – Cleese, Heath, Attenborough – '

'David?'

'No Richard – Dimbleby –'

'Richard?'

'No, David – Christie, Coe, Charles, Cousteau –'

'Wasn't he French, dear?'

'Was he!? Not him then – Farah, Ennis and, of course, the Queen.'

'Which Queen? You mean that television presenter Graham Norton?'

'Certainly not! He's an arse.'

'Why? Because he's a homosexuaol?'

'Not at all. Most of the Conservative Party is homosexual but I still vote for them. Graham Norton is an arse because he ridicules people in public.'

'So do you, Monty.'

'Yes, but I don't do it on purpose.'

'And why haven't you included Margaret Thatcher?'

'Because she sold us out to Europe. Stupid woman.' Mrs Major looks out across the ocean once again.

'What has any of that got to do with the sea?'

'Look at it, my dear. Look at the expanse of nothingness before us and tell me you are not moved by our own puny presence on this magnificent planet! I tell you, it's moments like this that remind me of my own mortal coil, my humble place beneath the stars, a mere dung beetle in the pecking order of the universe, above nothing more than the Germans and French and some animals. Verily, I say to you, travel does broaden the mind and reminds us of our place in this magnificent cosmos.' Mrs Major looks at her husband and realizes that, for all his faults, he still cherishing his childlike love of that special thing which is life itself.

'I'm going to the launderette, dear.'

'Outstanding! I'll be here when you get back – just marveling that we are here at all – turning gracefully round in the spin dryer of the heavens!'

'Alright then, Monty. There's a chocolate on the table if you fancy it.'

'I'll have it in a minute.'

'Oh, and apparently the people along the corridor have all got a funny tummies.'

'All part of life's rich tapestry dear. All part of our destiny. And they probably don't wash their hands properly after using the loo.'

The doctor has stationed his team on all the areas where the virus has been reported. They walk casually around, looking for clues which might lead to an explanation of the outbreak. So far, nothing has been reported. The sound of extensive wheezing in C298 was investigated and found to be attributable to an over-dose of snuff by a German still new to this peculiar indulgence.

The doctor himself is now pacing casually around on Canberra Deck and is about to return to his own quarters when he spies a curious thing. A gentleman emerges from a cabin near to the lifts and assists himself to the foyer with a stick. That's when it happens. He raises his stick and - to the doctor's horror - presses the 'down' button with its end. The doctor says nothing, but as soon as the portly gentleman has entered the lift and the doors have closed, he rushes to the controls and, without touching anything, bends down and inspects the button closely. It reeks of dog dirt.

'Oh, my goodness!' exclaims an elderly female voice behind him. He looks round to make contact with a couple in shock to observe a man in officer's uniform bendign over with his bottom in the air staring at the button.

'Oh, I'm very sorry – er, would it be possible to use the other lifts please? I'm just checking a fault.'

'What kind of fault officer?' asks the lady. 'Are we sinking?'

'No, not at all, ma'am. Don't worry. It's a tiny thing. But could you use the lifts in the next shaft please?'

'If we're not sinking then why can't we use the lifts?'

'You can. Just not these ones right at the moment.'

'I can't walk very far you know, Officer,' she retorts. 'I've got arthritis and I really don't think you should be making me walk miles to get to the next lifts.' Rather than continue the discussion, the doctor relents.

'Alright, I'll call the lift for you.'

'I thought you said it was broken.'

'Well, it's not very broken. It's safe for now.' He presses the button and they stand awkwardly awaiting its arrival.

'So what's wrong with it, then?' asks the man.

'I'm trying to find out. Don't worry, it's perfectly safe.'

'So why didn't' you let us use it in the first place, if it's safe?' Luckily the lift arrives, and the doctor darts in to press the internal button for the guests.

'What floor are you looking for?'

'Deck Nine – Canberra Deck.' The doctor looks at them uncertainly.

'This IS Deck Nine.' The elderly couple look at each other.

'Oh, so it is.' They get out of the lift and stand in the hallway for a moment. 'Let's go back to the room dear. Thank you for your help Officer. Good luck with your repairs.' As soon as they've gone, the doc scampers to the corridor on the starboard side and beckons one of his team to join him. Leaving his underling on duty, he instructs the steward to prevent anyone else from touching the buttons and races off to retrieve materials which will make it possible for him to take a swab.

When he returns the same couple are remonstrating with the steward about using the lifts. Now they want to go up to Deck 12 for a walk, and the Steward is working hard to prevent them from touching the buttons.

'Let me help you,' he says, and he presses the button with a sharp pen to minimize the contact with the button.

'Why did you do that, Officer?' challenges the elderly lady.

'Oh, I'm doing an experiment.'

'What kind of experiment? I don't like the idea of being a guinea pig for your scientific inquiries. We're not prisoners of war you know.' In the ensuing moments the doctor seeks to find a balance between discourtesy and closing the conversation down.

'I can assure you that the only experiment I'm doing is to make the lift better for you, ma'am. Now if you'd like to step into the lift my colleague will escort you to whatever floor you're going to.' And with that he ushers the steward into the lift and waits for the doors to shut. The last thing he hears is the lady rabbiting on about feeling like she's under the microscope. The only thing the doctor wants to get under the microscope is the small brown deposit on the UP button for the lift.

Monty is still sitting on the balcony when his wife returns from the launderette.

'How's your transcendental moment going, dear?' she asks.

'Oh, splendidly, madame Major. Splendidly. In fact, I'm thinking of getting ordained. What do you think about a nice thatched vicarage somewhere in an idyllic village on a river in Cambridgeshire? Sunday roast after the service, garden parties for the stain glass windows fund and an annual get together with all the other vicars at a spiritual convention in Whitby.

'Isn't that where Dracula comes from dear?'

'Yes but he's not invited. He's too busy doing deals with the Roman Catholics.' Monty notices that Mrs Major has a note in her hand. 'What's that – an invitation for me to conduct the service on beard this Sunday?'

No, it's better than that – an invitation to have dinner with the Captain tomorrow evening.'

'What? Outstanding! And about time too. This will be my opportunity to put a few things right on the ship.'

'Oh Monty, don't be embarrassing, please. Nothing about the Germans or French, and please don't tell him how to run his ship.' She looks hopefully at her husband.

'In that case, what would be the point of accepting the invitation? I owe it to the passengers – nay, I owe it to the Captain, to help where I can. After all, why else would they have invited us?'

Why else indeed – save for the fact that Monty and his beloved wife are the most frequently travelled guests amongst all 1,850 passengers on board this particular cruise. Although he doesn't know it, Monty has actually spent more days about the Spirit of Dogger V than the First Officer Ward. This obliges the A&G Line to take good care of him – for loyalty in the cruising industry is everything – the most sought after prize of all.

'Right, Mrs Major – this requires urgent action. Prepare for a shopping experience. We must make sure that YOU are the belle of the ball.' This news delighted Mrs Major who instantly calculates that an evening of likely embarrassment is a tolerable cost to pay in exchange for a new frock.

'Captain, I think I've cracked it.' Bladder raises his head and his eyebrows. That was quick, Doctor. What did you discover, or did our numerically gifted little virus step forward and confess its presence by means of algebraic equations?'

'No, it's better than that. I saw a man using the life with his walking stick.'

'And – '

'And once he'd gone in I took a swab from the button. Exhibit A.' The Doc places a small see through bag on the table in front of the Captain, who duly picks it up and inspects it from different angles.

'It looks like dog shit.' The doctor sits down and leans forward conspiratorially.

'Captain, that's because it IS dog shit. He's been depositing infected dog shit on the buttons.' The Captain leans forward too.

'Who has? Al Quaieda?'

'No, a passenger on Canberra Deck. He's been using his mangy walking stick to press the buttons. The dog turd is riddled with infections.'

'Are you sure?'

'Yes – I even took swabs from all the other buttons on all nine guest lifts – it checks out. The only one with the crap on them is the port shaft in the aft set. And it's turning up on his deck, as well as the Promenade and Lido decks because he's doing the same thing inside the lift too. One of the stewards was in the lift with him and saw him do it. Captain, he's our man. And anyone else using that lift with their finger just after him will be picking up a nice little dollop of disease.' Bladder looks at the doctor with admiration.

'If you're right, then this is a piece of investigative work worthy of Sherlock Holmes. Good job, my boy,' says Bladder, smiling. It only lasts for a few seconds. His face returns to a more frosty demeanour.

'Still, we will have to deal with this savage who sees fit to transfer everything his wretched stick pokes itself into onto the lift buttons. What a stupid thing to do.'

'In fairness, Sir, I wouldn't have thought about it unless I'd been looking. Let's not be too hard on him.'

'Hmmm. I'll make an announcement tomorrow, but could you possibly go and see the man tonight – get him to desist.'

'Aye, aye, Captain,' nods the doctor and prepares to leave and gently challenge the offending guest.

'Oh, and Doctor, good work. Very good work indeed.' The doctor smiles. Praise from Bladder counts as one of the highest accolades on the high seas.

Mrs Bitters has stopped vomiting. She continues to feel appallingly ill, and lies on the bed, wiping her brow with a sweat drenched towel from the bathroom, where she has spent much of the afternoon. Mr Bitters is busy downloading the photographs of her suffering onto his computer. When he has completed his action, he rifles through the newly created photo file with pride.

'These are brilliant – I deserve an award.'

'What about me,' complains Mrs Bitters. 'I made the pictures possible in the first place. Show me them.' Her husband ignores her plea, as he scrolls through his art work once again. 'SHOW ME!" she shouts loud enough for it to cause him to start. He half turns the laptop in her direction, but not enough for her to see. She sits up unsteadily and moves round. Unable to get a good view, she stands up and shuffles up to stand behind her husband.

'Look at this one, ' he says proudly. 'It's coming straight at the camera. It's a beauty.' His wife is silent for a few moments. She stares at the dramatic, blurred cascade of spew propelling itself towards the lens. Admittedly, it is a remarkable shot. 'I think I might be able to sell these to the Discovery Channel. Look - you can even see bits of carrot, they're the orange bits next to what I assume is cream.' Mrs Bitters leans forward a little, then vomits profusely, this time upon the computer keyboard. He sweeps the machine into his hands but it's too late. Some of the vile smelling bile has already found its way inside the machine, and the screen records the ingress with a psychedelic display of colours, followed by darkness and the sound of a shorted motherboard. ''Where did that come from? I didn't think you had anything left in you. Now look what you've done! You've broken it! You'll pay for this!'

'Sue me then,' she gurgles, before rushing into the toilet to continue her grim performance.

'I might just do that,' he mutters, without an ounce of irony.

The Doctor has arrived at C290. He knocks cautiously on the door. Sure enough, the savage with the stick answers.

'Mr Turdo?'

'No, it's T-Y-R-D-E-O, pronounced Trudeau.' The Doctor looks at his notes and concludes this claimed pronunciation is an act of self delusion, but he lets it go.

'I'm the ship's doctor.'

'Well, you've come to the wrong place. I didn't call you and we're fine.' Mr Tyrdeo starts to close the door.

'Um, I know you're fine, but it's not really about your health, sir. It's about something you're doing which is making other people ill.'

'Me? I think you'll find you're very much mistaken, ' retorts Tyrdeo, in his plummy Hampshire accent. In fact, I take particular precautions to quarantine myself and my wife from whatever viral booby traps may lie in wait in the public places.' The doctor decides a more assertive tone may be necessary.

'It's about that which I've come to see you. We know you're pressing the buttons on the lift with your stick.'

'Of course I am. What sane person would not? Those buttons are covered with infection. Hundreds of unwashed fingers jabbing at them hour after hour. It's an infection powder keg waiting to explode. In fact quite a large proportion of our neighbours are already afflicted. Only the wheelchair users who never press the buttons seem to have escaped this curse.'

'The thing is Mr TREAU-deau, you're causing the curse. You're putting the infections there. With your stick.' Mr Tyrdeo looks woundedly at the doctor.

'How very dare you! I don't know how you have the gall to stand there and accuse me of waging what amounts to biological warfare against people I am proud to call my friends. But let's not play games. We both know why you're here so don't take me for a fool, doctor.'

'Which is why exactly?' The doctor is genuinely curious now.

'You're here about the fact I haven't been using the disinfectant hand wash, aren't you?' The doctor is taken aback by this surprise confession.

'Really?'

'Come, come doctor. We both know that the hand wash is simply a way to continue to administer some kind of sedative to the guests - to make us easy to control. Well, with me you've picked the wrong chap!' The doctor looks past the stick man at his wife, who stands behind him blankly. She looks heavily sedated herself. He turns back to Stick Man. It's such a silly thing to say that the doc decides to ignore it.

'Please don't use your stick to press the buttons any more. It's really an order from the Captain.'

'Who are YOU to tell me that,' rattles Stick Man. 'I've paid for this trip and I can continue to do whatever I bloody well like. You, on the other hand, think you know it all about health just because you're a so-called 'qualified doctor'. Well, it doesn't rub with me. Statistically, people are more likely to die because they go to see a GO than they would be if they continued to stay at home.' The doctor is at a loss to respond convincingly without being rude.

'Um, that may have been the case 200 years ago, but I think you'll find medicine has come a long way since then. ' Stick Man looks sneeringly over is shoulder at his wife, who continues to look sedated.

'Hark at him!' Then he looks back. 'We only have your word for that. Besides, even if it were true, it's no substitute for common sense. I shall continue to act according to my own best judgement and will continue to do so whatever you continue to say to me.' The doctor recalls that his mother used to warn him never to trust a man who uses the same verb more than twice in a single sentence.

'Um, yes you can, sir but not on this ship. I have to tell you that if you insist on continuing with this practice, we will continue with plans to have to unload you at the next port.' The doctor smiles, and feels the authority of the Captain seeping through his words into the obstinate head of his adversary. The absence of an immediate reply further suggests to the doctor that he has finally got through to Mr Tyrdeo. 'If you feel at all ill please do contact me on 999. Don't leave your cabin, I'll come to you. Thank you for your co-operation.' Mr Tyrdeo shuts the door without another word. The doc stands there a little longer, knowing that he is being watched through the spyhole in the door. Then he gives a little wave and walks off, knowing the Stick of Death has been tamed.

'He showed resistence,' reports the doctor to the Captain. 'Quite a tricky character actually, if you ask me. Uses the word 'continue' too much when he gets angry.'

'Will he behave himself henceforth?'

'Yes, he will if you make an announcement. Make him squirm, Sir.' Bladder looks out at the sea and considers the sacrifices he has made in pursuit of his first love.

'Yes. It seems to me that this Turdo chap is as bad as any savage with a spear. Except that the savage with a spear tends to only be able to harm one personat a time. Mr Turdo has replaced this old fashioned method with his shit tipped walking stick which, by comparison, is a weapon of mass infection. What's wrong with these people,' mutters Bladder, mainly to himself. Then he turns to the doctor. 'I'll make the announcement now. And I'm not going to pull any punches.'

All across the ship, the tannoy crackles into life. 'Good afternoon, ladies and gentlemen, Bladder here, your Captain. I hope you are all having a pleasant sea day. But enough of the small talk. I have an important announcement to make about health and I must ask you to stop what you're doing, even in the whist drive, for a few moments and give me your full attention. As you may be aware, we are constantly striving to ensure your continued good health aboard the ship. It has been brought to our attention that a rather questionable practice has crept into the behavior of one or two guests. People have been pressing the buttons on the lifts with the end of their walking sticks. Unfortunately, this can have the effect of depositing dog crap on the buttons. That can make others ill. So if you see anybody doing this, especially in the aft of the ship on Deck Nine, please tell them to stop – or tell a member of the crew. And if you've done it before, then don't do it again. Thank you and whatever you choose to do on board for the rest of the day, wash your hands.' The captain takes his finger off the button and looks at the doctor. 'How did I do?' The doc searches for words.

'Yes, captain. Short of actually naming Mr Turdo you couldn't have said it any more directly. Is it company policy to use the word 'crap' in an announcement?'

'Crap? They're lucky. I was a breath of saying shit and bollocks. So, if they don't like it, let them put it on a feedback form.' Generally, any kind of expletive language is forbidden to staff, and the doc wonders if there will be complaints. Even as he stands there the phone rings. The captain picks it up. He listens for a minute and then responds.

'Put him through... yes, it's Bladder.' Bladder listens for a moment. 'Mr Turdo, yes I DID use strong language in my announcement. But then again, you've been spreading dog shit around the ship. Which is worse?' More talking from the other end. 'Alright Sir, I'll give you a choice. Either stop doing it or I'll charge you for every case we get in the sick bay. Let's put it at, say, 120 pounds per person shall we? In which case you already owe the firm just short of five thousand pounds. What's it to be Turdo? Trudeau then – but my pronunciation doesn't alter your options. Give me a call within the hour if you don't agree. Unless I hear from you I'll assume you're going to comply. But if you persist in your disgusting habit, my next announcement will name you in person. Good afternoon.' And with that the Captain puts the phone down and looks at the doctor. 'was that alright?'

'Um, courageous, sir.'

'Well, it's my last cruise. There's only so much I'm willing to put up with. If I could unload him, then I would. All the same, I've got a duty of care to the nice ones. Turdo isn't one of them, by the sound of it.'

'I'd say it's advantage A&G, captain.' Bladder pauses.

'Not really, doctor – just the containment of another prat intent on spoiling it for everyone else through his own selfishness. If he does it again, I've half a mind to urinate on his doorway myself. But I won't do it – only because I don't want to cause the extra trouble for the cleaning staff.' And with that, the Captain thanks the doctor and returns to his weather charts.

As the doctor walks along the corridor towards the aft end of the ship, he sees the same objectionable lady who insisted on using the lift approaching with her husband. She lifts an accusatory finger at the doctor and stops in the centre of the corridor, blocking his way.

'I saw what you did. You poked the button with a pencil. Captain says people like you are spreading infection. I'm going to report you.'

It's early morning and Dave is snoring again. Trev doesn't like it when Dave snores. Dave reminds him of a girlfriend he once had who sounded like a horse when she was sleeping. He looks at Dave with his open mouth and tomato red face and imagines that this is what a guppy fish would look like in a bed, though it must be said he's never seen a guppy fish.

Trev climbs over Dave and goes for a pee. He peers at his face in the mirror. He looks old – at least 35, and wonders if the salt sea air is causing the aging process to accelerate. Returning to the room, he looks disapprovingly down at Dave.

'Get up, mate.' Dave shows no sign of moving. Trev returns to the bathroom with a wine glass and fills it with tepid water. Then he returns to the bed and puts one of Dave's fingers, which are hanging over the dies of the bed, into the glass. Dave opens his eyes.

'What are you doing, Trev?' Dave realizes his finger is submerged and retracts it so suddenly that some of the water spill sonto the duvet. 'What did you do that for?!' grumbles Dave, his eyes peering out from sunburnt, hungover bags which are puffing up his face. Trev shakes his head a little.

'Someone told me that if you put a sleeping person's finger in water, then they'll wet themselves.'

'That's stupid, Trev.' Trev points at the wet patch on the bed.

'No it's not – look at that.' Dave sits up a bit and inspects the spreading wet patch on the bed. Then hi lifts the duvet and looks in.

'That's bollocks. That's the water you just spilt from the glass. Leave me alone, I'm still drunk.'

'Ah come on, mate. We're wasting every day like this and I want to explore. We're in a port today. Let's go and do something useful.'

'What like? Drink? That's all we ever do. There are no girls on board. Just you me and Captain Morgan. It's crap.' Dave tries to shrink back in under the duvet – but Trev whips it off the bed to reveal that dave has a mild erection.

'Dave! That's disgusting!'

'It's not my fault. Your stupid water experiment probably did that. Anyway, give me the duvet.' In the following scuffle Trev gives up and hands it back, not least because he feels slightly intimidated by Dave's aroused state. Instead, trev tries a different tack.

'Don't you want to have a look around?'

'Around where?'

'The port – Madras. We can have a curry. Maybe we can sneak onto one of the excursions for free and have a real good look around.' Dave emerges from underneath the duvete.

'You mean like an adventure?'

'Yeah, and we can get a curry too.' The two lads spend some time chewing over the possibilities, and the idea of getting something for nothing finally convinces Dave to emerge from his supine condition.

Up on the Bridge, the Captain is overseeing the docking procedure which is proceeding without incident.

'All stop,' he announces, and the vast power of the vessel is released from its propulsion duties. The Captain looks out at the sun soaked dawn. 'Ahoy the Tomatoes.' This is the phrase Bladder uses for guests who expose themselves to dangerously high amounts of solar radiation, in a bid to become browner than people who don't originate from the Home Counties. 'Why would a racist want a tan?'

'I'm sorry Sir,' asks First Officer Ward, who had been only half listening to Bladder, but who equally recognized the change in tone which indicated a question.

'Why would a racist want a tan, Ward? I mean, they spend half their lives objecting to the colour of a person's skin, and the other half of it trying to look like people they'd probably call 'darkies.' It doesn't make sense to me.'

'What, the sunbathing, Captain?'

'No, the hypocrisy. It's the contradiction that I find objectionable.

I once met a woman who told me she didn't like the Indian guests – but the thing is, she was darker skinned than the people she was whinging about.'

'Dare I ask what you said, Sir?'

'I told her to take a look in the mirror and that she should try not to hate anyone paler than she was.'

'What did she say?'

'Nothing to me. But she made a complaint to Head Office. They sent me a copy of it with a post it note saying 'keep up the good work. I think she had a reputation for complaining. Silly woman. Ironically, her surname was something like Cadogo. Doesn 't sound all that Hampshire to me.'

Trev and Dave have hatched a brilliant plan, borne directly out of the fact that they are still relatively inebriated from the night before. Dave has made it worse by brushing his teeth using swigs from a flat, half empty can of Fosters he found next to the bed. When he's finished he returns to find trev already dressed in a black T-Shirt with 'Stud Muffin' in white letters on the front.

'Are you going to wear that all day, mate,' inquires Dave.

'Why not, mate? It's true you know. And everything else stinks now. I think we should find out where the washing machines are, mate. When we get back.' Dave reaches out to offer Trev a drink from the warm Fosters can.

'Fancy a gulp? It's a bit rank but waste not, want not.' Trev looks suspiciously at the can.

'Where did you get that? Was it by the bed?' Dave nods, as he consumes another mouthful. 'Er, that's piss.' Dave sprays it out across the bed and over Trev. 'Dave! Have some manners, mate!'

'Manners? You're the one who's been pissing into lager cans because you're too lazy to walk four feet to the loo. That's disgusting.' Dave looks forlornly down at the can. 'I suppose under the circumstances that tasted surprisingly nice.

It's 0900 and guests are streaming down the gangway to the waiting buses. Trev and Dave are amongst them, casually implementing their brilliant plan, which is to sneak onto one of the excursion buses when nobody is looking. There are nine buses in total, and most of them have attendants who are carefully checking the tickets. They wonder between the vehicles looking for an opportunity.

'Dave!' whispers Trev urgently. 'That one, now!' Sure enough, right at the back of the fleet, a solitary bus sits unattended. Others are drifting on, apparently unchecked by Dogger staff. Dave and Trev look furtively round, and scamper as fast as they can towards the bus, merging into a dozen others mounting the steps. Within a few moments, they're seated at the back of the bus, grinning with a sense of achievement.

'Which tour do you think this is?' muses Dave.

'Dunno. Doesn't matter. It's free!' As the buses leave one by one, theirs remains steadfastly on the quayside. Presently, the portly driver wonders across with an officially dressed lady and not without difficulty steps aboard, seats himself at the font and starts the bus. After a few words in a language neither Trev nor Dave understand, they're off in pursuit of adventure and a free lunch. Dave cracks open a couple of cans which is a minor mistake, as they both belch acidly as they down their first mouthfuls. 'Madras here we come!' beams Trev.

Outside the bus, the sun soaked streets of Madeira flit past in light and shade, as the driver puts on some traditional music which serves to immerse the interior of the bus in an authentic Madieran spirit. They're on top of things and feel that, at last they're beginning to get the hang of the cruising experience.

Although neither of them remember falling asleep, Dave and Trev both wake up to the sound of silence. Dave is seized with the double challenge of a raging thirst and an irresistible need to go to the loo. The bus is empty. Outside, there is a vast orchard of vegetation the like of which neither of them has seen before.

'What time is it, Trev?' He grabs Trev's arm and looks at the watch. 'It's 11am! We've been asleep for hours! Where are we?' Trev runs his hands through his hair and gets up. He wobbles for a moment and then gropes his way to the front of the bus, where the driver is busy dozing underneath a local newspaper. Trev touches his arm, cuasing him to wake with a start and instantly confine Trev in a bone jarring arm lock. 'Oi, that hurts mate!' As soon as he hears the English language, the driver lets go.

'I ah sorry, Senor. In army manys years.' Trev ruds his arm more petulantly that is credible, making the driver feel a great deal better instantly.

'Where's the tour? Where are we?' The driver, now feeling the attractions of sleep overcoming and sense of remorse says something in his local tongue and points towards a shack about 30 metres from the bus. Trev mutters something like, 'thank euro,' in the way that British people do when caught between the logic of sticking to English and pretending they have a rudimentary grasp of a foreign language. 'Oi, Dave, get up,' he shouts down the bus. Dave is lying across the back seat and moves only slowly to an upright position. He considers arguing with Trev but decides this is an unwinnable dispute.

As they walk across towards the shack, Dave queries their situation.

'What exactly, is this tour, mate, do you think?' Trev, who is equally mystified, feels an urgent need to look in control.

'It's an economic tour of the country. This is where the Madrasians make the ingredients.'

'Ingredients for what?'

'Madras. It's a fruit.'

'I thought madras was a chicken.'

'Well, it's a chicken and a fruit. It' unique to the area, probably. We'll be going to see the chickens later.'

'Really? Are you sure?'

'It's what the country's famous for. Of course we will.' Dave looks at the unintelligible sign above the entrance to the shack. 'Is that Indian then? Are we in India?' Trev tuts.

'No, we're in Madras, obviously.' And with that he goes in. Inside, an old man is sitting behind a small desk, rolling what looks like an enormous cigarette. The shack smells strongly of smoke and is at a stifling temperature. Without stopping is preparation, he looks up at the two boys, and says something with a calmness and confidence which reassures the two lads.

'We don't speak, er, Madrasian.' The man raises an eyebrow and nods understandingly. He rises and shuffles to the door, pointing across to a distant corner of the orchard where wisps of dust are rising from unseen feet. 'Thanks amigo,' says Trev and with that they march off in the direction of the rest of the party.

The newlyweds have decided not to go on a tour. They're wandering around the streets of Madeira looking for a place to hold hands and be in love with each other.

'Oh, my husband, isn't this romantic.'

'Yes, it very much is romantic, and so nice to have a bit of time off the ship, don't you think. It's just us and each other! And that's our place.' He points at the entrance to a delightful looking tavern, with a sign outside saying 'Ful English Beekfast, bear gareden at our back. Welcome'

They seat themselves at a table in the milky noonday sun, and order a bottle of the local white wine. As they hold hands, they feel an overwhelming sense of togetherness and freedom from all their cares. They hear a familiar voice.

'Mind if we join you?' It is the unmistakable lilt of Mr Bitters, who has dressed for their on shore excursion in a pair of faded flaired blue jeans and an oversize T-shirt which has a picture of a Mister Man and the caption 'Mr Happy'. Next to him Mrs Bitters is wearing a sombrero and a kind of smock which makes her look the shape of a triangle. The newly weds nod without expression, for the arrival of Mr and Mrs Bitters is akin to the experience of having your grandmother walk into the bedroom while you are making love. The subtle disappointment is utterly lost on the twosome who now settle themselves down opposite Susan and Douglas.

'I don't think much of this place, do you,' says Mr Bitters with a tone that doesn't invite a response. 'I mean, it's impossible to enjoy a place this hot. I invariably sweat and then I'm thirsty. They wouldn't even give us a glass of water.' Douglas intervenes.

'Would you like me to get you a glass of water.' Mr Bitters shakes his head and looks at the bottle already on the table.

'Not really, I was hoping you would offer us a glass of your wine.' Mrs Bitter interjects.

'After all, that amount of alcohol isn't good for people your age, trying for a baby and that. It can make you impotent you know.' Douglas and Susan look uncertianly at each other. 'We're not scroungers you know. It's just that we haven't got any of the local currency and it seems a waste to change money when you just have to change it back at the end of the day.

The next half hour goes very slowly. Mr Bitters takes a long time explaining how the last time they came to what he insists on calling 'murderer' they got food poisoning and had to sit in the restaurant for a while afternoon before they got any compensation. Mrs Bitters adds her own unique flavor to the conversation by describing a dog which ate part of a sandwich in her handbag, leading to an altercation with the owner that only ended after they persuaded him to buy them a baguette and give them a lift back to the ship. By the time the bottle is empty, both Susan and Douglas feel a sense of injustice. Spurred on by the solitary glass of wine he has enjoyed from the bottle, Douglas makes a brave move.

'Mr Bitters, I rather feel you have stolen from us a precious moment in our afternoon. If you don't mind, we'll be leaving now.' Mr Bitters misses the point completely.

'I have no problem with that at all. Once you settle up with the barman, we can go and have a look at some of the shops.' Douglas waves to the barman with a credit card.'

'Oh, very flash!' moans Mrs Bitters, in the way people do when they wish to deride another's success on the basis of envy. The barman indicates that Douglas must go inside to pay with his card.

'Come on Susan, let's pay inside.' Without acknowledging Mr and Mrs Bitters, for fear of raising suspicions, Douglas wanders into the tavern casually, closely followed by Susan. Inside, he thrusts the necessary Euros into the barman's hand and whispers, 'keep the change.' With that Douglas takes Susan's hand and hauls her out of the tavern and up the street. Once a safe distance from the hostelry, he turns left and looks pensively back at the route they've just taken.

'Those people. I just can't see how they can live with themselves, let alone anyone else.'

'Do you think we'll ever be like that, Douglas?' inquiries Susan with flicker of worry.

'I very much doubt it, my darling. Unless you're planning to become some kind of scrounging anti-social zombie. Is that your plan?'

'Not really, Douglas. Having said that, perhaps those two were nice once, and became like that. Why do you think they even got married to each other?'

'So that two people could be miserable instead of four. Come on, let's get another bottle and sit somewhere they'll never find us – like anywhere that costs money.'

Monty and Mrs Major are sitting on a white wall as Mr and Mrs O'Jitters shuffle past.

'Hello thre old boy,' mutters Monty, wiping his brow as his wife looks in her large canvas bag for their bottle of tepid drinking water. 'Bit of a scorcher, eh?' Mr O'Jitters indicates assent.

'Aye. We've really only got off to buy a few postcards. The missus likes to send them back as a record of what we've seen.' Monty responds skeptically.

'Doesn't really work that way though, does it, old boy? I mean, you'll probably purchase a card with a pretty shot of a mountain or a beach you haven't even visited. If you were being totally honest, then you'd buy a picture of something like the local Burger King or a bus stop they used for the tour vehicle.' Mr O'Jitters shrugs and realizes his wife has maintained a steady pace towards the souvenir shop at the end of the street.

'I'b better catch up with the missus, like.' And with that he moves off. Monty inspects the dusty bleached buildings.

'This place hasn't changed much since the war. Never took itself seriously enough to do any proper fighting. If they had, then I imagine we'd have been able to get rid of all this and replace it with something more in keeping with Britain.' Mrs Major has finished with the water.

'So, Monty, would you have built here instead – a pub or a graffiti covered brick wall?'

'Let's see if we can find a shop which sells ice cream,' says Monty, realizing that once again he's out in the midday sun.

'Do you think all the excursions are like this?' Dave has just finished collecting another basketful of grapes from in the vineyard, and is sunburn is beginning to sting his forehead.

'No, I think the older people probably just get to ride about in the buses. I just think we got lucky.' Dave looks cautiously at the other people on the excursion, none of whom he recognizes from the ship. There's a couple of elderly ladies wearing headscarves, four children under 12 and a large contingent of men ranging from 60 to 85 years old. None of them speak English, but some of them are singing an uplifting ditty in their funny language.

'Why do they all speak Madras?' Trev has been wondering the same thing, but daren't admit it.

'Because it's a themed excursion, mate. This is the traditional way they used to collect grapes for the wine and that.' Dave looks at their fellow pickers again.

'But we ARE collecting grapes the traditional way. We're actually doing it. Where are the other people on the excursion? I mean, we can't be the only ones. And they've all got sandwiches. Where's our lunch?' Trev looks at his watch. They've been picking grapes for over four hours now and it's getting boring. The others all seem to know each other and apart from cordial smiles at the two lads, they've more or less ignored Trev and Dave since they arrived.

'Trev, mate, this is a crap excursion. I want to go back to the ship.' Trev feels a glimmer of alarm. The ship is due to sail at 17.30 and because they were both asleep he's got no idea how long it will take to get back. He goes up to the youngest man in the group, whose wrinkled skin tells tales of endless summers under the Madeiran sun.

'Excuse me, when do we go back to the ship?' The man looks at Trev blankly, and then laughs happily, patting Trev on the back, before saying something jovial which makes the others laugh. 'The ship – when do we go back to the ship?' Trev makes a wave like gesture, which initially confuses the man, who then concludes Trev is talking about the landscape. He nods and points at a distant hill, gesticulating as if riding a horse, to the amusement of the rest of the group. Trev looks at Dave. 'I'm not getting anywhere here. Let's go back to the bus.'

They arrive at the bus to find the driver fast asleep and snoring peacefully under the same newspaper he'd buried himself in hours earlier. Wary of his rapier like response earlier, he taps on the open door. The driver stirs lazily and looks at his watch.

'Excuse me, mate, we need to get back to the ship.' The man checks his watch again. Pointing at its faded face, he shakes his head and speaks in words utterly foreign to Trev and Dave. Trev takes the initative. 'Look, we sail at 5,30 – look FIVE THIRTY' – Trev shows this on his own watch. 'We need to go back, or we'll all miss the ship!' The man points at the number six on his watch.

'Back to then. This is when we going.' Dave pokes Trev in the back.

'Trev, I don't think this is an excursion, mate. I think we've been picking grapes. I mean for real.' Trev has come to the same catastrophic conclusion. 'Trev, what are we going to do?'

Moments later they are jogging up the drive towards what they hope will be a road. They're pouring with sweat and thirsty as hell, but the alternative is to miss the ship. Although Dave is very angry with Trev, he can't divert the energy to say so in this moment of crisis. Instead, he tries to adopt a scowling expression to display his displeasure.

At the end of the dusty drive, they find a poorly tarmacked road.

'Where are we even going? Madras? I mean which way? Up that way or down there?' They look at the clueless highway, and realize they're up the creek without a paddle. 'Trev, what are we going to do?' As they stand there, trying to figure something out, the low hum of an approaching car directs their attention to a speck in the distance.

'We've got to stop this car. It's our only hope.' Trev and Dave stand on the road preparing to forcibly flag down the vehicle. As it gets closer, they see it's a battered truck with an open back. The truck slows gently to a stop.

'Speak English, mate?' The blank expression is their response. 'To Madras? Lift to Madras.' The man looks at trev and Dave. He raises his fingers in the air and flashes them at him twice. 'Twenty?' Trev reflects the gesture. The man nods. 'Twenty Kilometres?'

'Euro.'

'You want 20 Euro for the lift?' The man nods and raises his fingers again. Trev looks uncertainly at Dave, who looks like he's going to cry.

'Ah, Trev mate, he's ripping us off! This is a nightmare!'

'Dave it's our only hope. Trev nods and tries to get in the car, but the man instantly locks the doors and holds out his hand. 'You want the money now?'

'Si.' Trev feels he has no cards to play. He shuffles around in his wallet and gives the man two 10 Euro notes. The man accepts it, smiles and points to the back. Dave moves round to join him, causing the driver to beep his horn twice. Dave looks in to see the man repeating the 20 Euro gesture.

'Trev he wants 20 for me too!' The man revs the engine slightly. 'Trev, lend us a tenner, mate.'

Having paid they climb into the back of the truck and look down in horror. The vehicle has clearly been used to transport some kind of manure product and fluid slurry forms a runny pond across the floor. As the man drives off, they both lose their balance and find themselves slithering in the noxious effluent without control.

The journey is in fact over an hour in duration. By the time they enter what they assume to be the town their ship is docked at, they are both covered with cow dung. Trev taps on the window behind the driver's head, and draws the shape of a ship using fingers covered in slurry. The man nods and carries on along a road which appears to follow the shoreline.

'How's he know we want to go to the ship, Trev?'

'He doesn't. I guess he's taking us to where the bus always goes from.'

Sure enough, presently they arrive on the quayside. They hop out of the back and with a toot the man is gone. So is the ship. Trev and Dave stand angst ridden at the sight of the stern a good half mile from the dock.

'Ah, Trev, what do we do now?' Trev looks at the vanishing hind of the ship and feels that sens in his stomach people get when a precious vase is falling to the ground. 'Trev, what do we do now?'

'Pray for a miracle, mate. Pray for a miracle.' And at that moment a miracle advances towards them.

'You on ship, senor?' Trev and Dave spin round. A man is pointing out to sea. 'You ship, no?' They both nod. 'You want back on ship?' Again, they nod. The man in grubby, oil covered overalls smiles politely and points to another vessel alongside the quay. 'Come, please.' They follow him to the tug. As they approach, they realize it's not a tug, but the pilot boat, preparing to collect the local navigator from the Spirit of Dogger V once it has arrived at the open sea. Trev looks across at Dave.

'A miracle, Dave, mate, a miracle.' They prepare to step onto the boat, but the engineer looks furtively around before raising his hand. 'One hunred please.' Trev is momentarily stunned.

'A hundred Euros!?'

'Each please.' Again, the engineer looks over his shoulder and now extends his hand towards Trev.

'That's all we've got! No way.' The engineer shrugs and prepares to board the ship without them.

'No negotiate.'

'Okay, Okay.' Trev digs deep and knowing that dave is cleaned out, hands over 200 Euros to the scruffy engineer. The man counts the money and smiles.

'Welcome here on board. Please, please.' They're ushered onto the boat and stand awkwardly on the deck, waiting for movement. The engineer vanishes into the bowels of the ship, and moments later a great puff of marine diesel smoke announces the departure of the pilot boat.

'That was a bit steep, Trev mate. Thanks for paying.'

'No worries, mate. We had to get back on.' They charge across the bay towards the Dogger and for a few minutes Trev and Dave are lifted by the exhilaration of the ride. As they pull up alongside the great ship, they both experience a sense of angst about the transfer from small boat to large ship. They've worried in vain. With an action carried out thousands of times before, the two lads are assisted off their little transport into the side of the huge vessel. An officer checks them in fills in a form, says goodbye to the pilot and looks at the lads.

'Judging by your sunburn being late's going to be the least of your problems.' Dave blushes but doesn't change colour at all.

'Sorry, Officer,' offers Trev. 'But we paid the price – I mean 200 euros for a 10 minute ride.' The officer's jaw drops.

'You paid them for that did you?' The officer shakes his head despairingly. Trev feels his wallet involuntarily and imagines the engineer laughing all the way back to the quayside. He looks at Dave who rolls his eyes towards the heavens. Trev turns to the Officer.

'Do you think we can get the money back? At all? Do you think? Officer?' The officer puts his hand on Trevor's shoulder.

'Ah, no. I think you should just put it down to experience. And next time? Don't be late. Whatever you choose to do on board this evening, just be grateful you're on board, eh?' Trev nods.

'Point taken. And thanks.'

'Upstairs at the Pennance Bar, Trev and Dave review their day over a couple of pints of lager.

'Look at my face, Trev. I look like a tomato!' He pats his face in an accidentally comical way. Trev stares at his friend's ruddy complexion and searches for reassuring words.

'I'm sorry, you're right Dave, mate. We really cocked up today, didn't' we? I mean, we spent 240 Euros to pick grapes for some wine company in Madras!'

'Maderia, mate. It's Madiera. It's not India at all, mate. It's part of France. That's probably why they've got all those grapes. I think.' Trev and Dave look quietly into their lagers.

'240 Euros. There was an excursion to a winery that cost 60 Euros each. We've rally cocked up today, mate.' Dave raises his glass to Trev.

'But we're here mate. Still on the ship. And somewhere in the world people will drink wine from grapes we picked with our own hands. Ha! When you think about it, that's been a funny day.' Trev smiles for the first time in hours.

'What language were they speaking then? '

'Two languages, mate. Rip off and French. And we deserved both of them.'

'Here's to Madras.'

'Cheers to Madeers, mate!'

And as the lights of Madeira fade into the night, Trev and Dave vow never again to stray from the safety of organized tours, courtesy of A&G. It's a commitment that will be blown apart by events in the days ahead. But for now, Trev and Dave lean their mental heads on the bosom of the Spirit of Dogger V. And the ship embraces them as a mother would embrace errant children whose main offences are an eye for a bargain and an endearing commitment to misunderstanding everything to do with that which is not English.

Chapter 16 :
My Beautiful Launderette

Violet Cryer has been cruising for decades. At the start, she tolerated the endless sunshine and beautiful views as a tedious and unavoidable element of ocean life. Then she discovered the miracle of the launderette. For reasons which are not obvious to the uninitiated, the launderette is the centre of a ship's communication system. People who, like Violet, have tired of yet another monotonous passage through the Panama Canal, or sink with the dullness of Manhattan, find sanctuary in the launderette, where they are able to create their own fantastic stories of who did what with whom and when in the soothing comfort of a steam filled cubicle all their own. This is the news factory – and she who controls the news controls the ship.

At least that's how Violet sees it. Others hold a different view. They regard an obsession with living in the windowless heat of 20 washing machines and dryers is an act of insanity, comparable only to their willingness to pay thousands of pounds for the privilege. They compare Violet's residence in the launderette as having a vampire-like quality, her skin artificially white in the strip-lit sterility of her chosen environment.

Violet has even carefully selected which launderette to inhabit. It's on Deck 5 – diagonally across from the Entertainment Director's office. Although this requires her to walk a long distance – her own cabin is on Deck 8 and at the far end of the ship – it's an effort eminently worth making. For this is the perfect viewing post to observe the comings and goings of the Ents team – and to record vital data such as the arrival and departure of entertainers, who's complaining and whether there's been an injury in the dance troupe. Her knowledge of ship borne matters is therefore effectively complete, for that which she doesn't know she can easily make up. Given the hunger for tittle tattle, her speculations are hungrily absorbed into the zeitgeist of the ship's population and, on occasions, even transported to land through the miracle of modern communication.

Today, Violet has a particular task. She has come to the view that the dramatic incidents which occurred in the Medusa Restaurant, leading to the death and apparent reincarnation of one Mr Morgan have a deeper meaning. It's been on her mind ever since her dramatic humiliation – in her own eyes at least – when the Captain appeared to raise Morgan from the dead in front of over 1,000 people. Violet has worked out the truth, and is just about to start sharing it.

'Hello Violet,' says Celia who's seen her on other ships at different times. 'How are you today?' Violet looks out of the door furtively.

'I'm fine, in fact, I'm a lot better than one other so called human I could name.' Her compatriot's eyes widen.

'You know the man who died in the restaurant? The one the Captain apparently brought back to life? Well he didn't. The thing is, that man – Morgan's his name – isn't what he seems.'

'No.'

'Very much yes, my dear. And do you know how I know that? Because there was no way he could have raised the dead just like that.'

'So how come he's alive – that Morgan?'

'He isn't. Morgan's still dead. He's a zombie.'

'How do you know?'

'Well think about it. He died in the restaurant, in front of lots of people. They took him to the on board morgue, and there he would have remained if panic hadn't started about that deadly virus. Then the Captain mysteriously has Morgan's body removed from the morgue and taken to the theatre. How can you freeze a living person without killing him, and then bring him back to life? The answer is: you can't.' Her friend is absorbing all of this. Celia feels compelled to ask another question of Violet Cryer.

'So what is he now?'

'He is part of the un-dead. Dead but walking around as if he's alive. I bet his skin is ice cold and that he has lost all of his personality. He's like a ghost in a body. And there's only one place that can happen – here.'

'In the launderette?'

'No, up ahead – in the Bermuda Triangle. That's why we've come this way. And do you know something else? Morgan isn't a Mister.

He's a Captain. Captain Morgan. He's here to do some kind of swap with the other Captain. I think they're trying to turn this into some kind of ghost ship.'

'Why on earth would they want to do that, Violet?' Violet shakes her head slowly.

'I don't know. But I'm going to find out – this evening at the Captain's reception.'

'I'm going to that too. Thanks so much for filling me in. This really is a very frightening situation.'

And so Violet Cryer spreads the news and by the afternoon rumours of a ghost captain are spreading from bow to stern.

Jack and Jane Jitters are on deck, drinking the non-alcoholic 'Mocktail of the Day,' called 'Barbados Breezer.' It's a delightful, creamy taste and Jack feels lifted and happy with the drink, the weather and his loving wife.

'This is lovely isn't it Jane?' Jane doesn't reply immediately.

'Ah, yes it is – isn't that the man who fell onto our balcony?'

'Where? Oh yes, I do believe it is. Oh, he's coming over.' Captain Morgan approaches the couple with a cold beer in his right hand. He changes hands and offers it to Mr Jitters.

'Sir, I just wanted to thank you for helping me out yesterday when I, er, landed on your balcony. I'd had quite a flight and was lucky not to get hurt. I am sorry.'

'Oh, don't worry at all Captain Morgan. These things happen,' says Mr Jitters, realising that if they do, they don't happen often. 'Anyway, we're glad you're alright.' And with that Morgan makes his excuses and leaves. 'What a pleasant fellow. Poor man. Obviously troubled.' Mr Jitters is aware of a lady fast approaching from the othe side of the deck.

'You don't know me, I'm Celia, and sorry for the intrusion, but I was just wondering if you might be able to tell me something which may sound a bit odd. That person you just shook hands with – was his hand warm or cold.' Jack doesn't understand why this is important, but nor does he see a reason not to answer.

'Well, I suppose it was quite, um, cold really. Very cold in fact.' Celia's eyes widen.

'Did he seem strange in any way?'

'Not as strange as yesterday, when he landed on our balcony and we had to let him back into the ship.' Celia is even more surprised by this.

'Where did he land from?'

'Up there, he came down from above us.' Celia needs no further clarification. So Violet Cryer was right. He's ice cold and, on top of it all, has descended to the ship from some other worldly location. She scurries off to report back to Violet in the launderette.

'What was that all about,' asks Jane.

'Jane, I have no idea. You know, his hand was only cold because he's been holding that beer. Some people ask the strangest questions.' Jack is mainly thinking about something else. 'Do you think anyone's going to come to our marriage renewal?'

'Oh I don't know dear. I do hope so, but really, I'm not doing it for them. I'm doing it for us.' She looks at Jack, a man who has been a huge part of her life for all of her adult life. No, more than that. He has been her life – and their children and grandchildren are their quiet contribution to the world. 'Jack, as long as you're there – as long as you're always there, then I'm going to be alright.' She leans forward and squeezes his hand. At that moment, they are at the centre of everything.

Chapter 17 :
Bride's head revisited

As lunch becomes afternoon, Captain Bladder looks despondently at his itinerary. He has to remarry an elderly couple. This is usually tolerable but he finds the false emotions difficult.

'The problem with these events is they're normally just a sham. You know, one partner wants to leave, the other makes her go on a cruise to try and breath life into something with the emotional robustness of a wet paper bag. I don't even know why we offer this service.' Ward doesn't share the Captain's scepticism.

'That's a bit negative Captain, perhaps even a trifle cynical if I may say so.'

' A cynic is is someone who's never disappointed. I'm frequently disappointed which means I'm neither a cynic nor wrong about people's motives for these things. But the Line demands it and so it shall be done. Come with me Ward. One day you're going to have to do this yourself.' Ward agrees to attend.

Captain Bladder and the relevant crew make their way to the small chapel – the location for today's ceremony. When he arrives there are 10 people in the room. An elderly couple dressed in their best formal clothes, and eight onlookers in various states of humour. Six of them seem excited and happy to be there. Two look like they've turned up for a funeral.

This is the day Jack and Jane Jitters have come on board for – to renew their original vows.

'Oh Jack, I'm actually really nervous. I feel like I've got the head and heart of a young bride all over again. I do hope I don't make an error.'

'Don't worry dear Jane – it doesn't matter if you do. I know we are going to have a delightful ceremony with our friends here.

Bladder goes through the wording he always uses for the ceremony. As the two life long lovers kiss, Monty pipes up.

'Look, those two even kiss in a Northern Irish accent!'

Mr Bitters jumps up.

'This is pathetic. Nobody really believes this is real, do they?' Jack and Jane look at each other in shock and then at the Bitters duo. 'How can this ceremony have any crebility? What right do you have to claim any knowledge of love just because you're the captain of a cruise ship? It makes me angry to see the institution of marriage reduced to a reality show for the benefit of Dinner Table 64.' There is an awkward pause, as Jack and Jane try to make sense of the bitter outburst. The Captain steps forward.

'Sir, never in my long and sometimes arduous seafaring career have I met two individuals as singularly objectionable as your good selves. I have performed this ceremony innumerable times, and I believe I am qualified to make a judgement on these matters. Demeaning the affections of others will not give you a love you never had yourself. I suggest that you take a long hard look at your own relationship and, if I may be so bold, ask yourselves: where did it all go wrong. As far as I am concerned – and I do not say this lightly – Mr and Mrs Jitters have what every person craves: a love which lasts a lifetime.' The others in the room erupt into applause, rather to Captain Bladder's surprise. As the room settles, Mr and Mrs Bitters are gone. Bladder turns to Mr and Mrs Jitters. 'Now, young lovers, I wouldn't normally do this, but under the circumstances and if you would allow me, it would be my honour to show you the bridge.' Ward watches the shocked reaction of Jack and Jane, a couple who have never asked for a special favour in their lives.

'Captain, we would be very delighted to see that, if we won't be in the way.' Ward smiles at a man whose life experience has eroded his patience of stupidity to nothing but which has never rusted his heart of gold.

Elsewhere on board, romance is also in the air. Dr Starwalker and Mystic Maria have agreed to go for a swim in the open air pool on Deck 12. The Doctor doesn't know Maria's dark secret.

'Come on in Maria, It's really warm.'

'I can't. I just can't. I'm sorry.' Lucas looks at her strangely.

'It's perfectly safe. And shallow.' Maria squats down and beckons Lucas to swim over. 'Yes?'

'I should have told you. My brother died of rabies, and ever since I've been afraid of water every since. In fact, I'm allergic to it.'

'How can you be allergic to water? Most of you is water! Come on, get in.' She looks around nervously. I can't. I just can't, Lucas.' Lucas looks around to see if anyone's listening to the conversation. He suggests she enters the water using the ladder, slowly and carefully. Eventually, she reluctantly agrees. As she lowers herself in, she keeps stopping. After some moments, she's up to her waist. And then she starts screaming. He's right next to her and people look at him as if he's assaulted her in some nefarious fashion. He's too busy trying to help her get out to worry about that. As he's pushing her up the steps an elderly gentleman puts his hand on Lucas' shoulder.

'What did you do to her?'

'Nothing!'

'that's what they all say. Leave her alone.' Lucas stops pushing Maria up the steps, and this causes her to start screaming again. By this time everyone is watching. Following an ungainly scuffle in the pool between Lucas and the do-gooder, he finds a way to push Maria up the ladder with one hand while keeping the gent away with the other. As soon as she's out of the water, she calms down.

'Who's this man, Lucas?' the gentleman stops harassing Lucas.

'Oh, he was just trying to help.'

A few minutes later Lucas is helping Maria dry off away from the pool.

'If that's how you feel about swimming, why did you agree to it in the first place.' Maria's jaw drops.

'Because you asked me to swim with you. You didn't ask me if I'd freak out about it.' Lucas is defeated by the logic, but somehow beguiled by this irrational and warm hearted innocence – which has now caused everyone else who witnessed the incident to regard the doctor as a sexual opportunist. 'Anyway, Lucas, do you fancy a drink instead.'

'I do, but you can't have one. They're full of water – and you're allergic to that, remember?'

'Oh, Lucas, not all the time. Only when it suits me,' and she smiles in a way which baffles him in the way that female logic has baffled men of reason for centuries.

Bladder swallows hard. Although he had a pleasant time with the unassuming and courteous manner of Mr and Mrs Jitters, the

Captain's receptions are the thing his dislikes the very most. He has one this evening and there's no escape from it. It's an opportunity for all the guests to meet him and his top team. The guests cram the atrium and, as ever, Captain Bladder must say a few words and then garner applause for each of his Senior Officers. Bladder keeps it short, welcoming every on board, discussing the clement weather and then introducing the senior officers one by one. The whole process takes about 15 minutes, but despite his longing to disappear back to the relative privacy of the bridge, he knows he won't get away that lightly.

Sure enough, once he's done, the usual suspects descend upon him to ask a series of questions ranging from the odd to the ridiculous. 'Captain, how many miles per gallon does the ship do?' 'Do the crew still sleep in hammocks?' 'Do you catch the fresh fish on board?' 'Has the metric system made any difference to the performance of the ship?' 'Is the top of the ship waterproof like the bottom?' He handles each question in turn, directing some guests to other members of the senior team who are better equipped to explain the cubic capacity of the cylinders and whether the vacuum toilet system can suck a fat person's guts out.

Violet and Celia are standing at the back near a steward with drinks when Celia spots Captain Morgan holding two fresh glasses of champagne.

'There he is.' Violet spies him too. She rushes across and extends her hand.

'Hello, you must be Captain Morgan.' Morgan struggles with his two glasses and, in desperation, downs one and puts the flute on a nearby tray.

'Er yes, and you are?'

'Violet Cryer.' Their hands meet. Shock briefly wafts in and out of her expression and she withdraws her hand quickly. 'I'm told you landed on board in a rather unconventional way yesterday.' Morgan goes red.

'Oh that, I was hoping that would have been kept quiet. I did, yes, but really, I don't think I want to talk about it. It's not the sort of thing people would believe.' Violet is silent, hoping to draw out still more information. It works. 'Yes, I could have died – again so to speak! You only live twice and all that!' Violet is staring straight at him now.

'Er, I don't know you if you're aware of what happened to me the other day…?'

'Oh yes, I know all about it. Yes, yes. Now, I must go Captain, I'm so sorry.' Violet scurries back to Celia. 'He's just admitted the whole thing. He's been on some kind of flight around the Bermuda Triangle, and his hand is freezing! It's obvious he's a zombie – there was no life in those eyes at all. I'm going to confront the Captain.'

Celia and Violet edge up towards the Captain who's trying to explain why Spirit of Dogger V would not work well as a submarine. Eventually, the conversation is over and Bladder turns to Violet.

'Ladies.'

'Ah yes, Captain,' Violet draws close and grabs his arm. 'We know about Captain Morgan. But the question we're asking is: why is he here, on this ship? What's going to happen?' Bladder rolls his eyes.

'He's just a guest, like you are. He's not a Captain of this ship as such, but I understand he has had a seafaring background. In fact, I believe he's here, you may want to talk to him yourselves.'

'Yes, yes, never mind that. What is to become of him?' Bladder knows a little about Morgan's difficult personal situation but doesn't feel he should share it.

'I think we can just say he's here to find himself – as we all are. And I'm sure we will all find ourselves one way or another! Now you must excuse me and have a wonderful evening.' Bladder turns to leave only to be apprehended by Mr and Mrs Bitters who are complaining that the champagne is too flat.

'So Morgan is here to find himself. So that's where he died – the Bermuda Triangle.' Celia ponders the other part of the Captain's comments.

'And I'm sure we will all find ourselves one way or another! Where is he taking us? Violet, we need to get off this ship!'

They look across at Captain Morgan who has just managed to grab the last flute of free champagne. He waves at Violet and feels a little embarrassed at having been spotted. Morgan gestures at his drink and indicates with a finger motion across his neck that this last drink could kill him. Then he laughs, causing Violet and Celia to turn as white as ghosts.

Just before Bladder leaves, he is approached by Mr and Mrs Jitters, who are holding hands and still dressedin their 'wedding clothes.'

'We just wanted to thank you for a most wonderful day Captain,' says Jack. 'I have to say that we could not have imagined a more lovely way to celebrate our many years together – or a kinder person than you to preside over our afternoon ceremony. I know it's not much but please accept this bottle of Whiskey from us. I don't know if you drink malt whiskey, but I'm afraid we took a wild guess.' He hands it to the Captain, who is deeply touched by the unexpected gesture.

'Mr Jitters this isn't necessary at all. And it was my pleasure.' Bladder says it like he means it. 'And, as for those two rude individuals who turned up for your ceremony, please don't let them spoil your cruise. I don't really like people very much,' admits the Captain. 'But you're like normal people. You're as easy to get on with as frozen lamb - which, er, sounds a little strange, by which I mean – oh just have a great evening!' As Bladder leaves, he instructs a steward to provide the Jitters couple with two cocktails of the day: 'Angostura Bitters.'

Chapter 18 :
The Drill

As the rising sun begins to beam into his cabin, Monty is very determined to hear all of the Captain's broadcast this morning. He has tuned the television to Channel 1and Bladder's dulcet tones have just begun to bathe the ship with information.

'Mrs Major, my darling, it would be prudent to listen to this.' The announcement from the bridge indicates there will be an emergency procedures drill for the crew at 11am, and that this is a necessary part of the crew's regular training. When the explanation ends, Monty shakes his head. 'I imagine it's to do with pirates.'

'Pirates!' Exclaims Mrs Major. 'Whatever do you mean Monty?'

'Think about where we are, my dear. These islands are very, very dangerous. Any kind of scallywag and opportunist scamp can conceal their pirate ship in a balmy bay or a covert creek, waiting to pounce like wild animals on decent folk like us. As soon as they know that there's a ship full of Brits about, they'll be swarming round the Spirit of Dogger rattling their spears faster than you could say 'Achtung Schweinhund!'

'Now why would the pirates be speaking in German, darling?'

'Because a lot of war criminals came here - to escape justice after they lost the war. And don't underestimate these scoundrels. They've all changed their identities to local names - like Abdul and Hashim, but don't be fooled – a leopard can't change its spots.' Mrs Major makes a calculation.

'If they're Nazi war criminals, they'd have to be well over 80 years old. Do you honestly think they'll still be effective in the pirate world at that age?' Monty looks out across the glistening seas pensively.

'Oh yes indeed my darling, age cannot change the heart of a savage beast. Besides, because these islands are mercifully outside the so called European Union, they're not subject to the ludicrous employment legislation that would otherwise force them to retire. They can carry on being pirates for as long as they like.'

'No dear, I meant, don't you think being a pirate is a bit too physically demanding for an octogenarian?'

'With modern technology anything's possible. If you have no morals and can use an English phrasebook, you can fleece an Englishman with ease – I mean, just look at the French…'

'I hear there's a mountain in France with a U.F.O. in it.'

'I very much doubt it dear. If aliens from other worlds are smart enough to get to earth, I expect the last thing they'd want to do is land in the World's worst country. Unless, of course, their home planet is in the grip of a shortage of onions.'

In keeping with the spirit of the drills, the cruise Director is currently announcing that today's featured cocktail is called 'Man Over Board' or 'M.O.B' and consists of a potent combination of Tequila, Drambuie and a sickly sweet energy drink plus crushed ice. He exhorts guests to 'sign up to the M.O.B this afternoon.'

Trev and Dave are more hungover than usual. The Friends of Dorothy event turned out to be a blast. Although they singularly failed to convince anyone that, unlike the rest of the group, they were straight, nobody really cared. By the end of it Dave had collapsed into a peaceful stupor, as Trev finished off the night with a couple of large vodka shots and a sing song round the piano with Geoff and the others. The announcement about the drills scheduled for 11am was a muffled drone which doesn't cause them any disturbance.

Suddenly, their room is thrown into brightness – causing Trev and Dave to curse and blame each other. Then they spot their steward at the door, stalling the moment he sees the two lads sprawled unfetchingly on the bed.

'I'm very sorry sirs – it was the sign you left to make up the room. I'll call back,' and with that the room descends into a booze saturated darkness. Trev turns on the table lamp.

'Dave, mate, you must have put the do not disturb sign in upside down you plonker.' Dave responds by racing to the loo and honking up. The smell is so bad it causes Trev to want to wretch too. After short while the room has become uninhabitable, even to the likes of these likely lads. They pull on shorts and T-shirts, and shuffle out of the room. Across the way, the lady who spoke to them yesterday is leaving her room. She is visibly shocked by their appearance and volunteers assistance.

'Do you need any help, boys? Have you become ill?' Trev shakes his head.

'No, no, thanks lady. It's self induced.' She looks at them and, noticing the pungent odour now emanating from the room, makes her excuses and leaves. The steward also notices the emergence of the lads.

'Do you need a doctor, sirs?'

'No thanks, mate just the hair of the dog, I think.' They laugh gormlessly, and both realsie for the first time that their hair is mutually hilarious, and twisted into a prize-winning styles by gel and sweat. The steward responds.

'We don't have dogs on board, I'm sorry.'

'Eh?' Dave twigs. 'Oh no, it's just a phrase, mate. Sorry about the smell.'

'No problem, sir. I've had worse,' he lies.

Trev and Dave enter the Winners bar on Deck 7. There's only one other person in there, a portly fellow with a sad expression, and clearly already well on his way to the wrong side of drunk.

'Hey, Trev, that's they guy who died, isn't it?'

'Yeah, look at him now.'

'Er, I think we look like that too, Trev.' They introduce themselves and realise they have two things in common. They're all hungover, and they're all keen to drink at 10.15 in the morning. Mr Morgan has quite a story to tell, which sheds light on his recent behaviour. A former captain of a fishing vessel in Swansea, Morgan had retired to spend more time attempting to save his creaking marriage. The cruise was meant to be a 'win back' gesture, and he'd even booked them in for a renewal of their wedding vows. Just days before departure she informed him that she was very much 'casting away' from the relationship. He decided to come anyway.

'The rest is history.' Dave and Trev listen sympathetically, with Dave offering the first comfort.

'Aw, mate, that's got to be tough. Is that why you died on the ship?'

'I didn't die – apparently I threw up in the restaurant and I can't really remember anything after that, except waking up in a packed theatre full, pissed out of my head on a trolley in front of the captain. Ever since then, everyone's been calling me Lazarus.' Dave is not familiar with the reference.

'Is that the footballer?'

'No, you're thinking of Gascoigne. Lazarus is the guy who came back to life in the bible.'

'Was he hammered too?'

'Shut up Dave,' says Trev. 'Never mind, Gazzarus, here's to our new mate Captain Morgan!'

'To Captain Morgan,' echoes Dave, and in some perverse way, the retired Captian feels briefly loved. After the toast, he becomes reflective.

'Actually, it's just as well I was so drunk on stage because I tend to suffer a bit of the old 'morning glory' usually, that that would have been even more embarrassing.' Trev looks down at his pint.

'Too much information,' he mutters, but Dave carries on regardless.

'What's morning glory?' Captain Morgan looks down at his drink

'Um, it's an erection.' Dave absorbs the information.

'Trev, you get that.' Turning to Morgan he continues, 'we're sharing a bed on the ship.' Morgan shrugs.

'Well, it's more than I'm getting, you lucky buggers. Let's go out and take some holiday snaps.' This sounds like an exceedingly good idea, and they wobble off towards the deck.

The bridge is ready to operate the drill. It's a 'man overboard' drill – a vital and regularly practiced procedure which has saved lives in the past. Various factors determine the survivability of an accidental fall into the sea from a ship. These factors include the temperature of the water, roughness of the sea, speed of the ship, local ocean currents, physical stamina of the victim - and whether you get eaten by a fish. Survivability therefore ranges from good in warm, calm waters on a gently moving vessel, to virtually nil in an icy Atlantic storm.

The final preparations are just about complete for the drill. First Officer Ward makes the announcement. 'For Exercise, for exercise, for exercise – man overboard. Would Blue team proceed to forward port Deck 7.' The sirens blast and the crew swing into action. There will be a series of further announcements as the exercise proceeds.

Dave Trev and Captain Morgan are playing with a life ring, taking it in turns to hang it round their necks with Spirit of Dogger V emblazoned upon it. The pictures are terrible because none of them can hold their camera phones steadily enough to take a picture which isn't blurred. Captain Morgan is, for the first time on board, actually happy. It's his turn to be photographed. Dave tries to figure out how the device works, moaning that Blackberry phones are terrible compared to his iPhone. As trev unhelpfully helps Dave, Morgan, wearing the buoyancy ring around his waist and underhis arms, clambers up backwards to sit on the top of the railings, spilling an appreciable portion of his drink over himself in the process. At last, Dave is ready and lifts the camera phone.

'Say cheese mate,' he chirps. Morgan raises his nearly empty glass, shouts 'cheers' and falls backwards out of view. Trev and Dave look at the empty space which has just become vacant. They look at each other. Then they lunge forward to look for Morgan, who is nowhere to be seen. Then, seconds later, a bobbing form appears, already a shockingly great distance behind the ship. Dave shouts to Morgan.

'Mate, what good will that do? We've got to tell someone.'

'Trev, I can't believe what just happened,' he says, and considers trying to take a shot of Morgan in the sea. By now Morgan is almost impossible to see in the water. 'Shall I try and keep an eye on where he is, and you go and tell them.' Trev speeds off back into the bar, while Dave makes a futile effort to track Morgan's receding location in the sea.

Trev returns to the bar, because he knows there's a staff member there – the guy who served them.

'Hey, mate, er, man over board!' The Steward nods immediately.

'How many. Sir?'

'Just one. Hurry. I'll wait here.' As the steward swings into action, Trev knows he's done the right thing. A couple of minutes later the steward returns to Trev and hands him a drink. 'Thanks,' he says, signing the form. 'Are they coming?'

'Are who coming? I have not seen your friends since you left with them some minutes ago.'

'Yes, but I said man over board.'

'And you have one sir,' says the steward gesturing politely towards the drink. 'Today's cocktail.'

'What, THIS is a man overboard? No I mean there's a man overboard, a real man, really overboard. It's an emergency!' judging by the state of Trev, especially his hair, the steward decides he needs to be reassured.

'Let me put you on the phone to someone.' At the bar the steward calls an internal number and hands the phone to Trev who tries to explain as best he can.

'Oh thank goodness, yes, we've just had a man overboard and, well, it's terrible. You've got to come up and see now.' There's a silence at the other end. Then the voice speaks reassuringly.

'I'm very sorry to hear it. My advice is that you don't have another one.'

'Another what?'

'Another man overboard.' Trev has no idea what the man's talking about.

'I mean – a man has fallen off the ship. Into the water. He's out there in the sea! You've got to do something.' The voice remains calm.

'Sir, there's nothing to worry about. As we said this morning in the daily announcement, it's just a standard drill, just for exercise. However, I do thank you for your concern.'

'No NO! It's REALLY happened,' pleads Trev, 'a real man. Captain Morgan.'

'What, like the rum?'

'Well, not he really is called Morgan and he used to be in charge of a fishing boat in Swansea. At least that's what he told us. He fell off the rails! We got a picture.' There's a silence on the line and the voice asks Trev to hand the phone back to the steward, who listens for a moment and then puts the phone down. He asks Trev to wait there.

Shortly afterwards, the Cruise Director arrives at the Winners Bar. He, too is visibly shocked by Trev's appearance, but asks him to recount events. Trev does his best, and this causes the Cruise Director to go white. He makes a call. Immediately another announcement is made – this time proclaiming the drill is no longer a drill. The ship immediately begins a turn to port, in a great arching swing in an effort to retrace its steps and find the waterlogged guest – now miles behind the vessel. By now, a number of staff are assembling in the bar – and they move en masse to find Dave on deck. Dave is gone too. Trev fears the worst.

'Oh hell, I bet he jumped in to try and save Captain Morgan.'

'Why would be do that?'

'I don't know, because he's a good guy.' The Cruise Director sends a runner to send a second message about another man overboard. Moments later, Dave re-appears on deck. Trev explodes at him – 'where the hell did you go you dick?'

'You were away for ages and I needed a pee.'

'Show them where you last saw Morgan.' Dave looks back into the distance, and raises his hand, swinging it in a wide arc from left to right.

'Back there. I've got a picture.' Dave starts fumbling with the phone, which the Director firmly prises out of his hands. And sure enough, there's picture, supriisingly sharp, of Morgan in the processes of departing the deck backwards.

'At least he's got a buoyancy aid. Was he suicidal?'

'No. I'd say he was pissed.' The Cruise Director suddenly realises this must be the same man who threw up in the restaurant.

'Lazarus!'

By the time the ship has return to the approximate location of Morgan's fall, there's nothing but water. In the time it has taken to get back amounts to about 20 minutes, but in that time the ship and Morgan are more than least 3 miles apart. With the wind and currents the processes of recovering a soul from the sea is at best hit and miss, and at worst little more than a guess.

Hours pass, and as they do, new rumours abound. While most people have heard the official line – that they are searching for a man overboard – others suspect that they are in fact, lost and that the ship's captain has no idea which way St Lucia is. The officers have to contend with a barrage of complaints, the most irksome generated by Mr and Mrs Bitters who say they are finding the search for the missing person 'boring.'

There comes a point in every search where the chances of success are regarded as vanishingly small. By now, a helicopter, two small fishing vessels and a lifeboat have joined the effort. As night falls, as it does suddenly around 6pm, further efforts are considered futile. Captain Bladder makes a difficult announcement.

'Ladies and gentlemen, as you may have heard, we unfortunately had a mishap earlier on today, when one of our compliment accidently fell overboard. We are all hoping of the best, but at this time we cannot proceed with a search in darkness. As such, I have to report that we will resume our cruise. However, given the incident, I have to inform you that instead of St Lucia, we will for various reasons have to divert to Barbados, which is very close to our current position. I expect we will be alongside at a berth we have secured in the port of Bridgetown at very short notice within the hour. Our thoughts are with the missing soul.'

As darkness falls, the gentle northerly breeze conspires with the tide to drift everything on the surface of the balmy Caribbean waters south. This includes Captain Morgan, who hasn't felt this sober since he parked his car in Southampton, and until now had never expected to end his days as a shark snack.

Chapter 19 :
Time and Tide

The docking proceeds without incident. A lot of guests are pleased to arrive in Barbados because they tend to feel safer in places they've heard of, like Bermuda, New York and Beirut. Some have heard of St Lucia but know nothing about it, so there's a certain familiarity here on an island often referred to by people trying to impress they're neighbours. After tonight, they can say it too. One-upmanship is a great motivator in the cruising world.

All the same, it's a difficult night for Captain Bladder. He may not like his guests, but he doesn't want to kill them either. His decision to divert here is based on a very practical consideration. The Dogger V and others spent the lion's share of the day looking for Morgan's body in the water - and the A&G Line take incidents like this very seriously. He will, in any event have to answer to their regional office here in town at dawn. Furthermore, anybody joining the ship for the inevitable inquiry will - as a matter of course - do so through Barbados. Had he not diverted here, the press, who appear to have become obsessed with the supernatural goings-on on the Spirit of Dogger V, will concoct some further story about the incident, and he'll never hear the end of it. He also hopes that, with a little imagination, he can fiddle with the itinerary and cover the island they missed today.

He has one more reason for coming here – a tenuous seafarer's hunch. The wind and tides did them a favour, giving them a few favourable knots towards port. Morgan was very unlucky to fall in the sea in the middle of a 'man overboard' drill. But what's been good for the ship, might possibly also be good for Morgan's corpse. The failure to recover a dead body is regarded as almost as bad for public relations as the incident itself.

As guests come and go off the ship, Bladder is studying the drinks menu. He's appalled at the crassness of a cocktail of the day called 'Man Over Board,' and has requested a full list of all cocktails planned for the bars of the ship across the 104 days of the World Cruise. It's just as well he asked.

Al Carr, the restaurant Manager knocks on the door. Bladder signals him to sit down.

'I don't pretend to know much about catering, but I know a little bit about common sense. I want to talk to you about your choice of cocktails names. Now, just for the sake of argument, I'm going to grat out a list of cocktails and as I do, I'd like you think about why they might be an issue on a world cruse - on a SHIP which takes people all over the world. Ready? Here goes: 'Bermuda Die Angle,' 'Captain's Log,' 'Collision Collada,' 'Columbia High,' 'Cranbury Capziser,' 'Gin & Titanic,' 'Hurricane Force 12,' 'Death by Stingray,' 'Dogger's Surprise,' 'Lost at Sea,' 'Pirates' Passion,' 'Shark Attack,' 'Sun Stroke,' 'Suez Crisis,' 'Tequila Tidal Wave' - and of course, 'Man Over Board.' So any idea why I might read that list to you, Al?' Al knows very well what the Captain's getting at, but he daren't risk a reply, in case his guess is even worse than the Captain's. It isn't.

'It's because they're all inappropriate. I mean who's going to go on one of our beach tours in St Kitt's after having ordered a 'Shark Attack?' What's the waiter supposed to say when someone orders a Gin & Titanic: 'would you like ice with that?' And tell me please, what images you were intending to conjure up with the concept of a 'Pirates' Passion?' Bladder stops. 'Well?'

'Er, they were meant to be comedic, Sir. A sort of light hearted take on nautical events.' Bladder rolls his eyes.

'Oh I understand now. So sharks, piracy and sinking are supposed to be funny are they? Look at my face.' Bladder points at his puffed up face, which in itself is comical to Carr. 'Am I laughing?' Al was tempted to laugh himself because Bladders reddening complexion.

'No sir.'

'That's right. No it isn't funny. Fix it - and from now on I want to approve any new hilarious ideas you may have for cocktails personally.' Al Carr leaves the Captain's office and for some reason can't help bursting out laugh in the corridor, causing the Captain to open the door and stare at him purposefully. It's a tense moment, ruined by the fact that Carr breaks out laughing again.

'I'm sorry Captain,' he splutters out as he laughs with uncontrolled mirth. The Captain looks at him and shakes his head.

'You can be a real idiot sometimes, Carr.' Carr is still creased up and apologises between guffaws.'

'Yes, I know, Sir, I'm sorry.' The captain looks at his wretched Restaurant Manager and lets himself down - by smiling.

'Al, keep 'Dogger's Surprise' on the menu. He pats his still laughing Restaurant Manager on the arm - and feels an uncharacteristic moment of camaraderie with a man who has to face all the guests every day of his working life.

As dawn approaches, there is a resumption of the efforts to find Morgan out at sea, though everyone now accepts this is now only a search for a body. Meanwhile, the Captain visits the A&G Line office for a brief and frank exchange, in which it is generally agreed that while it takes a modicum of common sense to survive on a ship, sense is not common. After the meeting is over, Bladder beckons four of his men over.

'We're just going to take a look at something. Sort out a car.' His crew are far too loyal to question the order and presently they're procured a substantial truck and driver who knows the island well. The Captain directs the driver to a place none of the others have heard of, and they set off.

On board, Trev and Dave have decided not to drink today, as a mark of respect for their departed friend. They lie in bed silently, contemplating their best move.

'He was alright, wasn't he, Dave mate?'

'Yeah, that could be us in forty years' time. I really felt a connection with him.' Trev looks at Dave curiously.

'You mean you're saying that would be a good thing?'

'Yeah, 'course it would be mate. He had a great life. I mean, imagine having done a fishing boat and all that. And having enough money to come on a cruise on your own like he did. What a way to go.'

'And being eaten by a shark at night on your own in the sea? Yeah, lucky guy.' Dave thinks about this for a moment.

'At least he's famous now, Trev mate.'

'How's that then?'

'Well, I found a way to send that picture of him falling off on Facebook and also it looks like I sort of filmed it by accident. It's only

a few seconds but you can see what's going on. I put it on YouTube.'
Trev can't believe what he's hearing.

'Dave, do you realise that means all his friends and family will find out he's dead from YouTube and twitter?'

'So? It'll probably make his wife feel bad for leaving him, which serves her right, and everyone else will see he died having a good time.'

'Dave, that's a bollock stupid thing to do. How many people have viewed it so far?' Trev's question is accusational.

'One or two mate.'

'How many?'

'13 million.'

'Oh bollocks.'

Monty is mulling over yesterday's events too.

'Ghastly business, don't you think?'

'Yes darling,' replies Mrs Major.

'I wonder if he even survived the fall.'

'Does it really matter? I suppose at least that way the end was quick.'

'Yes. Apparently he was wearing one of those buoyancy rings. I wonder if something like would give a shark indigestion. And whether if they eat a scuba diver the oxygen tank makes them break wind.'

'I think it's all very sad, Monty. It should make us appreciate what we've got.' Monty sighs.

'That's true, dear lady. But what we haven't got is St Lucia.'

Monty's observation is technically correct, and points to an age old problem in the cruising world – disruption to programmes. There are always a proportion of individuals with their hearts set on a particular destination. If that destination is abandoned for any reason, there's hell to pay. The tour organisers and desk staff are invariably in the front line. Mr and Mrs Bitters are at the desk right now, and Mr Bitters is concluding his monologue.

'And since we haven't been able to go to St Lucia as clearly outlined in the itinerary be bought and paid for, we expect these unscheduled days to be refunded to us forth with.' The staff member struggles to explain the reality of the situation.

'I do understand your concerns, Mr Bitters, but as you know, we had to deal with the emergency. Also, the Captain is seeking to reschedule the next few days to get us to St Lucia, but just on a different day.' Mr Bitters' eyes bulge.

'That, madam, is the whole problem. A different day is NOT today, and on a point of principle it is not the same thing. I could have had anything pre-planned on St Lucia for this – and only this- period. For all you know, you've ruined the whole purpose of my cruise.'

'Did you have anything planned for St Lucia, sir?'

'No, but that's not the point is it? Your cavalier attitude to our holiday is just not good enough, and this isn't the last you'll be hearing about.' The receptionist bows her head in ritual supplication to the complainers. But the temptation to ask one final question back is irresistible.

'Oh, did you receive the sea view by the way, sir – after we left Southampton?'

'Er, we did for a while, yes. But it's gone again today, hasn't it?'

'I'll see what we can do, Mr Bitters. Have a nice day, Sir.'

'Under these conditions, that is self-evidently impossible. Especially in a place as hot as Bermuda.' Mr Bitters walks off proudly. His wife is shaking her head.

'They really don't care, do they?'

'No they don't, and they're just making it worse for themselves. By the time we've finished with them, we should be making a nice little profit.'

In the universe, there are some things which are probable. Others are improbable. But statistically speaking, nothing is impossible. Sometimes very unlikely things come to pass. One such event is taking place on a sandy beach on an island. Sunburnt and flaking, a portly face flickers into life, suspended as it is by a great white and red buoyancy aid. By conventional wisdom, Captain Morgan has survived his most intrepid voyage. He's exhausted, hypothermic and thirsty as hell. But this is either heaven or a bloody lucky escape from hell, or both. He tries to stand, only to be knocked down by the boisterous wave. After a few attempts he crawls this deserted island paradise. He savours the moment of redemption and says a quiet prayer to a God he, until now, believed had forsaken him. He has the impression that he was brought here by some other force greater than himself.

Normally, one would attribute his survival to four factors. Firstly, he happened to fall in wearing a life ring. Secondly, the tides and winds were favourable to guiding him to this shore line. Thirdly, he was so drunk when he fell in he didn't break anything. And finally, the odour of booze in the water warned predators to stay away for his comfort and everyone's safety. But in his own mind he has a strong sense that he was carried here by some kind of force field – surely it wasn't aliens?!

He returns to his circumstances and contemplates his fate. Tears begin to sting his face. How long will our latter day Robinson Crusoe have to live on this deserted island, eeking out a humble existence from nuts and berries and the fruit of the sea? For how many years will his friends and family mourn his loss – and will they never discover his miraculous redemption? Will he meet another human being again?

'Are you alright?'

Morgan opens his eyes. A man in naval uniform is looking down at him.

'Yes.'

'Have you finished with that life ring?'

'Er, yes. Where am I?'

'Bermuda.'

'How did I get here?'

'Everything that ends up anywhere usually ends up here. It's just a thing that happens round here. Can I have it back then please – the life ring?'

'Of course, Captain.'

'Did you get attacked?'

'Well, a bit. A shark seemed to be sniffing about but it hit it on the nose with my bottle and he buggered off.' Bladder nods.

'Frankly, the way you smell would probably have been enough to keep them away. As a rule, sharks don't tend to eat alcoholics.' Bladder smiles. 'It's said that time and tide wait for no man; but I think they've made an exception just for you, Sir.'

Apart from severe dehydration and sunburn, Morgan is relatively unscathed by his ordeal. The Captain had a feeling Morgan would turn up here – he knows this area better than almost anyone else on the high seas. However, he wasn't sure whether he'd be meeting a person or a corpse.

At the hospital he sits quietly with Morgan.

'You know, Captain Bladder, I'm a seafaring man, and I can't help feeling I was saved by a, er, flying saucer or something.'

'Rubbish, Morgan. You were hallucinating thanks to a combination of cold, booze and thirst.'

'No, I -'

'Catch a grip man, or you'll have everyone talking about it. Now listen up. If you come on board again, there have to be limits. I'm taking away your right to buy alcohol aboard.' Morgan nods. 'And no more stupidity climbing onto rails.' Morgan nods again. 'Come on then. Let's get you back.

As they leave the hospital a throng of photographers pictures Bladder resplendent in his white uniform and Morgan looking tired but happy walking out of the building with the life ring which Bladder has firmly insisted is not a souvenir for Morgan, but company property. To shouts from reporters, Morgan says only one thing.

'The ring probably didn't save me anyway. I think it was something from above.' Morgan makes a spinning shape with his finger which could be anything, but, of course, the press interpret this as a space ship. A reporter shouts out 'How did Bladder know where to find you?'

'He just knew – maybe he has a direct line with up there!'

Next day, under the heading 'So endeth the lesson,' a story in the New York Times begins: 'Move over Neptune! A modern day Jonah hails Captain Bladder as the new King of the Sea.' The story infers, but does not say explicitly, that Morgan has experienced some sort of religious conversion thanks to Captain Bladder and was saved through a spiritual event. Tabloids take a different view: 'Calling occupants of interplanetary craft: sea are your friends.' And probably the most pun ridden title of the day: 'Bladder's run saves Captain Morgan from a rum fate.'

As they walk up the gangway, the ship erupts into applause from all the open decks. Bladder shakes his head as Morgan walks on board like a sunburnt tramp. A final article in Barbados paper Post pictures Morgan in his dishevelled state next to Bladder: 'Captain Sensible saves Captain Morgan from that sinking feeling.' Bladder has become a global sensation.

Chapter 20 :
Bitter words

There's been increasing unrest following the skipping of St Lucia on the way to Bermuda. As usual, a skipped destination creates secondary complaints, as guests seek avenues to express their displeasure. It's not even about the location – most people have no idea what St Lucia does or doesn't offer. They just feel in some way robbed by the absence of a visit. Senior Officers wait and see what form this anger will take. There tends to be a herding instinct, and people will complain about broadly the same things.

The first complaints aren't really complaints and occur at the Reception in the atrium, midships. Four people come in to discuss whether they can rebook for other coach tours in lieu of the ones which were cancelled in St. Lucia. The staff have long ago learned to deal with such inquiries with the utmost care, in order not to provoke the situation further. By and large, this works.

The next couple have a concern about the temperature of the Jacuzzi, which they regard as too hot. Immediately behind them, a man has concerns about the toughness of the steak.

'Normally, I have it rare, and unfortunately on this occasion it was far too well done. The steak has damaged my dentures. Look.' The man removes his teeth and offers them to the surprised receptionist who attempts to deal with the gentleman's issue without being ill. Next up are another couple who are unhappy because the Jacuzzi is too cold.

This steady stream of complainants dribbles on till about lunchtime when, inevitably, Mr and Mrs Bitters turn up. This time they're supported by a small number of other people who step forward as a whole group.

'We demand to speak to the Restaurant Manager.'

'May I ask what it is about Mr Bitters?'

'It's about the condiments. We have become aware that your ship is taking wreckless risks with our health by not providing the condiments in individual pre-packed portions. One man has already died on this ship and I would have expected you to have taken appropriate measures to prevent another such death.'

'Mr Bitters, I'm not aware of any deaths on this cruise.'

'Don't be ridicuclous,' retorts Mr Bitters. I saw the whole thing with my own eyes.' The receptionist has to make a calculation. She eyes up the eight guests and quickly concludes that this is a scene best avoided in public. Asking them to wait, she goes into the back room and pages the Restaurant Manager, Al Carr. They agree a meeting in a room near the bow where others won't see them.

Minutes later, the Restaurant Manager arrives with one assistant, who's primarily there to act as a witness in case things turnugly. The Bitters are well known to the crew already, having so far submitted eight verbal and six written complaints since leaving Southampton.

'Mr Bitters, sorry to keep you waiting. Now, how can I help?'

'Yes, it's about the condiments – you jeopardize life and limb by failing to safeguard us from deadly diseases which have already killed one man, before our very eyes.' Bitters rambles on about disease and human contamination for a while. When he stops, Al Carr decides to take a fairly firm line.

'Firstly, Mr Bitters, nobody has died. As you may know Mr Morgan has been seen all over the ship since that incident.'

'We only have your word for that. There are those who think he's an impersonator -'

'Or a zombie,' adds one of the other ladies.

'A zombie?' Al Carr is genuinely surprised by such a ludicrous suggestion.

'A zombie Mr Carr.' Celia continues. 'We've heard what goes on in this part of the world. The Bermuda Triangle is a very dangerous place for law abiding Christians like us, and we want to know what's going on.' Al Carr realises this woman is being very serious, and decides to handle her claim in a non-commital way. 'Can we come back to that once we've covered the condiments issue?'

'As long as we do – and I don't want any lies, mind.' Celia is satisfied she's made her initial point forcefully. Carr tries to settle frayed nerves about the condiments.

'Look, I've been in this business for 30 years man and boy, and I can reassure you in all that time we haven't had a single case of the spread of infection from a condiment. It just doesn't happen.' Mrs

Bitters chips in.

'Yes it does. My friend's brother in law died from contaminated mayonnaise two years ago. It developed into septicaemia.' Al Carr knows this is a lie but what does he say?

'Er, Mrs Bitters, I can categorically state we haven't had a single case of condiment related illness in the history of A&G Line.'

'Well,' snorts Mr Bitters, 'you would say that, wouldn't you? It's typical of you jobsworths to always protect your practices.' Her husband delivers the coup de grace.

'Yes, this is why, with the power vested in me by this cross section of the on board passangers, we have raised thispetition of 86 signatures calling for your resignation.' Bitters hands over the petition to Al Carr, who accepts it with dumbfounded shock. 'Take your time to consider our five just demands – listed there. We will give you 48 hours to comply after which time we cannot be help responsible for our actions.' Carr looks up at Mr Bitters.

'You're being serious, aren't you?' Mr Bitters nods. 'In that case I'll, er, take your requests seriously.' He reads the list:

1   We demand all the condiments to be provided in individual
     pre-packed packs.
2   We demand that rare steaks and other poorly cooked meat
     be banned forthwith.
3   We demand input to the daily menu schedules.
4   We demand the right to inspect the kitchens for cleanliness.
5   We demand to know the truth about the dead man.

'Right, then, thank you for this. Give me a couple of days to consider it and if you'd like to pop downto reception to fix another meeting I'll be, happy to do that, then.'

Celia speaks again.

'And don't think we don't mean it. We've been messed around by your company before – like the time you cancelled the visit to Christchurch in New Zealand.' Al members the incident.

'You mean just after that earthquake which destroyed much of the city?'

'Yes – it was terribly disappointing. And then when the Haifa visit was pulled at the last minute.'

'Because of the – um uprising?'

'Yes – again all at the last minute. So now we're making a stand.'

Al Carr says thank you and eventually manages to clear the room.

'What is it with people like that – why do they bother travelling?'

'Well, Sir, I think you were very patient.'

'That was the easy bit. I'm going to have to tell the Captain.'

There is one other particular complaint who has been demanding a certain amount of attention all to herself: Mystic Maria.

'Hello, Maria,' says the Cruise Director. 'I understand you have had a couple of issues this morning.' Mystic Maria breathes loudly down the phone.

'Yes. Once again, I had to order my own breakfast. I understood that we had discussed this. Also, I have a slight concern that a special leaflet has not been distributed to guests explaining my presence on board.' The Cruise Director has never heard such a request.

'Well, you are included in the Daily Programme, and as you'll see you have quite an impressive biography.'

'Well I'm not happy with what it says about me.'

'But Maria, you wrote it yourself.'

'Well, it's not good enough for a lady of my stature. I'm a television star you know. I've been on loose woman – twice!' The Cruise Director tries to figure out how to manage her expectations.

'We really do value your presence on board. Let me have a look at those things for you and call you back this afternoon.'

'You'll find me on Deck 12 with my people. Many thanks.' The Cruise Director puts down the phone and realises that Mystic Maria just wants to be loved. He picks up the phone again and punches in a number.

'Maria, I just want to tell you I really love that you're on board. Thank you Maria – thank you on behalf of the Captain and crew, but more than anything, on behalf of the passengers who depend on you for their knowledge and inspiration.' He can hear her weeping quietly. 'Don't feel anything less than our angel, Maria.' When he finishes, he knows that she is ready to do what she's on board to do.'

'Bladder is wide eyed with annoyance.

'Those bloody fools. Apart from the fact most of what they're complaining about is absolute rubbish, to have the audacity to tell us how to do our job is – well it's just plain offensive. And as for this nonsense about Morgan….' Al Carr hesitates to tell Bladder the rest but he ought to know.

'Captain, they're now saying that Captain Morgan is some kind of zombie who's on board to make contact with The Other Side in the Bermuda Triangle. There's really no point in even trying to reason with them – anything you say is taken as a conspiracy.' Al Carr sighs. 'I don't know what to do.'

'I do,' says Bladder. He goes over to the tannoy, lifts up the microphone and presses the button. 'Ladies and gentlemen, this is your Captain speaking. I hope you are all having a pleasant afternoon. I just wanted to make a special announcement to inform you that, as a result of a request by some of the passengers, all condiments in the restaurants will henceforth be supplied in sachets to those who want them - on written request. We are doing this to accommodate those guests who have requested this. In addition, for the comfort and safety of all on board, let me categorically deny that we are heading towards an area of intense sea monster activity. However, should anyone see anything peculiar then I would be very grateful if you could make your observations known to the main reception. Have an excellent afternoon.' Bladder puts down the microphone. 'Now, let's see what happens to the complaints.'

Within 20 minutes a long queue has former at reception, each couple claiming to have seen 'something in the water.' All thoughts of condiments and rare steaks have vanished as the guests concern themselves with thoughts of giant squid and ship eating colossans. Strangely, nobody is scared. Instead, everyone is excited. Even Celia is seen scanning the horizon for signs of activity.

Captain Bladder summons the energy to take a brief walk around the Promenade Deck. He is repeatedly stopped by passengers, all asking the same question: 'are we in the Bermuda Triangle yet?' His answer is unchanging. 'You'll know when we are. You'll just know.'

That evening Al Garr is still grumpy about the petition calling for his resignation – even though he knows it will not be acted upon under the circumstances. He watches as guests come in, largely talking about the unconfirmed sightings of scary monsters of the deep. Not one person has anything bad to say about the food, the service or the menu.

Towards the end of the evening Al Garr is sitting by the front desk of the Medusa Restaurant. He's impressed with the elegant manner in which Bladder provided a focus of attention to the ship's passengers. Bladder may not particularly like people, but he certainly knows how they tick. A waiter attracts his attention.

'I am sorry to disturb, Sir. We have a complaint - about the brand of margarine.' Al sighs heavily. OK, I'll go and have a chat. Which table – no, let me guess, Table 64?'

'No, it is table 22.' Al is amazed.

'I can't believe it's not Bitters.'

Chapter 21 :

Mystic Maria and the Starman

Mystic Maria had been somewhat 'diva-like' since she boarded the ship. Her expectations have included fresh flowers every day, breakfast in bed consisting of caviar and rye bread, plus – most inconveniently of all – a courtesy call from the Captain every morning. This last act become a chore for First Officer Ward, as Bladder simply refuses to do it. That's led to a comical five minutes every morning on the bridge, when Ward has attempted to impersonate his superior's northern accent, to the stifled laughter of the other bridge crew.

'Good morning Miss Maria. This is the, er, Acting Captain, here, and I'm just checking that you slept well and that everything on board is to your satisfaction.' Each morning Ward continues in that vein for a few minutes, listening to the woman's latest list of requests.

'Would it be possible to achieve a greater amount of fruit, especially with vitamin C in it. I'm coming down with all the symptoms of scurvy.'

'We can look into it.'

'Also, I need extra moisturiser - the sea is drying my skin out and shrinking my clothes.'

'Again, I'll see what we can do.'

'Finally, could you go a bit slower – the vibration from the engine keeps me awake.'

'I'll pass it on.'

'Oh, and what day is it?'

'Tuesday, as you'll see from the Daily Programme. As you know, you're scheduled to give a talk today at 10am – which is in just under an hour.'

'Am I? Oh, right then. Where is it?'

'In the Red Curtain Theatre – in the bow.'

'Is that the middle of the ship or the back end?'

'Um, it's the front end – the bit which is going through the water first.'

Ward's patience has paid off. She's quite popular around the ship, and has willingly agreed to reading people's palms. However, her predictions on every occasion have consisted of one of three things: 'I see love', 'a financial opportunity will present itself next year' and 'You are going on a long journey'. She also performs a ritual to the sun every day, which has attracted a small audience.

The one outstanding issue is that Maria continues to claim she is making a 'fly on the wall' documentary. As far as everyone can see, this consists of her filming herself around the ship, talking to the camera while holding it at arm's length. She has attempted to interview some guests about the Bermuda Triangle. Her posh accent has also raised suspicious whispers, as one lady clearly remembers that Maria went to a Comprehensive school in Scunthorpe with her daughter and that her parents were local.

It's 10.00am - and the main event in the Red Curtain Theatre is about to start. Mystic Maria – fortune teller and astrologist – has arrived on time. Thanks to a cheeky decision by the Ents crew, Doctor Lucas Starwalker, the Astronomer, is talking at 11.00 in the Chances bar at the far end of the ship. He's come to watch Maria's performance - because it is bound to impact on the mood of the audience he'll receive for his talk immediately afterwards. Also, he fancies her despite her flighty nature.

After an upbeat introduction by the Deputy Cruise Director, Mystic Maria takes to the stage. Her act begins with a dramatic light show, during which she prances round the stage in an odd and unintentionally entertaining performance. As the dutiful applause dies down, Maria addresses the audience.

'You are interested in the unknown; the unexplained; the supernatural. That is why you are here. Let us go forward on a very strange adventure, just as we ourselves steam remorseless on towards... the Bermuda Triangle!' A gasp emanates from the audience.

As her set proceeds she performs various mind reading tricks.

'I close my eyes and I see a name – the name is – Jane. Is there a Jane in the audience? 50 hands rise, and there is a smattering of applause. 'Good, I have a message for one of you, it is from someone called, 'Daddy' or 'Papa'. The message is that he is fine and very proud of something you did earlier this year.' A lady shouts out:

'That's my late father. Is he safe?'

'Yes he's very safe, but he says his hair is as grey as ever.' The woman is shocked.

'He was bald when he died – does that mean he's younger now?'

'Ah, yes. He is much younger. And he is well.' More applause. She shuts here eyes again. 'Now I see another name – Geoffrey – is the a Geoff or Geoffrey here in the room.? About 35 hands rise up. 'Yes, and for one of you there is a message from a four legged friend – a pet, a dog. Has anyone lost a pet in the last 12 months?' Six hands remain raised. 'Rex?' All the hands go down. 'No, no, it's clearer now it's – Patch,' still no hands 'or Shep.' one hand rises. 'Yes Shep says he's fine, and looking forward to seeing you again. The man's face drops.

'When will he see me again? Does that mean I'm going to die in the Bermuda Triangle?'

'No, he doesn't look forward to seeing you again soon – not for a long time.' Another voice shouts out.

'Do all pets go to heaven?'

'Yes.'

'Even bad ones which were put down because they attacked a child?'

'No, not those ones.' Maria remains embroiled in a continuing dialogue about the criteria relating to pet entry to Heaven. In an effort to shut down the debate she says 'All the pets have now gone back to the other side,' but not before some smart alex shouts 'that was champion, Miss!' She cues some music to drown out the on-going questions about Fido and pet fish and dances her strange dance again. 'Now, it is time to look into your future.' She shuts her eyes and the lights go down as mist swirls onto the stage 'Are there any Aquarians here? I have a vision – you will be going on a long journey.' A voice shouts out:

'On a ship by any chance?' causing a ripple of laughter in the room.

'No – on a plane, from far away.' The voice shouts out again:

'Yes, I've already got the ticket.'

'You will land safely. I also have a message for any Sagittarians here this morning. Your will meet a stranger who will offer you something which may be useful to you.' Following that, it's on to the finale of her act, a séance. She invites five people up on stage to participate round a table with her. The lights darken and she begins her chants. She raises her hand.

'Is anyone out there?' The table knocks and a murmur wafts around the room. People are genuinely interested now. 'Put your hands on this stone and let the spirit guide us.' There's a great screen which will show any words which are generated by the board. After a few moments the glass begins to move. Initially it spells nothing coherent, just letters which don't add up to words. Then come two words on the screen tracking the actions of the Ouija board. 'I LIVE.' The audience is fully engaged now. 'Who are you?' Maria asks. 'CAPTAIN MORGAN.' Many in the audience, who saw Captain Morgan's 'reincarnation' thanks to Bladder in this very theatre, whisper excitedly to each other. Violet Cryer in the audience digs Celia in the side and looks at her knowingly. Mystic Maria continues. 'Oh spirit Morgan, what else can you tell?' Again the stone begins to spell words, which shows up on the screen behind the séance: 'SAILING TO WORLD'S END.' The stone stops moving. Everyone is looking at the words on the screen in silence. Then they look at Mystic Maria.

'It is a message of hope.'

'What's hopeful about it?' asks one of the passengers on the stage.

'Wait! There's more!' She hums in an unusual way and suddenly the stone begins to move again. 'CHANCES AHEAD.' The audience continues to stare at the words. 'Please give a great round of applause to our séance team!' She signals to the band to start up again. As the crew remove the table, another voice shouts from the audience.

'What chances?'

'I believe the spirit knows the answers will be given in Chances bar.' There's a smattering of applause. Maria thanks everyone for coming, finishing of with another odd dance. As she leaves the stage the Deputy Cruise Director steps on the stage.

'Please show your appreciation once again for our wonderful astrologer and fortune teller, Mystic Maria!' Maria makes a brief appearance and departs behind the curtain once again. The Deputy Cruise Director continues. 'Now it looks like we have a mystery to solve. Over at Chances bar our other on board astrologer Dr Lucas Starwalker will explain the secrets of the cosmos and explain the meaning of this mysterious message.' Starwalker rolls his eyes. 'That starts in just under 10 minutes over at Chances at the far end of the ship. See you there!' Doctor Starwalker knows that, thanks to the Deputy Cruise Director's comments, Starwalker is now guaranteed an enormous attendance, and incessant questions all about the 'message from the other side.'

90 tonnes of humans shuffle out of the Red Curtain Theatre towards Chances. 1,100 people migrating from bow to stern in one coordinated activity causes the vessel to shift in the water by a tiny amount. The stampede has been caused by the enormous interest that Mystic Maria and the deputy Cruise Director's comments have caused amongst the audience. Since they know that Lucas Starwalker is a 'doctor' they are determined to attend his talk and find out the truth behind what they've just heard from Maria.

Starwalker is about to start. As he paces up and down at the front of the smaller Chances auditorium, he notices Mystic Maria on the front left side, sipping a fruit juice of some sort. He goes over.

'I came to your show.' He kneels down and lowers his voice. 'What's with all that I live Captain Morgan stuff?'

'You've heard the rumours about that zombie guy. Too good an opportunity to miss.'

'And the end of the world message?'

'I knew they'd all come to see you if that happened. And I like you.' She smiles disarmingly and he's wrong-footed by her charm. 'Good luck!'

Starwalker begins his talk with an explanation.

'Ladies and gentlemen, let me begin by asking you a question: raise your hand if you've just seen Mystic Maria's – remarkable – show in the Red Curtain Theatre just now.' Everyone puts their hands up. 'Ah, right. Well, should explain what I do is astronomy, not astrology. I'm all about stars, not star signs or predictions.' Celia shouts out.

'Can you explain how the dead man - Captain Morgan – was able to send a message if he's still alive?'

'He's not dead, I don't think, madam.'

'So how come he communicated through the Ouija board?' There's an old rule on cruise ships which effectively forbids one performer from rubbishing another. It's the sort of etiquette which no artiste, however under pressure, would dream of violating. Starwalker is cornered.

'Well, maybe it was a different Captain Morgan. The one on board is -'

'A zombie!' shouts out Violet Cryer. 'And what does the message mean? You said the world would end and so has the spirit. We have the right to know!' The level of noise rises until Doctor Starwalker has to tap the microphone to restore calm.

'Let me try and explain what I know. Firstly, there is no such thing as the Bermuda Triangle. It's not real. It's just three lines on a map.'

'Yes, that's the definition of a triangle,' says Celia.

'Well, yes it is, but it's not real. Things don't happen in the Bermuda Triangle because of it. It's a made up myth. And as for the message, about the end of the world, there's a perfectly rational explanation.' An elderly man half way towards the back raises his hand.

'Are we going to die like Captain Morgan?'

'No. Of course not.' Celia intervenes again.

'We don't want to die in the Bermuda Triangle! We demand a statement from Captain Bladder – to prove Morgan is not sailing us to our deaths.' There is applause and people begin to talk amongst themselves. Starwalker has lost the room. There's a ragged exchange of accusations as people become agitated. Eventually, it's obvious he's not going to get any further.

'Thank you very much everyone and I'll be happy to carry on talking with you after, er, afterwards.' He rips the microphone off and walks across to Mystic Maria. 'Well done. Now you've got all the guests believing this a ghost ship which is going to be taken over by the infamous on-board zombie Captain Morgan to sail us to our doom in some fog bank in the non-existent Bermuda Triangle.' Maria smiles.

'Oh they prefer this. It's more fun than silly planets and so called science. Can I buy you a drink?'

As the room clears, the newlyweds stand at the back and survey the nightclub.

'I didn't know this was here, darling husband.'

'No, me neither, dear wife. Perhaps we'll meet some other young people here.' Right on cue, a young gentleman walks up.

'Hi, I'm Christian.'

'Hi, we're Susan and Douglas. We've just got married.' Christian looks at the two of them, and his eyes well up. He steps forward and hugs Susan, then Douglas.

'Thank you Susan, thank you Douglas.'

'What for Christian.'

'For being under 30 years old. I'm the DJ.' Christian has been working on Spirit of Dogger V for three years. The average age of the clubbers is around 61, seven years younger than the overall average age on the ship. DJ Christian lives on a diet of Elvis, Buddy Holly and Christmas Number 1 singles.

'I once played the Spice Girls and received complaints from the cabins above the nightclub for what was described in the official report as noise pollution. So what can I play you two young people, dudes?' Douglas and Susan look at each other.

'Do you have anything by Madonna?' DJ Christain goes through his mental library.

'Yup, but not just yet. Maybe tonight. But for now, I could do you a Barry Manilow classic?'

'Her name was Lola, she was a showgirl

With yellow feathers in her hair and a dress cut down to there

She would meringue and do the cha-cha

And while she tried to be a star, Tony always tended bar

Across a crowded floor, they worked from 8 till 4

They were young and they had each other

Who could ask for more?'

'Fancy lunch,' says Doctor Starwalker to Maria.

'Oh Doctor, I didn't see that coming.'

'Not much of a psychic are you then, are you?' And there's romance in the air. 'So what star sign are you, by the way, Maria?'

'Virgo. What star sign are you?

'Guess.'

'Um,' she looks closely at his eyes. 'Either Pisces or Saggitarius.'

'No, I'm Capricorn.'

'I thought so! You seem nice, Lucas, that's the main thing.'

This evening, Celia and Violet compare notes in Celia's cabin.

'Celia, did you see how the Doctor and Mystic Maria talked

together? I followed them and they even had lunch! After that they went to the Entertainments Department together, and then I followed them to the posh restaurant and they booked themselves in for dinner!'

'It's obvious they're both in on it. They know something which we do not.'

'Yes Violet, but how do we get to the bottom of it?'

'Be vigilant my dear. We must keep our eyes and ears open - right to the horizon. Nobody will confuse us with the fog of propaganda.'

It's true. As the evening becomes night, Maria and the Doctor are still consorting, ending up in Chances bar again, this time to the strains of Madonna. Only two people are dancing – the newlyweds. The rest are watching them as if they have been provided as an act for the benefit of the others.

The activities on the ship run long into the night, eventually winding down as people drift back to their cabins. With all this entertainment plus the lure of alcohol, the danger of social embarrassment remains great. This is an ever present hazard of cruising, as every veteran knows. Starwalker and Maria are about to prove this very point.

'Would you like to come back to my cabin, Maria?'

'Why not,' she says with evident delight. They wander off, vaguely holding hands and humming the strains of Barry Manilow's Lola classic. She hasn't seen this coming either.

However, whatever the mood which will accompany the sober morning light, a far more sinister danger lurks before Spirit of Dogger V, drifting quietly in the water. For now, the giant twin propellers – or 'screws' in nautical terminology – power the graceful vessel relentlessly forwards at around 20 knots. Everything is steady as she goes. All that will change in the darkness of a Bermudan night - but not just yet.

A modern cruise liner is a combination of idiosyncratic tradition and evolving technological ingenuity, not all of which works very well. Let's come to that in a moment. For now, we briefly hark back to the glorious seaborne past, honoured by crew members who have never lost their respect for legendary pioneers of opulence and reliability such as Cunard, the White Star Line and P&O. These are names which still carve their mark into the oceans of the 21st Century.

Back in the fledging decades of the 20th Century, passenger carrying vessels had grown to stupefying size, funnels proudly signing their soot laden signatures across skies above every one of the seven seas. While the motive power for the ships of yore may be relatively historic compared to the heavy duty modern alternatives, they nevertheless represented some of the most powerful machines ever built by the human race. Deep within the towering iron-clad sea palaces, enormous, red hot furnaces contained fires stoked by anonymous men charged with satisfying a remorseless appetite for coal worthy of Dante's Inferno.

The heat created by all this toil boiled billions of litres of water to superheated temperatures. Entire reservoirs were provoked into agitated steam. These superheated atoms coarsed fanatically through metal pipes to sustain tremendous turbines in fearful spins. The irresistible force of these revolving shafts propelled gigantic, reptilian blades in their relentless revolutions. And so the bible black waters beneath the hulls foamed in seething, unseen froth. Such was the intensity of the process that the water couldn't cope; it frequently broke down into bubble filled clouds of salt water and vacuum – a process known as cavitation. While not good for efficiency, this combined empty space and brine to leave a turbulent wake and cause some of the vibration effects which so dogged passengers in Steerage, doomed to shake their way across the Atlantic in accommodation located above the resonating transmission shafts and propellors.

But, taken together, even with these shortcomings, the vessels were a triumph of human ambition and confidence. They would plough ever forward, hour after hour and day after day, as passengers rich and poor shared the united experience of traversing vast distances in search of amusement or work or love, each with their own story to tell of tragedy or hope or unplanned destiny. Whether wearing the starched collars that defined a man of the gentry or the more humble attire of those who could only just afford the least alluring passage, all could stare across the ocean's fickle plane and dream of horizons as yet unseen.

As these stately, oak lined vessels crossed the temperamental oceans in all their elegant glory, the mix of wood and gin and fire down below combined as an anachronistic transition between the 'old' and the 'new.' Remarkable speeds were achieved which equal or exceed the cruising knots of modern ships. The privileged unity which a giant ocean liner confers to her temporary residents without prejudice or fear or favour was a matter of record. All were subject to her hesitating but unstoppable responses to sea state and velocity - and the vaguaries of the atmosphere which can levitate or suppress the vessel in almost imperceptible ways, according to wind and pressure.

The main thing that happened to alter the equation between past and present was the advent of relatively minor improvements, one of which concerns us now. It's true that methods of propulsion have changed considerably. However, except for engineers and watchers of the smoke from funnels, these revolutions have occurred in private, below deck in places never visited by the conventional voyager. Collectively they add up to a big step forward, but nothing in the league of the original invention of the steam turbine. Few passengers will devote much time to comparing the quality of 24 knots achieved through the miracle of the diesel electric engine versusa more arcane design such as the coal furnace. It should be said that tremendous improvements have occurred in electronic tools for navigation. These have made cruising considerably safer. Thanks to them, the few accidents which have occurred in recent years have owed more to human error than mechanical failure.

There is one invention which has been noticed on board cruise ships. It's a revolution that has been anything but quiet – carrying with it the unique and displeasing howl of a suddenly induced vacuum. For cruise liners have new bowels. The Queen Elizabeth II, or QE2 – arguably the most famous of all ocean liners - employed the services of conventional toilet technology which owed everything to the game changing imagination of the late Sir Thomas Crapper - a man whose legacy has not been rewarded kindly in the English language. It was he who recognized the miraculous advantages of a latrine capable of whisking away human waste using the medium of flushing water. Countless lives have doubtless been saved by his hygienic and inspired design – and one which has stood the test of time. Indeed, ships down the ages were entirely dependent upon his methodology, employed to great effect for generations.

However, over time some believed that was not the best way to extract crap from cabins. Eventually, some genius proposed a new, if not utterly dissimilar, way of removing the colossal quantities of seaborne fare from the bathrooms of thousands of defecating guests – the 'vacuum system.' This system took the opposite approach to Crapper's design. Instead of spiriting excrement and urine away in a carousel of swirling water, suction would be used to do the trick. There are two key advantages to this system: firstly, it uses a lot less water. Secondly, it makes a funny and emphatic sucking sound which virtually berates the user for having the audacity to eat to such excess – a siren warning against avarice.

The Spirit of Dogger V is blessed with a vacuum toilet system. And, on the whole, it works extremely well. On average, it flushes away no less than 9 tonnes of crap and wee per day. Across a world cruise that's enough to fill 5,000 baths with the obnoxious and toxic effluent, though it is not at all clear why anyone would want to.

But there's also a problem. Vacuum systems are vulnerable to stupidity and very large turds. For some reason which evolution hasn't addressed, human beings have a compulsive tendency to drop unfeasibly silly objects in the toilets – and to create horrendous quantities of crap when cruising on the high seas. This has occurred as long as kitchens have existed at sea. Cruise liners do not escape the insane inexactitudes of a citizenship which feels compelled to test any lavatory system and its own belly to well beyond its design limits.

'Captain, we've got a problem.' Bladder looks up from his beloved weather charts. He's already in an irritable mood. Every time he treads the boards of the promenade deck he is worshipped in ways which makes him feel uncomfortable in the extreme. Furthermore, there isn't a decent storm within 1,500 miles of their course. The passengers are doomed to enjoy calm seas and hot weather.

'What's the problem? No, let me guess. Someone else has died and the deceased has asked for me in person. Have we experienced an alien abduction? No, someone has been aducted by aliens. Or better still, a great sea monster has eaten all the steamed jam pudding. Please do tell.' The First Officer swallows hard.

'Vacuum system.' Bladder puts his pen down and looks out the small porthole to the left of his desk.

'Oh. The vacuum system. The brilliant invention which was to upstage a trusted old design which has flushed away billions of tons of crap for centuries. A vacuum system which works on the premise that a suck of wind can expunge the sins of gluttony which has characterized life on a cruise liner since the first time a passenger had the temerity to succumb to the kind of overwhelming five course self-abuse which causes them to crack the very pan which A&G has so generously and naively provided to its customers since the first days that this fine line injudiciously offered its guests an infinite supply of food instead of a tolerable gruel and a shot of rum.' Bladder looks back at the First Officer. 'Do you think over a trillion tonnes has been shifted by the old way? Probably not, I suppose. Alright, what are the symptoms this time?' The First Officer hesitates to respond for fear of further provoking his superior. However, he knows his Captain to be a fair man who respects the truth, and decides to tell it like it is.

'Deck 11, Sir. Aft on the port side. Apparently 40 guests have simultaneously complained of flushing problems. Clearly it's another blockage. We're going to have to take it apart and see what's inside.' Bladder breathes in deeply, holds the lungful in rather the same fashion as a cigar smoker would keep the fumes in his person for a melancholy and self-indulgent moment. Expelling the breath he uses it economically.

'Alright. Keep me posted.'

There's a lot of commotion on Deck 11 by the time Ward arrives. Guests are standing in the corridor arguing with another officer. The strong smell of effluent invades the atmosphere like a rancid cackle. And already Ward can identify the ring leader – a man with a remarkably tedious voice. Ward makes his way to the centre of the remonstration.

'I'm First Officer Ward. I'm very sorry about what's happened, but please let me assure you –' but the ring leader intervenes.

'No, let me assure you that we are not going to stand for this clear and present danger to our health and, it must be said, to our on-going enjoyment of this cruise, Mr Officer. The fact that they send you instead of the Captain tells us all we need ot know about the seriousness with which you take this current crisis, Sir.'

'As I say, I'm sorry about the situation, and – could I ask your name?'

'Bitters. And I could equally ask you the same question. And also why your once proud line believes that we're not even worth a proper flushing toilet, but instead are forced to suffer the slings and arrows of some Jonny-come-lately system which can't even remove a semi-digested steak without exposing an entire deck to this kind of tragedy.' The others are nodding quietly and awaiting a response from Ward.

'Er, could I ask which cabin you're in? Can I have a look?' Mr Bitters raises his head pompously.

'No you cannot. That is a private matter, and frankly, none of your business – which is to fix the problem, not to try and force your way into another man's private space.' Ward is exasperated but knows these situations must be handled sensitively.

'I'm not trying to intrude, Mr Bitters. I'm just trying to help. I just want to have a look and then we can sort out a remedy. You do have a cabin which is affected, don't you, Sir?' Bitters looks at the First Officer in a fashion which indicates a loss of confidence.

'Officer, I don't need to be in an affected cabin to observe the distress these fellow travelers are experiencing. They have every right to invite an expert like me to support them, and that is exactly what I am doing.' Ward inadvertently shakes his head, mystified by the apparent need for this man to interfere in another person's business.

'Um, well, would anyone be willing to allow me to have a look?' Before anyone can answer, Bitters raises his hand.

'Ladies and gentlemen, I strongly advise you not to comply with this demand. There is no reason for you to make it easy for them to fix a problem they have evidently caused. As soon as you show the first sign of weakness, any chance of conversation will fade into insignificance. We have to stand together or not at all.' Others in the group of 10 look awkwardly at Ward and then at the floor. Ward takes a risk.

'Alright, it's like this everyone. If you're willing to spend the rest of the cruise living in your own shit, then don't let our maintenance staff have a look. On the other hand, if you actually want us to solve the problem then perhaps you'll let us take some kind of look.' At this point a passenger raises his hand and offers to allow Ward and his team to investigate their toilet. Bitters shakes his head menacingly.

'Well, Officer, you win the battle, but you will lose the war.' And with that he marches off, leaving the others to conclude that he is something of an idiot.

'Captain, I have the report on the Deck 11 problem. And, well, it's a little bit odd.' Bladder likes odd. It's more interesting than normal. He leans back and awaits Ward's exposition. 'Basically, we found quite a lot of things which could have caused the issue.' He looks down at his list. 'Amongst the recovered objects are… a towel, a pair of men's underpants, a pornographic magazine – an onion, a banana skin, 30 used condoms –' Bladder interjects.

'Are there any newlyweds on Deck 11?' Ward nods and they both roll their eyes.

'Yes Captain, though interestingly all the condoms are flavoured and that made one part of the vacuum system smell of chocolate. Er, anyway, the other two items were a slipper and a possum.' The Captain raises his eyebrows.

'A possum – as in the animal possum?'

'Yes Sir. It was dead – needless to say. And we suspect it came from the room of a man who's given us trouble in the past. He's previously been connected with toilet blockages involving a beaver, a rabbit, a carp and an uncooked chicken.'

'Was the carp still alive?'

'No sir. It was dead.'

'What would possess someone to flush all of that down the toilet? Is he some kind of pervert?'

'I don't know, Captain. But I think so. He's travelling alone and a couple of days ago the smell of women's perfume was coming from his room.'

'What does that prove, Ward?'

'Er, nothing, sir. It's just information.' Bladder thinks for a long time.

'OK, go and see him. My money's on the possum.'

Ward doesn't mince his words at the door of the startled guest.

'I understand that you flushed a possum down the toilet, Sir.' The man looks confused. He looks quizzically into a space above and behind Ward, as if trying to remember some distant memory of a funeral.

'I'm not sure I get your drift, Officer,' he says with a laughable lack of plausibility. Ward hasn't really got time for this.

'We found a dead possum in the vacuum toilet system. You'll recall that in previous cruises we've also recovered a beaver, a rabbit and uncooked chicken and a carp. You've made a bit of a habit of flushing wildlife down the loo, haven't you sir?' The man widens his eyes.

'I don't know anything about the carp.' The two men stand in silence. Having solved one mystery, Ward feels even more perplexed about what he believes to be both an admission and a plea of not guilty on one charge.

'Could you stop doing it please. You're wrecking the toilets.'

'Sorry.' Ward pauses.

'By the way, why do you do it? What's the thinking?' The man looks up and down the corridor, then addresses Ward in a hushed voice.

'Hypnosis. I was on one of your ships a few years ago and there was this hypnotist. He put me under and instructed me to come out in a hot flush if I saw a mammal. Only I mis-heard him, see. Now, every time I see a mammal I feel a need to flush it down the toilet. And carp aren't mammals. But – well, there it is. Nothing I can do about it.' Ward is amazed to hear this explanation. But it has the ring of truth about it.

'Why can't you get unhypnotised then?'

'Dunno. I just don't seem to be able to stop myself.' The two men stand in silent contemplation. Eventually, Ward concludes with a compromise.

'Look, if you get tempted to do it again, can you give us a call and we'll try to sort it out?' the man nods.

'By the way, Officer, is the story true about the fat lady who flushed the toilet while she was sitting on it and it sucked her guts out?'

'Um, I believe it to be untrue, sir. But I don't recommend that you try to test the theory. That would also block up our toilet system. Although you are a mammal, it strikes me that under any circumstances flushing yourself down the loo would be a bridge too far.' The man ponders Ward's observation.

'Hmmm… I'd never looked at it like that. And sorry I can't help you with the carp.'

'Yes, the carp is a problem. Not a mammal and a horribly boney fish. Virtually inedible. Have a good day sir, and thank you for your candor.' And all at once there's nothing more to say. Ward bows in an awkward way, as if departing from a royal audience. Realising his action to be inappropriately deferential, he adds 'and don't do it again, please.' This seems an over compensation. The man looks at him curiously.

'I've never done it on purpose. It's just that I'm very suggestible. If you told me I'm very sleepy nad that I want to piddle in the pool when there's a blue sky, I'd probably do it. It's just how I am. People like me make the world go round, really.' He shrugs in an unanswerably honest way, prompting a short chuckle from Ward.'

'Where do you get the mammals, by the way?'

'Deputy Restaurant Manager, I think he's called. Always comes and offers me these dead things. Says he gets them from a man in France. I don't know, maybe I'm paying him too much, but it's just this thing.' Wards face stiffens into anger. He makes a split second decision not to pursue it further with the man, and not to tell Bladder everything just yet. But he's certain that there's a bit more work to be done on this with the potential culprit.

'Thanks for your cooperation, Sir. Have a wonderful afternoon.' Ward departs purposefully down the corridor with a difficult explanation to pass on to Bladder and a note to self to add an extra instruction for on board hypnotists: 'do not talk about flush, flushes or flushing.' He's also got some unfinished business with the Deputy

Restaurant Manager.

'Oh bugger.' This is the mantra employed by Bladder every time he sees 'Captain's Dinner' on his itinerary. It's not always terrible. Occasionally, he has had the pleasure of sharing an enjoyable couple of hours with the likes of retired sea captains or accomplished owners of abattoirs with whom he can while away hours on the subject of frozen lamb. However, on the whole he is obliged to spend the evening romancing people who appear to have an insatiable appetite for revisiting the same general conversations, the same general destinations and the same ships. Indeed, at this time the Spirit of Dogger V has no less than 233 individuals who have previously made the very same voyage in the past. 52 of them have done it at least twice. Captain Bladder is forbidden by a specific letter from company headquarters to remonstrate with guests about their motivations for such behaviour. Instead, and by way of empathy with Captain Bladders known disposition towards such matters, he has been invited by no less than the Chef Executive Officer - who has a high regard for Bladder's seafaring talents - to 'listen as patiently as you can and absorb their feedback and questions in the spirit of a martyr.' Bladder also likes the Chief Executive Officer – the only man who might be able to persuade Bladder to bite his tongue on occasions such as the forthcoming dinner.

'Double bugger.' Bladder has just spotted a familiar name on the guest list. Monty and Mrs Major are amongst the very small number of voyagers who have traversed the globe on the Dogger not once, not twice, but five times. Indeed, he has met them before on other ships belonging to the A&G line, including the Spirit of Biscay, the Spirit of Fastnet and the Spirit of Rockall. He doesn't like Monty because Monty invariably insists on mercilessly hammering three subjects into submission: the increasing number of people with tattoos on board, the increasing lapses in dress code, and the Germans. There will inevitably be an additional conversation about the French, whom Monty regards as a subset of the Germans.

'I will not miss these dinners when I retire, Ward.' First Officer Ward, who will also be attending the dinner, takes a different view. He knows their regular clients are both the most loyal and most opinionated of all their paying travellers. He actually enjoys listening to them simply because it is a simple matter to remind himself that they pay his wages. Privately, he bashfully admits to himself that he harbours a kind of morbid fascination for supping with people who spend approximately one quarter of their lives at sea – and are willing to pay for the privilege.

Meanwhile, in Monty's quarters, he's busy writing.

'What are you doing, dear,' asks Mrs Major absently, as she focusses on her make up in the mirror next to the television, which is switched on the Sky news channel. 'Can we have some music?'

'Certainly not on an evening such as this, dear!' Monty wants to keep up to date with any developments of significance in the news, lest the Captain attempts to undermine him with highbrow talk of world affairs instead of responding to the list of topics Monty himself is determined to address. 'And as for what I'm doing, I am preparing an agenda – something I ought to have done years ago. I made all those suggestions last time and I'm beginning to realize that the only way I have a chance of achieving results is by holding them to account in a more formal way. Treat kids like kids and they might grow up to be adults – that's what I say.' Mrs Major ponders Monty's aphorism.

'But you're just about to treat an adult as a kid. Won't that make him act like a kid back?' Monty looks up. He stares out the window at the water.

'Childishness isn't about age. It's about outlook. That Bladder is used to having it all his own way. He doubtless regards himself a some kind of oceanic emperor of the high seas. People like that need to be taken in hand with a firm grip. And then there's the question of his name. It sounds a bit Gallic to me.'

'Gallic!' blurts Mrs Major. 'Bladder's about as British as you can possibly get!'

'Gall Bladder isn't very different to Gallic Bladder, my dear. There are weaknesses in your argument.'

'But he's not a Gall Bladder, or a Gallic Bladder even. He's just a Bladder. Come on Monty, now you're just being silly.' Monty turns his wife's rebuke over in his head.

'We'll see, my dear. We'll see. At any rate, you must admit he always sulks when he meets me, and I'm going to have to take a parental attitude to ensure he understands that such an attitude is not especially acceptable.' This sparks a shower of thoughts in Mrs Major's head, ranging from the learned works of a man called Eric Berne who wrote a book about Transactional Analysis, to entertaining a a sense of dread that this evening could end badly.

'Have you ever heard of Transactional Analysis? The idea that if you treat people like children they will act like children? And what do you think would happen if you sought to be complimentary to the Captain instead of telling him off?'

'Complimentary?! What kind of loose talk is this? For me to take such an approach would be to ensure he loses all respect for me. I cannot allow these circumstances to occur under any circumstances.' Mrs Major tuts.

'You used circumstance twice in that sentence. One might argue that was bad suntax.' Monty is taken aback, but he is a fair man.

'Technically correct I suppose. Perhaps I ought to have said that I cannot allow that eventuality to occur under any circumstances.'

'Much better, dear.'

This is what Monty's agenda looks like:

20.30 Greet Captain Bladder

20.45 Establish content of menu (and check for French spelling)

21.00 Disucss tattoos – what is A&G policy? Make suggestions.

21.30 Dress code lapses – propose sanctions for failing guests

21.45 Discuss Germans (and French)

21.45 Any Other Business

22.00 Depart

Monty looks at his agenda and sees that it is good. He is ready for action.

It's 20.30 and this is the time Captain Bladder most misses a drink. However, he has, since his early days as an officer, applied a self-denying ordinance, preferring instead to maintain a sound and sober mind when charged with the lives of thousands on the earth's mercurial oceans. It is not the oceans which cause him to crave the sanctuary of alcohol. It's the guests. He recalls very clearly the last time he had to dine with Monty and Mrs Major. While the lady was nothing less than an object lesson in charm, her husband appeared to believe that, by virtue of a few decades in the fighting forces, he was qualified to run the ship as well. The evening ended badly when Bladder suggested to Monty that perhaps he would have more credibility as a commentator on maritime matters if he could swim, causing Monty to retort 'the Desert rats couldn't swim, but they won the bloody war for us, which is more than you did!' However, irrational Monty's response, it caused the other guests to side with him for reasons that were clear to nobody at the time.

'Ready Captain?' inquires First Officer Ward, who feels a great personal sense of responsibility to protect Bladder from the worst excesses of ignorance which his superior is likely to experience in the proceeding hours.

'No, I'm never ready for these things. I'd much rather be able to eat the cargo than to eat with it. Come on, let's get this over with.'

They enter the reception to discover that all the guests have arrived early. Bladder tends to forget the exalted status these dinners enjoy in the minds of the guests and feels a tinge of guilt not to have been here to welcome his diners individually upon their arrival. As well as various officers, the guests comprise; a couple of property tycoons from Dorset; an astrologer and an astronomer who are, apparently, guest entertainers; a dapper looking man and his enormously glamorous wife who possesses an extraordinarily loud laugh; a couple who own an abattoir in New Zealand; and Monty and Mrs Major. Bladder realises all conversation has stopped on his arrival and that all eyes are upon him. He feels obliged to speak.

'Good evening, guests.' He is greeted with a spirited response and, for no reason that is obvious to him, the glamour girl bursts into cascades of laughter, causing an echo of mirth amongst the other diners. At a loss to suggest anything else, the Captain continues: 'shall we take our seats?'

To Bladder's horror, Monty appears to be sitting next to him. He leans across to Ward who is sitting opposite and whispers 'why's he next to me?'

'He's not meant to be. He must have changed round the place settings.' Bladder leans back and looks accusingly at Monty.

'Did you fiddle with the place settings?'

'Of course I did, Captain. They'd accidentally put me at the far end of the table. I sorted it all out. Now, I've got a few things to discuss with you.' Monty removes his agenda from his pocket and begins to bore Bladder with is views on tattoos. After a few minutes the Captain interjects.

'I don't see why you have a problem with other people's tattoos. What possible difference does it make to you if a man has an anchor on his arm?' Monty puts down his knife and fork deliberately.

'Captain, the difference it makes to me is standards. If you came home to find your neighbour has painted the front of his house with graffiti, would you not have something to say about it? After all, it could even affect the value of your house.'

'How does a man's tattoo affect the value of your holiday?'

'I find it offensive. And that impoverishes my poolside experience.'

'As I recall, you can't swim. What poolside experiences are these exactly?' Monty is surprised that Captain Bladder remembers that Monty is not a swimmer. He looks for an appropriate response.

'Well, I probably would be able to swim if it weren't for all that body art round the pool. Indeed, should we founder, I am more likely to drown specifically because of the tattoos which you allow your passengers to flaunt across the length and breadth of the sun deck!' By this point, the others at the table have stopped talking to listen to the fractious exchange between Monty and the Captain. The Captain looks at Ward for assistance.

'Bon appetite, everyone!' says Ward cheerily.

'Yes, bon appetite,' adds Bladder. Monty's eyes widen as the glamour model bursts into rapturous laughter causing another ripple of bemused amusement amongst some of the other guests. Monty decides to skip the other agenda items on his list and goes straight to his ethnic challenge.

'And where, might I ask, do you hail from, Captain?' Monty says this so loudly that the table is stunned into silence. Bladder looks up to realize that for some reason the moment has become a stand off.

'I come from Wotton, just outside Northampton.' Everyone looks at Monty who attempts to trap Bladder into a confession.

'And what proportion of your heritage is French, might I ask?'

'Sir, although it would matter if there was, I don't happen to have a Gallic bone in my body. And might I add that your attitude towards these matters is not one I take kindly.'

'Captain, it occurs to me that a Northamptonshire chap would not be employing the use of phrases like 'bon appetite' or such like. Furthermore, the fridges are German and the wine is generally French. I put it to you that there's little point in pretending – we're effectively at the mercy of the Franco-German axis and as far as I can see, the A&G Line is no exception.' This is too much for Bladder. He turns to Monty, waving down First Officer Ward's attempts to calm him.

'I find your wife's company absolutely charming. I also acknowledge that you spend a great deal of money with the A&G Line on an annual basis. This is the reason you are at this dinner. However, it appears to me that your Britannic spirit prevents you from recognizing that we are neither at war with the French or Germans, nor in competition with them for nationalistic superiority. The main course is chicken chasseur. This is a French dish. I notice you also finished your pate – another gallic delicacy. If you cannot bring yourself to enjoy the evening in a more civil and less sectarian manner, I'm going ot ask you to leave – though your wife is more than welcome to stay.'

The room is frozen. Only the distant sound of waves occasionally colliding with the bow breaks the silence. Monty looks at his wife. She looks down. He looks back at Bladder.

'Well, Captain, I find myself in a socially compromising position, where you appear to be challenging the etiquette of my right to assert British values on a British ship. What is it you wish me to do?' Bladder breathes in deeply.

'Well, Monty, what I'm asking you to do is to desist from offensive commentary without just cause. What have the French ever done to you?' Monty hesitates. He looks at the critical eyes round the table. He shudders with the pressure of confession and takes a drink of the ample glass of French red wine before him.

'Well, Captain, the French collaborators, the friends of the Vichy Government, tortured and killed my father. As I understand it from eye witnesses, they did it for no military purpose, but rather for fun. I qam informed he bled to death from a hundred cuts. Subsequently, my mother passed away from what I can only describe as a broken heart.' And with that, Monty rises from the table and departs from the room. Mrs Major, her eyes welled up with moisture, removes her napkin.

'Excuse me, please. I'm so sorry.' She leaves to find her husband. Bladder looks at Ward, who nods for Bladder to follow.

'Excuse me, please continue ladies and gentlemen.' Bladder leaves the room to find a steward outside the room. Without needing to be asked he indicates to the Captain that Monty and Mrs Major have both exited to the deck by the nearby entrance. Bladder breathes in hard and geos out the door.

Outside, in the balmy, salty darkness, Mrs Major has her arms around Monty, who in turn is looking down at the ocean's moonlight spray, generated by the bow's patient undulations as the vessel presses forward. Bladder does something completely out of character.

'Sir, I have instructions not to be provocative, but in all honesty I can't apologize because it would not be sincere. Frankly, I don't really understand people. This is my domain, the ocean. It's like this you see.' Bladder searches for the words. 'Perhaps we might try to accept each other's blind spots with a little more generosity.' Monty continues to look down at the waves.

'I feel more comfortable with institutions than people. This makes my wife a saint – something which I most certainly am not. I can never forgive the French. Too much pain there, old chap. Thank you for the invitation to dinner. But I think I should go back to our quarters now, before I ruin it for everyone. My wife will stay.'

Bladder steps forward and , as every instinct screams at him to step back again. He puts his hand on his shoulder.

'In that case, you shall miss a most delightful sirloin steak.' Monty stares down at the froth at the bow.

'I recall it is chicken chasseur.'

'Under the circumstances, I believe we can make an exception,

Sir.' Monty finally looks towards the Captain. ' Monty's face is that of a man who has not cried for years.

'I can only be who I am.   What can I do?'

'I know. Hence the steak.'

'Bugger you, Bladder.'

'Bugger me, Monty.'

The hand shake that follows is the beginning of a healing which will take a significant part of the rest of two lifetimes.

Chapter 22 :
Silent running

Of all the weather phenomena in Nature's extensive arsenal, there are only two which Captain Bladder actively dislikes: ice, for its considerable accumulation on the frame of a ship can cause it capsize; and fog, which robs seafarers of the most important defence against danger – a forward view.

As the pre-dawn light begins to permeate the cracks in the curtains on a thousand balconies, something else seeps in too: that unmistakable humidity of Bermuda fog. The waters are like glass the air windless and saturated, and the horizon has been replaced by a single shade of grey.

Up on the bridge, crewmen are straining to see anything at all. In reality, the ship is at the mercy of electronics – the radar and radio and depth gauges drawing a mathematical model of what no eyes can see. Bladder is always a little more tense in these situations. He even considers slowing their forward progress, but in a sense this is a meaningless gesture. A collision at 15 knots is barely any less calamitous than one at 22 knots. Barring some additional reason, he opts to maintain the original cruise speed.

'How long is it scheduled to last,' asks Bladder.

'I'm afraid there's no news on that Sir, except that ships a hundred miles ahead are reporting similar conditions.'

'At least five hours, then, unless the sun can burn it off. Alright, keep me posted if you see or hear anything at all which might conflict with our track.' Bladder departs to rest. He wants to take a kip when he can. If there is any risk of proximity to another vessel, he will, as a matter of course, take the helm – and responsibility.

Down on Deck 8 Violet Cryer has pulled back the curtains.

'Look! This is it – the Bermuda Triangle. It's started!' Her second husband has long since abandoned his efforts to find simpler and rational explanations for Violet's theories – for the simplest explanation of all is that Violet has too little to do and therefore fills her hours by generating self-important fantasies that serve to elevate her to the status of a bard at the same time as colouring her dreary and unchallenging life with ghosts and goblins and killer bugs from Outer Space. Thus it is that the grey outside provides an ironic, multicoloured opportunity to build supernatural dangers in the mists. She grabs some washing and heads for the launderette on deck 5.

'Good morning, Mrs Major,' chirps Monty.

'Yes dear.'

'What splendidly calm seas,' he remarks before pulling back the curtains. 'Bugger me!' he exclaims in vivid enough tones to cause Mrs Major to stir. 'Fogged in, and that's a fact!' For some reason, the fog genuinely catches Monty by surprise. In the vein of military professionals, he considers the options available to the Captain to ensure safe passage.

'Is this because we're in the Bermuda Triangle, dear?' enquires his half conscious wife.

'Bermuda Triangle my arse! In fact, my arse is far more real than the Bermuda Triangle, which is about as plausible as the Loch Ness Monster, UFOs and the End of The World. Fog is about moisture, not conspiracy theories. But no doubt we'll hear it all today from the same people who brought us all that tripe about the Captain raising the dead.' Mrs Major likes the fact that, for all his bombast, her husband is reassuringly rational when it comes to matters of science and reason.

Trev and Dave have woken up without a hangover, mainly because they ended up in a long and protracted argument with two men from Friends of Dorothy in Winners Bar about whether 'sea monster' could only be used to refer to creatures which have yet to be formally categorised and can make a roaring sound if attacking a ship. Inexplicably, the application of logic caused Trev and Dave to drink less quickly.

'What time is it Dave, mate?' Dave looks at his phone.

'It's 11am in Britain, mate, so whatever it is here less than that.'

'Er, are we five hours ahead or behind?'

'Dunno, mate. But that means it's somewhere between 6am and four in the afternoon.' Trev picks up the phone and calls reception.

'Hello, yes – er room A116. Yes, you can, what time is it please miss? Thanks. No, that was all. Bye.'

'So what time is it then Trev?'

'Not telling – to teach you a lesson about not keeping your phone up to date with the time. And it's 7am.'

'What? That's amazing. Let's get up and do something useful like sunbathing then.'

Dave and Trev arrive up on deck 12 to find all the deck chairs are free. The fog swirls forlornly between the railings and across the deck in patterns that create an eerie impression. Water drips from the metal frames, as the moisture brushing across the structures. Dave and Trev stand there like spirits in the grey mist.

'Let's see it's the same up there.' The ascend to the highest point on deck, where the swirling effect takes on an even more dramatic dynamic. The fog horn blairs out, scaring the two lads out of their skins.

'Bugger this, mate. Let's have breakfast.'

Mr and Mrs Jitters have woken to the sound of silence. This distresses them slightly.

'Does it sound different to you today, Jack?'

'Yes it does, Jane.' Jack gets out of bed and pulls back the curtains. 'Oh. We seem to have lost our view to fog.' And it's true – somehow fog makes the sounds of sea life seem different – as if the airborne water has shrouded the vessel from almost every sound. He turns round and looks at his wife. 'I have an excellent suggestion. Let's just stay in bed and have a nice cuddle!' His wife giggles like a young girl, as Mr Jitters snuggles up to his reason for being.

Mr and Mrs Bitters react differently to the fog.

'Now look what they've done to us,' he moans. 'I suppose that's because it's the Bermuda Triangle. We could disappear in this and nobody would know. Or come out in a different time zone or something. I don't want to spend the rest of my life in 1500B.C. or on another planet.'

'Does that sort of thing really happen then?'

'Well, you never hear anyone come back from these things and say it didn't, do you? And I met a woman in the launderette who says there's a ghost on board and that we're all going to meet our dead selves. That's not very good, is it?' Mrs Bitters thinks about that.

'I wouldn't want to meet myself, I don't think.'

'Why not?'

'Because I don't really like people from Birmingham very much, do you?'

'Not really. Do you thinkit's going to be foggy in the ship?'

'I don't think so – because they'll have people to deal with that sort of thing.'

'I hope you're right. I don't want to have breakfast if I can't see my own plate. They might try and rip me off, see.'

Trev and Dave are sitting in their room, doing – nothing. Dave is flicking through the channels, and has settled on the forward view of the ship's direction of travel. It's pure grey.

'Trev, mate, what are you looking at that for?'

'Sea monsters.'

'Ah come on, mate, don't be such a plonker. Sea monsters. I think this is the time for us to break open something to make you sane again.' Trev reaches under the bed and pulls out his suitcase. 'This!' Trev is brandishing an unopened bottled of Sambouca. 'Ta daa!'

'Trev mate are you sure? Strange things always happen when we have that stuff.'

'What else is there to do? Come on.'

An hour later, Dave and Trev are hammered on a drink which causes them both to experience significantly altered states.

'Let's explore, mate! Let's go in that door. The Crew one. Come on – what's the worst that can happen?'

Trev and Dave walk along the corridor in a conspiratorial kind of way. They reach the door which says 'Crew only – no admittance' just as the lady from across the way is passing.

'Now what are you boys up to? Naughty, naughty!' Dave feels like challenging her assumptions, but given their nefarious intent, he remains silent. Once the corridor is clear, they test the door: it's unlocked.

'Now! Whispers Trev. They dive in the door. As they stare along what looks like an endless, neon lit corridor, the door closes behind them in a final kind of way. 'Come on.'

10 minutes later they're still walking along deserted corridors. Down some steps, the descent seems never ending. The light changes, becoming darker and more sinister.

'Trev mate, I'm not sure we're supposed to be here.' Trev ignores

Dave's concerns and presses on. A few minutes later, there's an enormous door in front of them. They push on it together and as it opens, they can't believe what they see. 'Wow.' Before them is what looks like a giant forest. There's a river and tall trees. The sound of the leaves as they rustle under their feet does not seem to disturb the wildlife. A small herd of deer stands in a clearing nearby. Dave nudges Trev and points to the left.

'Cows! So the steaks don't come from fish.' Trev is overwhelmed by the spectacle.

'I can't believe this mate. It's like Noah's Ark!' they stand there trying to figure out how large the woods are. 'What's that noise?' They run to hide behind a tree. It's Al Garr and another member of his team, walking through the woods. As he stops, the birds land on his shoulders and the deer run to him. Al feeds them with something from his pocket. Then he starts singing;

'I see trees of green........ red roses too

I see em bloom..... for me and for you

And I think to myself.... what a wonderful world.'

Dave steps out from behind the tree, and Trev's too late to stop him. Dave starts walking towards Al Garr. The animals run away. The singing stops. Al waits until Dave is right next to him.

'What are you dong Dave?'

'It's all just so beautiful.'

'You shouldn't be here Dave. Is your friend here?' Dave points to the tree. Trev steps out and waves. Al gestures at Dave and Trev. They're suddenly surrounded by crew with angry dogs, barking and straining to approach the boys. 'Take them away – put them in the freezer. They can be tomorrow's steak!' Dave and Trev start screaming as the crew carry them away towards a large white door. The door is opened and inside are the icy remains of the dead animals which keep their lonely vigil in anticipation of their moment of glory in the many restaurants above. Dave and Trev are pushed inside. The door is shut and it is pitch dark.

'Trev, mate, I'm cold.'

'So am I Dave. I'm sorry.

'This is the end, isn't it?'

'You were a good mate to me. Take care pal,' Dave sings 'Always look on the Bright side of Life,' as the two of them descend into a hypothermic coma, the precursor to death.

'Look!' screams Violet so loudly that her husband prepares for a collision. 'A sea monster! She snaps away at the balcony for 10 seconds and then reviews the effects. 'There! Se it rising up!' Sure enough a great dark object is protruding from the sea in the picture. 'This is the proof we've been looking for!' She dresses to leave the cabin.

'Where are you going, Violet?'

'To the launderette – the ship needs to know the truth!'

Up on the bridge First Officer Ward speaks to Bladder.

'Well, Captain, we finally have a confirmed sighting of a sea monster.'

'Really, that didn't take long.'

'Would you like to see it?'

'A picture too. Certainly.' Ward presents a photocopy of Violet Cryer's photograph. Bladder looks at it in detail. 'So the sea monster is Violet Cryer's finger in front of the lense, is it?' Ward nods. 'Excellent. That should keep the complaints about everything else down to virtually zero.' Ward never ceases to be impressed at Captain Bladder's grasp of the human condition – which appears to be inversely proportional to his disdain for having to actually meet the passengers.

Dave and Trev wake up in bed.

'What just happened Trev, mate?'

'We had Sambouca.'

'I dreamt etc.' Trev stares at the ceiling.

'So did I.'

'Bermuda Triangle, Trev mate.'

'Na, Sambouca. Fancy another?'

'Don't mind if I do. I want to see what happens next.'

What happens next is not very good at all. The Bermudan night is about to bowl a curve ball to Spirit of Dogger V – and it's going to be a very close scrape... literally.

Chapter 23 :
Unlucky Strike

It's all steady as she goes up on the Bridge. It's 0400 local time and even the wildest revellers have now succumbed to their beds. Bladder is on watch, as he likes to be in the small hours, engrossed in the technicalities of the dials and gauges which report on the engineering state of the ship. With thousands of metres of water beneath the hull, he feels secure in his location and with no indication of any other vessel in the vicinity; everything's looking good for Bermuda's Hamilton port in approximately 26 hours.

There have been unconfirmed reports of some piracy in these seas recently. It's a worrying development. Until now, cruise ships have had little concern about such issues in these waters. But times are changing and Captain Bladder has heard talk of the apparent disappearance of a 27 foot yacht over the last couple of days – a vessel which nobody has heard anything from since. Often, these mysteries are quickly solved when the small craft reappear with radio failure in some port or other, or they deliberately and irresponsibly fail to report their location through some misplaced sense of machismo. But Bladder is concerned and he takes the risk of piracy very seriously.

Bladder is thinking about the future. He's weary of this cruise and Dogger V's complaining guests, but on the other hand the ocean is a compelling domain for him, and even transporting people is better than living on land. He hasn't worked out what to do with his life at that time when there cruise returns to Southampton. His wife has long since died and, having enjoyed a love which led to two wonderful children and 22 beautiful years, he has seen no reason to remarry. But in less than three months this journey is over and he has no new journey to cherish or wish for. The darkness ahead is as un-illuminating as the future. Like the future, there are occasional glints of light, other vessels which rise and fall and hint at the expanse of what lies ahead. Beyond this promise of the ocean's continuation, there is no more information in those blinking, silent lights.

A Junior Officer steps up to the Captain.

'All quiet in the Bermuda Triangle, Officer,' says the Captain, with a karmic tone of voice which makes his subordinate feel calm. At times like this Bladder emanates an aura which appears to connect him to the sea as if he's a spokesperson of the oceans themselves.

'Safe and true to track, Captain.' Bladder pauses.

'True to track indeed, young man, but never safe. Never completely so. The dangers which nature spares us from mankind have found an equal in those which mankind has replaced them with. A voyage is only safe at the final port – which is why we so often indicate the nautical miles to run to that port throughout each leg of the voyage.' Standing with Bladder at these peaceful hours is often an education and, for those willing to listen with humility, a gentle joy. Bladder asks a further question to the junior without averting his eyes from the view ahead. 'Will you be comfortable to mind the bridge for 10 minutes. My namesake requires a brief relief.' The junior is only too willing to step up to the plate. 'You have control.' Only now does Bladder look away, patting the officer on the shoulder as he passes. The junior suddenly feels a rush of pride, as tens of thousands of tonnes and 4,000 souls are in his careful custody.

Bladder enters the loo, and shuts his eyes briefly. He's been on for quite a few hours, and this evening he's feeling a little tired. Another hour and he'll hand over the watch entirely. The low hum of the toilet is in some way soothing, one of those whip sounds he's known all his life. The distant throb of the engines has been the soundtrack to his life since he was a teenager. He notices that the loo roll is nearly finished.

A dull thud shakes the vessel slightly. He hears a scraping and the vibration which started at the bow returns from the stern. Bladder is entirely awake immediately and urgently, running into the bridge just in time to see the dials on for the port propulsion system dip momentarily, and the ship shake in a manner which he knows means only one thing. Without looking up from the dials he issues orders to his junior and the others on the bridge.

'Sound the alarm for the engineers, he says,' contact the engine room for the port engine immediately and tell the Chief Engineer we've had either a prop strike or a blade separation. Send the assessment crew to the stern watertight compartments.' The bridge springs into urgent life. Everyone is now in a different mode, going through checklists and within seconds people are appearing on the bridge till the numbers there have almost doubled.

'Captain, I have the Chief Engineer.' The officer hands Bladder the phone.

'I'm sure it's a blade, can't be the whole thing – otherwise it would have over revved. Not so, thus we have an asymmetry which would indicate prop trouble rather than engine trouble. That's as far as I can go without speculating. Let me know.' He puts the phone down, and only now realises the Junior Officer is still standing at his station, paralysed with shock. Captain Bladder stops his urgent inquiry and goes across. 'Fredrick, did you see lights ahead?' Fredrick shakes his head. He looks at the Captain with fear.

'No Sir, absolutely not. And there was no proximity warning either. Sir, I didn't see anything.'

Alright Fredrick, what you need to understand is that this wasn't your fault. You're not to blame. Do you hear me? It is important that you grasp this point. Even had I not needed to relieve myself at that moment, it would have happened anyway.' The officer is not accepting of this, and Bladder can see this. Leave it for now. We can return to this, alright?' With that they get back to the task of diagnosing what went wrong, and Bladder knows he'll have to hold a longer conversation on this later.

Around the ship few have noticed the incident. Those awake will have noticed a brief unusual vibration and almost immediate change in engine tone. The vibration in the stern cabins is briefly quite pronounced but little different to the changes in tone which occur as the ship plows through significant waves, which create a similar effect. The ship is not listing, and for the next few minutes the Captain is willing to await reports – most importantly from the Chief Engineer.

This is not long in coming. The immediate provisional verbal update confirms Bladder's suspicion.

Bladder calls a meeting and invites the Chief Engineer to explain to everyone what they know. Something has happened to the drive shaft rather than the engine itself which shows normal function. Most likely the propeller has lost one or two blades, causing it to wobble. The cause of this can be only one of two things: structural failure due to a weakness in the metal, or an impact with a solid object. The Chief Engineer will betting on the latter.

'Right, the Chief Engineer has told you his assessment – and this concurs with my own. We heard an impact at the bow, followed by scraping and banging along the length of the ship. I believe we hit a solid object, and that it was sucked into the line of the port screw, where it impacted with one or more blades.' Silence in the room indicates assent. 'There's no breach to the hull and the engine appears in good working order. However, we're down to half power at the business end of Dogger V. Any questions?'

Ward asks one question.

'Where do we check it, Captain? The blade? We can't really do it out here.'

'The nearest place we can – Little Epsilon South.' Epsilon is a known island in the Bermuda chain, but Little Epsilon South is not a familiar destiantion. There's a questioning in the room. The Captain is firm. 'Politically, it's a restless little place. Mechanically, we have no choice. We're going there now, and at our current speed of 10 knots we'll make it there in 27 hours. I'll make the announcement to the guests at 10am today – six hours from now. For reference, and for the record, this occurred on my watch and I am fully responsible for it.'

The meeting disperses. The Junior Officer who was there when the incident occurred is leaving.

'Frederick. The record will show it happened on my watch. You're out of the picture.'

'But it didn't sir. I was responsible.'

'I'll tell you what happened young man. We hit a container – one which fell off a ship. It wasn't a yacht because our blades will cut through fibreglass, and we'd hardly notice the impact. And it wasn't the sea bed as we're in thousands of feet of water. This is my last cruise and you're just starting out. Alright?'

'Thank you sir.' Bladder smiles.

'Thank you Frederick. We had two options: an accident on the bow or an accident on the bridge. This latter eventuality is far less embarrassing for me.'

Bladder may not like his guests, but he loves his crew. It takes a brave man to take responsibility at the twilight of a spotless career. Bladder would never have even considered doing it any other way.

Chapter 24 :
Troubled waters

Spirit of Dogger V is operating in a stable though compromised condition. Instead of the customary 22 knot top speed, the vessel is confined to a performance envelope which barely exceeds half of that velocity. The seas have become rougher and the swell makes the vessel roll to left and right according to the vagaries of the ocean swell. Chief Engineer is determined to ensure they don't end up with a second failure, which would convert this drama into a crisis.

The Captain has determined that the nearest British owned port is the most logical one – and that turns out to be the diminutive island of Little Epsilon South – the southern most island far beneath the main band of islands which traditionally are considered to make up the famous Bermudas.

Dave wakes up in the darkness of their inside cabin. There's no way to tell the time of day in here. Dave has been snoring all night, which initially kept Trev awake. Now Trev is continuing to snore. He looks at Trev's dribbling, unshaven face and decides that evolution has not been kind to Trev. Trev Also wonders whether it's time to start worrying about the fact the ship is only going at half speed. But he can't get his mind around this.

'The thing is Dave, mate, if anyone on board was late for anything, they wouldn't be on the ship in the first place – because we're only going back to where we started in the first place.'

'Oi, Trev. Should we get up and see if the bars are still working mate?'

'I don't think the pubs are powered by the propellors.'

Trev and Dave eventually get up and decide to go onto the rear deck. When they get there, they're surprised to see a lot of other people there too.

'Why are these people overcrowding our pub,' questions Trev.

'Na, they're looking at something.' Trev and Dave get their pints of Fosters and join the viewers at the stern. Sure enough, there's a small boat approaching the ship from behind. 'Hey, that's nice. Well wishers.' Monty happens to be there too.

'Well wishers? Think again my boys! These people wish us anything other then well. These are pirates!' Trev and Dave are excited.

'Cool. Pirates of the Caribbean! Jonny Depp and that fit bird.' Monty is appalled at their ignorance.

'Don't be so damn foolish, lad! These people are not glamorous! They're old Nazi war criminals who've been on the run for decades. They'll just as likely torture you for secrets as they are to steal your watch.'

'What secrets Monty?' Monty ponders this.

'On second thoughts, you're probably safe. If you found a secret, you'd probably drink it.'

Captain Bladder is looking pensively at the situation.

'We can't outrun those damn buggers. It's a very serious situation. Make sure you keep the Line posted – they'll know what to do. For now, we ought to protect ourselves as best we can. I won't make the announcement yet. However, perhaps we ought to congregate all the wheelchair users in one place. They tend to be easy targets for these swine. In fact, yes, take them all to Pretender's Bar - it's got the best open floor.' Bladder considers how to make the announcement and decides to just put it out there.

'Ladies and gentlemen, this is your Captain speaking and I'm sorry to disturb your mid-morning activities. I trust you are making the most of this glorious Caribbean sunshine. I have three announcements which may be of interest. Firstly, in about five minutes we will be overrun by violent pirates and those of you at the stern will have an excellent view of the approaching boat. At our current rate of knots there is little which we can do to outrun them. Secondly, can I ask all wheelchair users to make their way to the Pretenders' Bar where we will ensure you're very well looked after during the pirate invasion. Finally, the un-hosted chess club event has been moved from noon to 2pm this afternoon due to necessary maintenance in the Billabong Room - I do apologise for this change of timing, and I hope this does not cause too much inconvenience. Thank you.' Bladder looks at Ward who is staring at the Captain. 'They need to know, Ward. Better they have a bit of a panic now and a bit of calm later.' Ward shakes his head.

'I doubt that's possible Captain – I mean you've just moved the chess club fixture by two hours. That's likely to cause a mutiny.'

Mr and Mrs Bitters have never felt so bitter. After everything else they've had to complain about now they've got pirates as well. They listen mournfully to the Captain's announcement, Mr Bitters at the window, his wife sitting on the sofa.

'With all this palava I really think we ought to deserve a full refund. It's outrageous. You'd think they'd have planned for this.' Mr Bitters stands with his back to the room.

'I think something fishy is going on here. This is just too much of a coincidence. First the propeller breaks. Then, lo and behold, a lot of scrap metal merchants happen to be passing by.'

'Scrap metal merchants?' inquires his wife. Her husband turns round.

'What I'm suggesting is the pretty obvious fact that they've set whole thing up themselves. Perhaps this is about stealing the propeller which must weigh hundreds of tonnes. Now they're going to sell it for hard cash to these barrow boys to make thousands of pounds for themselves. It's a scam and I bet Captain Morgan, and the two astrologers, are in on it. That's what all that rubbish was about.' Mrs Bitters curls the sides of her mouth down into resentful anger.

'They must take us for fools.'

'Yes – but we can call their bluff. We need to go upstairs. We need to be there when these so-called pirates meet the Captain to hand over his share of the cash.'

The pirates are nearly upon them now. Crew members are at the back, encouraging the guests to return to their cabins. The pirates have not one boat but two. One a twin-engined powerboat, behind it a sailing boat on tow – and clearly spoils from an earlier attack. There are 12 pirates, all armed and pumped up with enthusiasm. As they board the ship, those guests who see the activity begin to panic. All the pirates are dressed in the same way – stripy tops, headscarves and unkempt beards.

'Look at that, Trev, they look just like cartoon character on the telly! This can't be right, mate.'

Monty looks down suspiciously, but says nothing. Only Mr and Mrs Bitters take a proactive view.

'See, it's not real. If they expect us to believe that then they're even more stupid than they think we are. Come on, and check you've got your camera and the sunscreen. We've got to get down there.'

The head pirate climbs up a rope they've slung over the back of the ship followed by the others. They hop at the back of Deck 7. They're armed with guns and immediately start shouting at the guests, pushing and shoving them into big groups. Within minutes they're marauding the public spaces, demanding jewellery and possessions from the terrified passengers.

The Captain races down to the deck to confront them with a contingent of crew. By the time he apprehends them, they're just about to enter the Pretender's Bar where the wheelchair users have been assembled. The Captain steps in front of them.

'I can't let you do that.' The pirate is shocked by his boldness. He squares up to the Captain, but the Captian is resolute. 'You're not going in there.' The pirate looks Captain Bladder up and down. Then he speaks to two of his people, who immediately point guns at the Captain and indicate he will have to walk with them. 'Ward, I'm putting you in charge. It's a kidnap situation.'

'Captain!' exclaims First Officer Ward. 'We can't let you go.' The Captain stops and looks round, catching the pirates off guard as they keep walking.

'You'll be OK. Save the ship.'

The pirates have returned and are hustling him to the stern of the ship. They pass Mr and Mrs Bitters, who look at the Captain and immediately follow on. At the stern, Bladder is instructed to go down the rope ladder by the pirates. He doesn't offer resistance. There's no chivalry in getting shot. However, just before he goes down, Mr and Mrs Bitters tap the pirate on the shoulder.

'We're coming too,' demands Mr Bitters. The pirates are confused. They've never experienced this before – volunteers to go with them. Then they suspect this is a trick, that these people know more than the others. It's suddenly become a game of brinkmanship. The pirate can't figure out the nature of the game, but clearly these two are valuable to someone, and in some strange way they're being offered as collateral in lieu of others on board. As long as they have the Captain, they'll be guaranteed a good ransom. Mr and Mrs Bitters are just a bonus. They're signalled to descend the ladder after the Captain. Soon two pirates, Mr and Mrs Bitters and the Captain are all aboard the pirate boat. The third remains on board to guard the top of the rope ladder.

Down on the pirate craft, Bladder asks for permission to have a look at the back of the boat. The Bitters couple object – Mr Bitters knows this must be to do with the handover of cash to the Captain in exchange for the propeller blades - and even possibly a share of the booty from the on-going robbery.

'We demand to see what the Captain is doing in the back,' says Mr Bitters in his monotonous Birmingham accent. Mrs Bitters talks at the same time, confusing the pirates with their insistent whinging. They're on strict orders not to kill hostages in full view of the ship during a raid: that might embolden other passengers if they believe there's nothing to lose by 'having a go.' So the pirates try to shut them up by shouting back – an utterly futile strategy when it comes to this particular pair.

Meanwhile, up on Spirit of Dogger V, nine pirates enter the Pretender's Bar. They're stunned by what they see. The leader has never seen anything like it in his life. The fact he's not familiar with wheelchairs or motorised scooters causes him to chatter to his colleagues and fiddle with the machines - much to the annoyance of their occupants. In the rolling seas the room creaks tensely, as if reflecting the mutual tension.

'Don't touch that!' shouts an elderly gentleman, as one of the pirates releases the break lever, just as the swell tilts the floor. The elderly gentleman's wheelchair flies across the room, gaining speed towards the uncomprehending chief pirate. Within moments, he's fatally crushed between the feet of the chair and the wall of the bar. There's no further delay as all the other wheelchair users respond in kind. They release their brakes and accelerate their vehicles to full speed.

The next few seconds are carnage. As the mayhem settles, one solitary pirate is left semi-conscious, moaning and injured on the floor. All the guns are now in the possession of the wheelchair bound guests, every one pointing at the one surviving pirate. Mrs Wilson, aged 84, wheels herself up to the pirate and pulls him up by the ear. She eyeballs him:

'Go back to your people and tell them what happened here.' Then she turns to her husband in a motorised buggy. 'He's all yours darling.'

As the posse of wheelchairs arrive at the back of the ship, towing the dazed and injured pirate behind them, they're shocked to see another well armed pirate. Then, spotting his colleague in ragged tow, he raises his gun to threaten them, uttering words none of the pensioners understand. This is a moment of peril for all concerned. The pirate demands his dazed friend is brought to him, and the injured man staggers his colleague's side. As his pirate friend crosses the railings, holding on to his colleague for support, the able bodied pirate also mounts the railing and takes aim to fire at Mr Wilson. He begins to squeeze the trigger... only to be smashed by an enormous man in a manual wheelchair. The pirates lose their footing and fall down into the sea, leaving the wheelchair users shocked but relieved by the sudden events as the two criminals splash into the water.

Meanwhile, the pirate boat is roped up to the stern of the still moving Dogger V. They can see two pirates and two guests apparently involved in a shouting match. Suddenly the yacht behind the pirate boat seems to slip its rope and fall suddenly away, as if deliberately released, causing the pirates to break off from the argument and start gesticulating and threatening whoever is on board the rogue yacht.

'It's Captain Bladder!' exclaims Mr Wilson. 'We've got to help him. There's nothing we can do.' The pirates in the boat are preparing to shoot at Bladder and seek to hole him before the water line, when they spot their two colleagues in the water. Their two pirate friends have become collateral currency requiring a quick calculation by those in the small boat.

'Do you think they'll die?' asks one of the wheelchair users, as they watch the commotion down in the sea.

Mr Wilson, looks down.

'Well, I know we're supposed to be fair minded and all that. But, frankly, if they can't even beat a group of disabled pensioners in wheelchairs – well, it's hard to respect them as pirates, isn't it?' They watch in silence as the remaining pirates in the boat fumble with the rope ladder, which has now become a tugging match between some of the other wheelchair users on the deck. Eventually, they abandon the rope ladder and spend yet more time unlashing themselves from the back of the ship.

The bridge has seen what's going on and has restarted the damaged prop, which now begins to cause colossal, thundering vibrations through the decks and walls of the ship, as if the entire vessel were passing through an automatic car wash in which the soft bristles have been replaced with hammers and roaring metal rollers. Within seconds, the broken prop sends irregular and enormous plumes of spray into the air, making it impossible or the pirates to control their small craft. Eventually, they cut free, disorientated and far from their compatriots. There's little chance they'll be able to recover both of them alive, let alone catch up with the ever resourceful Captain Bladder who is already making full use of the feisty force 6 wind which continues to unsettle the restless ocean surface.

Back in the Pretender's Bar, First Officer Ward is surveying the carnage and has reassembled the wheelchair users for a comprehensive debrief.

'Was all this killing strictly necessary?' he asks. Mrs Wilson responds for them all.

'We didn't kill them on purpose, did we? What were we supposed to do? Anyway, Captain Bladder can bring them back to life just as he did with Captain Morgan.' There is general agreement.

'And the two men overboard?' challenges Ward.

'Officer, I don't know what's happened back there - but consider the situation young man. They're violent. We're disabled. They had guns. We have wheelchairs. They were preparing to shoot at Captain Bladder. We need a captain. Officer Ward, if doing what's right for this ship and the safety of its crew and passengers is our crime... then, Sir, we are guilty. Ward looks at the assembled group – wheelchair users, the nemesis of Bladder's tormented life as a Cruise Captain, who it seems took great risks in his defence. He ponders the events of the last 30 minutes.

'I see your point. Thank you, ladies and gentlemen,' says Ward. 'You saved the ship.' Mrs Wilson raises her finger.

'That's as may be Officer Ward, but I think I speak for many of us when I say none of the events in this room compare to the gratuitous shifting of the Un-hosted Chess Club event to 2pm. This day will live in infamy.' Sombre applause and shouts of 'Hear! Hear!' fill the room.

Chapter 25 :

Danger Island

Spirit of Dogger V limps into the harbour of the island known as Little Epsilon South at an achingly slow speed. This is the closest island to their position with a deep sea port. It's not a conventional tourist destination. Being some distance apart from the rest of the Bermuda archipelago, it is regarded as something of a frontier island, with little law and a tendency for wayward political behaviour. With one propeller – or 'screw' as it is technically called in marine terms - out of action, the performance of the ship is intolerably slow for the world cruise. It must be repaired immediately. And acting Captain Ward wants to do it immediately rather than risk a longer journey - and greater cost - in Bermuda 'proper.'

They approach the dock cautiously. They haven't been in here before – and there's always the prospect of further damage to be added to what's already been incurred.

Ward edges the ship close to the concrete harbour. The local harbour staff watch on, leaning against their beat up cars, drinking beer. As they get closer, an ever increasing number of men appear to be turning up on the dock. It looks like many of them have guns.

'Captain, they've got guns. Are you sure this is altogether wise?'

'No I'm not sure. In fact, we might be finished, but we're committed now.' Ward judges that they're too close to docking to change the plan. Futhermore, it would be utterly irresponsible to sail with one blade out of action. Another container strike would lead them dead in the water and at the mercy of the elements – and more pirates. They can't afford to risk that scenario. 'We've got to go in even if they impound the ship. There's a lot of danger out there for us just now. At least this place is meant to be friendly.' A few of the men on the quayside point their guns casually at the ship.

'That inspires confidence,' mutters his junior. 'I'm not scared.'

'Speak for yourself. But we're here and we must get the repair team to work straight away.'

The ropes are lashed and Ward makes an announcement.

'Ladies and Gentlemen, many thanks for your patience as we deal with our minor technical issue. I'm delighted to report that we have docked safely, and our team of engineers will now be able to replace the damaged prop blade in the course of the day. We are going to meet the relevant authorities and seek to arrange an opportunity for you to visit the, er, delights of this island, whatever those may be, as the repair is being made. Please do listen in as I hope to make an announcement about possible tours within the hour. In the meantime, have an enjoyable day. Thankyou.' Ward stops and shuts his eyes. 'That was terrible. They'll all know we're in trouble.' Ward's right. Everyone knows there's a problem and that the bridge has no idea what reception they'll receive on the island. Nobody will have to wait for long to find out.

Ward is preparing to leave the bridge to talk personally to the authorities. They save him the effort. He is invited to open the bridge door, which he debates with himself briefly before realising that if there's any problem a door isn't going to hold anyone with explosives back for all that long. He opens the door.

Three men smoking rancid smelling cigarettes and brandishing guns enter the bridge. Their darkly tanned skin and belts of bullets is mildy impressive, but they're credibility is somewhat reduced by the fact that one of them is holding a bottle of beer and another is reading a copy of OK magazine. In broken English the apparent leader of this motley trio reads a prepared script. 'Lady and Gentman, I am to be vowed for ship to this republic no wit controlled of seaman to us.' Ward is visibly annoyed with the incomprensibility of the statement.

'What? Give me that,' and he snatches the paper out of the man's hand. Before he reads is out he signals at the cigarettes and shakes his head. 'NO SMOKING.' The three look at each other uncertainly and falteringly extinguish the cigarettes with their boots. 'Thank you, gentlemen.' Ward studies the note – which, it turns out, the man had read out accurately. 'No, I still don't understand. What is it you want? Are you by any chance the engineers?' A long pause ensues, until the three consult with each other in their unusual language. Then, the ring leader turns to Ward.

'I get else,' he says and they leave. Ward stares at the open door in disbelief.

'What the hell was that all about?! Look, let's get going with the repairs, and I'll deal with that elite force of linguistic plonkers once

I understand what they actually want.' Ward issues the relevant instructions and adds, 'bleep me if you need me. I'm going to catch up with The Three Amigos to find their leader.' Ward doesn't have to work hard to achieve that. The mystery gunmen have found themselves lost and confused only a few paces away from the bridge. 'Where is your leader,' he says slowly to them. They stare blankly at each other and one of them offers Ward a cigarette. 'No, I'm not asking for a cigarette, thank you. I'm asking to know where-is-your-leader?' Again, no comprehension. Ward takes the initiative by walking past them and signalling them to follow. 'Come with me.' They duly oblige. They've all started smoking again and Ward stops and turns. 'NO SMOKING!' Again, they put them out, but as they do they have to catch up with Ward who reckons he knows where the leaders are most likely to be.

Sure enough, Ward arrives just in time to see about 10 men with more guns and cigarettes in the main reception of the area, mid ships. They're all smoking too, causing the three he has on tow to light up again. He stops on Deck 7 and looks down to Deck 5 through the open space there. It looks like there's about to be a confrontation: Monty appears to be limbering up to another member of this mysterious militia. For some reason, Monty is wearing his medals and some kind of military uniform. Monty is about to speak.

'You, yes, you, are you in charge? IN CHARGE?' The man shakes his head. Who's in charge of you then? The man points to a paler looking fellow at the reception. Monty thanks the man, and, before leaving him adds 'in a way I agree with you, Sir. I think the smoking ban is bloody ridiculous as well – though I never really smoked much myself.' The man nods at Monty pointlessly, but Monty is already marching towards the ring leader. Within seconds he taps the man on his back. 'ARE YOU IN CHARGE?' he asks slowly and deliberately. The pale man nods. 'Good. Now, DO YOU SPEAK ENGLISH?' The man nods again. 'Very good. NOW WHERE DO YOU COME FROM?'

'Peckham,' replies the pale man in a broadly East London accent. There's a gasp in the atrium.

'PECKHAM? Well, in that case it's much worse than I thought. I'd rather deal with proper revolutionaries. I suppose that means

I'm dealing with a man who has suffered a comprehensive school education,' he speculates.'

'What's that to you?' retorts the pale man.

'What's that to me? Well, it's simple really. If you had a private schooling then there's an outside chance you might have got a job which would have made you able to afford a cruise on this ship. Your selfish behaviour in harming the progress of our cruise would indicate an oikishness regarded as intolerable in the public school sector. Sir, you have no idea how much trouble you are causing us with your preposterous and uninvited visitation.' There's applause in the room, causing the pale man to get angry. He grabs Monty's lapels.

'No listen here geezer, Britain's dead to me. This is my home and you've just managed to sail yourselves right into the middle of a military coup, that's what you've done. Get it?

'A coup? What kind of coup? You expect me to believe a man from Peckham has the initiative to lead a coup in the Bermudas instead of making bogus benefit claims back home? If you had that much leadership ability, why didn't you get on your bike and manage a street stall in Stratford – or even in the Elephant & Castle.' This causes a titter amongst the onlookers. The pale man is very annoyed now.

'Listen here, granddad, there's my way or the highway. And nothing you've said yet convinces me you can out talk a gun.'

'So, sonny, if you've got it all arranged, what is it you actually want from us?

'I want your ship, your cash and your, er, ladies.' There's tutting and cries of 'shame on you,' causing the pale man to raise his arms – 'well, OK not the ladies but the ship and the cash anyway.' Monty's having none of it.

'Bugger off with your stupid demand for our ship and our. You're nothing more than a baffoon' the pale man raises his gun at Monty and says something in the same incomprehensible local language.

'Tell all the men to come quietly with us, or we'll start shooting.' Monty doesn't need to say it, because everyone's heard it. People are looking to Monty for guidance. He makes a judgement that his position is, in practice, quite uncertain.

'Choose 200 of us, and I'll make sure we come peacefully.' As soon as the pale man begins counting, Monty knows he's made a mistake. There aren't 200 men in the entire atrium. This means it will look like the rebels have 'won' in some way. Nevertheless, the pale man continues to count.

Upstairs, Ward is concerned to plan ahead for what's looking like some kind of effort to seize the ship. He has to get back to the bridge. The problem is, he's still being guarded by the three smokers, right next to him. He decides to try something.

'I'm going back to the bridge, see you in a few minutes.' They nod, and return to following the unfolding drama downstairs. Ward can't believe it and stalls for a few moments, causing confusion on the faces of the three men, one of whom offers him a cigarette once again. He looks down and this time takes it, allowing the gunman to light it for him too. He coughs violently at the first puff, causing the gunman to slap him on the back. 'Thanks, I'll be fine, he splutters, and shuffles off out of view, where he kills the cigarette before it kills him.

Back on the bridge, Ward issues three instructions. Firstly, be polite to the intruders at all times. Second, don't smoke any of their cigarettes because they're disgusting. Thirdly, inform the Line about what's happened and keep them posted on a minute by minute basis until it is no longer possible to do so.

Ward has no doubt the pale man will be up here soon. That will be the time to find out what's really going on, and why. In the meantime, he dispatches his people to different parts of the ship and ensures they're all in communication with each other through mobile phones and their paging system. And now he waits.

Sure enough, within a few minutes, the pale man arrives on the bridge. Ward has left the door open because he needs to make this particular contact and this is no to what the pale man expected.

'I've been expecting you, Mister Bond,' says Ward. The pale man stops at the door.

'It's not Bond, it's Cox. President Cox.'

'Look, what is it you want from us?'

'Simples – your ship and your cash and a ransom to release you.'

'How much?'

'A hundred million U.S. dollars,' he says menacingly.

'NO seriously, how much – we might have it on board if it's not too much – or you can ask for a silly amount and then we'll have to get the Royal Navy in.' The pale man looks around at the officers.

'Alright, how about, er, ten thousand or, no, a hundred thousand dollars?'

'No and no. I'll give you $5,000 if you'll get off this ship once it's fixed.' The pale man shakes his head.

'No deal – no can do. Revolutions cost money see. You've just blown the negotiation.'

'Hang on a moment! YOU started at a hundred million Dollars and dropped it down to ten grand. Now you say my counter offer isn't enough. I don't mean to be rude, but have you ever done this kind of thing before?'

The pale man blushes slightly.

'Well you started it with your poorly considered counter offer.'

'Anyway, I really want the ship more than anything else.'

'What for? Are you considering starting a cruise line? Because, frankly, no offence but with a reception like this your island would not be most people's first destination of choice.'

'Actually, I intend to use it as my Presidential palace. And as my official transport.' Ward looks around at his Officers, pointing at President Cox.

'Get a load of this guy. He's going to go to the international conferences on board the Spirit of Dogger V. Everyone else – like the American President and the Chinese Premier - turns up in Jumbo jets and Airbuses. But oh no, our friend President Cox from Peckham here turns up on… a cruise ship. That's practical. I suppose you're going to ask them to hold all the global summits in places like Southampton and Majorca - so when they fix an emergency meeting about world peace they'll have to wait a fortnight because you can only do 22 knots.' The pale man blushes even more. He decides to take affirmative action.

'No more games.' He says something to the others in the local tongue who clearly don't understand any of it. After a series of hand gestures by President Cox, Ward is escorted out of the bridge with his officers.

'Where are we going?' asks Ward. One of the guards pokes him with his gun. Ward suspects the answer is 'prison.'

Trev and Dave are still in bed, as usual. They've heard none of what's going on, because they had another heavy night with their new mates from the Friends of Dorothy, who've suggested a joint entry to the talent show, scheduled for the next day. Trev and Dave willingly agreed to this – and spent the rest of the evening chatting through the alternatives. After five ours of drinking, they decided on an original and creative solution: a rendition of Village People's immortal song 'Y.M.C.A.'

'What time is it Dave, mate?' Dave doesn't even open his eyes.

'Sleeptime.' Trev is quiet for a while.

'OK.' The darkness sooths their tired bodies – exhausted after unremitting days of drinking and revelry. Trev drifts off with a dream about a pool filled only with Fosters lager. Dave is dreaming he has a headache and a mighty thirst. There's a banging in the corridor. 'What's he doing now? Usually he waits till noon. 'Come in!' shouts Trev. Their steward has become tolerant of Trev and Dave's indolent sleeping habits. There's a knock at the door. 'COME IN!' shouts Trev again. Another knock. 'Let him in,' mumbles Trev.

'You do it!'

'You're closer.' With feigned annoyance Dave gets up in his underpants and opens the door slightly.

'There's a man with a gun here.'

'Er, then let him in.' A tanned man with a gun is smoking a cigarette and extremely surprised to see the door open behind him. The butt of his weapon had been casually tapping their door. Now he has to act. He wonders in as Dave backs off. Trev raises his hands. 'Is this about all the noise?' The man looks at them blankly. He clearly has no instructions for this kind of situation. 'What do you want?' He looks suspiciously at Trev and Dave – then starts fumbling in his pocket. Trev and Dave gulp in anticipation for what is to come. The man offers them both a cigarette, which they accept immediately. He lights them and the two lads breathe in deeply, hold the smoke in their lungs, and then begin to cough violently for many seconds.

'Are you tying to kill us?' splutters Dave between wheezing fits. The man shrugs. Now the man points his gun at the boys and marches them out of the room.

Ward arrives in the prison, to find over 100 male guests already in there.

'Captain!' hollers a familiar tone. It's Monty. He's in a cell with 10 others, all of whom appear to have been plucked from the atrium, as they are well dressed. Monty is still wearing his medals. Ward and his officers are thrown into the neighbouring cell. There's some shouting between the captors and then they leave. Ward tries to take control. He raises his voice.

'Is everyone alright?' There's a general and subdued murmur. Someone shouts that they're hungry. Another asks 'will we still get scones in the afternoon while we're here?' Yet another asks 'who are we backing? The old regime or the man from Peckham?' Ward realises he's in no better position to answer all but one of these questions – which he now applies himself to.

'I'm afraid there probably won't be any scones this afternoon, sir.' The gentleman replies.

'Oh dear – that is disappointing. Monty gave us a contrary impression.' Ward looks at Monty.

'Yes Captain, in my old job in the military we were always told it was important to open lines of communication with your captors. In this case I have done just that.'

'Oh.' Ward is genuinely surprised. 'What did you negotiate?'

''Well, to cut a long story short, we agreed that the inmates would receive tea and scones at around 3pm as long as we are good.' Ward tries to process this.

'What des good mean?'

'Oh, you know the usual things in this situation. Don't try to break out, don't kill anyone.' Ward is a little worried.

'So what's your plan?' Monty leans towards Ward and lowers his voice.

'Well that's the clever thing, you see. I very much doubt they have the capacity to provide sufficient scones and tea for thisnumber of people. These island rebels probably haven't seen a raison in their lives – and I know the man from Peckham certainly won't have. They'll be up the creek by 3.15 and then we can try and break out and kill whomever we like.' Monty is evidently pleased with his gambit – Ward less so.

'By the way, why are you wearing your medals?'

'Oh I always do on the third Saturday of the month. You know, lest we forget. Lucky really. For a while our cockney cannibal thought I was in charge of the ship. This lot really don't know very much about revolutions, do they?'

'No, about as much as I know about their language, Monty.'

'I thought everyone was supposed to speak English round here. This isn't English – it's Rubbish.'

Trev and Dave are now standing in their underpants on the keyside. The rebels are highly entertained by their appearance. They point at the boys' white complexions and laugh at their pasty skin.

'What are we going to do Trev?'

'I'm thinking, I'm thinking.' Trev looks up to see Dorothy from the health spa looking down from open deck 12 with her friends. They're obviously fascinated by what's going on. Trev looks around the quayside. This is more confusing. Apart from the attention being paid to the two of them, everyone else seems be allowed to come and go with no checks whatsoever. A few of the rebels are even offering some kind of touring arrangement to some elderly people in exchange for American Dollars. 'What kind of coup is this exactly?' he muses. 'What do they want?' Before he can ask anyone, Trev and Dave are suddenly bundled off into a jeep.

'Trev, where are they taking us?' squeaks Dave. Trev hopes for the best and fears the worst.

On board, the intercom crackles into life. The pale man is on the bridge with a handful of his people.

'This is President Gary Cox – President of the People's Republic of Little Epsilon Island and I have some announcements to make. Firstly, welcome to my island. My new regime means that I give anyone from the ship freedom of the city and the island. You can also apply to be citizens of the People's Republic of Little Epsilon South, especially the able bodied men and also all the ladies. Thirdly, in keeping with international sea rules, the ship now belongs to me and that is punishable by death – I mean taking it without my permission is, and I won't give you permission. So no funny business, right. OK, that's all for now, and have a good stay.' Cox takes his finger off the intercom and looks at his rebels. 'That was good, yes?' They indicate agreement, because it's easier than admitting they really don't have any idea what he just said.

Chapter 26 :
Rebel yell

Trev and Dave finally arrive at what looks like a tatty, camoflagued portacabin. On top there is a pole and a fluttering piece of material a cross between an African flag and an improvised painting of a banana.

'Hey, Trev, this must be the banana republic I've heard people talk about. Do you think this is their headquarters?'

'Dunno, mate.'

They are told to enter the hut. Inside, there are 10 men, all with guns and combat fatigues. They point at two chairs at a fold away table in the middle of the room. The chair opposite them is empty. Everyone is smoking apart from Trev and Dave.

'Do you think they're going to torture us Trev, mate?'

'What for? What can we tell them? If they want the run down on Britain's top football strikers I can help them a lot. If they want us to tell them all about politics, I think it's true to say we're pretty much screwed.'

'Let's cooperate. Let's just give them what they want.' Trev shakes his head.

'I somehow don't think it's going to be quite that easy. For one thing, they've got this weird language. I thought everyone was meant to speak English in Barbabos.'

'We're not in Barbados. We're in, Bahamos I think. Like the Triangle.'

'The Bahamos Triangle. There's something wrong with that, Dave mate. Isn't it a square?' Their dialogue is halted by the arrival of a self important looking man who looks like the pale one but isn't. He sits down in front of them. He reads something on the table. Then he looks up.

'So, how's tricks lads?' he says in the kind of accent you get in the bit of Manchester halfway between the centre of the city and Chorley.' The lads are taken aback.

'Eh?'

'Fancy a beer?'

'Er,' Trev looks at his watch, 'aye.' The man chucks them both a warm can of Carlsberg and opens one himself. As the lads pull the openers, the cans spray over them, causing everyone in the room to laugh politely. 'Ta mate.' The man continues.

'I'm General Gaz, and this is our revolutionary headquarters. I know it's not much but if we win then we'll save up for a better place.'

'You're English then? Asks Trev.

'Ah, sort of. More Manchester really, or Chorley.'

'How'd you end up here?' General Gaz leans back in his seat.

'It's more to do with my mate, you know President Cox. He's been here a while and wanted me to join him.' He leans forward again. 'Now, what we're needing to ask is you for your cooperation.'

'Er, in what way?' asks Dave nervously.

'Cooperation. Assistance. You know. The thing is, we've got a bit of a revolution going on here and it's not easy. What we're actually trying to do is take over the island and set up our own kind of dictatorship. We're calling the island the 'People's Republic of Little Epsilon – or Espilon, I can never remember which – South. President Cox says that's PROLES for short which he says means something but I can't remember what that's about and he wasn't too sure either. It's to do with the Boer War – ever heard of it?'

'No, replies Trev. 'Sounds boring.'

'I see your point. Anyway, what happened was this war over a century ago and what President Cox says is if the Boers had won then the island would be free or a part of Africa or something. That's why they speak that language they do which is meant to be from Africa,' and at this General Gaz leans forward to whisper, 'though between you and me President Cox made it up himself and he was always crap at languages in school. He went to a comp. I think it sounds like when people pretend to speak a foreign language and just make up words and that.' Trev is curious.

'Can they understand each other?'

'No! All these guys come from all differenet places but President Cox makes them speak his language which he calls Prolean all the time. They're just making it up as they go along. Anyway, this revolution means we're not owned by the Queen any more, and everyone will be free.'

'What changes then?' asks, Dave, genuinely interested.

'Well, President Cox gets the big house in the middle of town where the Governor lived at the moment, and we can have our own currency, which we're calling the Prole Dollar, which is worth the same as an American Dollar.'

'So what's the point of having it then?'

'Because it's going to have a picture of me on it. So, do you want to be on our side?' Trev looks at Dave and himself still sitting in their underpants.

'Will we get uniforms?' asks Trev. General Gaz indicates assent. 'Yeah then.' Gaz is delighted and chucks them two more cans.

'And I suppose we could have a go at the language.' Trev throws his can across the room and straight into the bin. General Gaz is impressed.

'Show me that again!' The rebels spend the afternoon drinking at cans and throwing them with incredible accuracy at bins and other targets.

'Where did you get so much Fosters?' asks Trev after an intense period of boozing.

'Washed up on the beach in a container which had a blade stuck in it, mate.' Trev and Dave look at each other.

'Can we see it?'

'Sure, fill your boots. We can't drink it all.'

Meanwhile, it's 2.55pm back at the prison. The officers, led by Ward, are planning a break out. The Governor is sitting in a corner of his own cell with a small notebook, recording these historic events. Scones are scheduled for 3pm, and if they're not there by 3.15, then this plan will be put into action. It's complicated. One of the Officers is to pretend to fall ill, to encourage a guard to come close. Then they'll overpower the guard, with lethal force if necessary, unlock the cells and fight their way back to the ship. It's a high risk strategy and could lead to casualties, but Ward will accept full responsibility. At 3.15 the scones still haven't arrived. Monty grabs Ward's arm.

'Listen old boy, you're overcomplicating things here. Let me implement my plan.'

'Monty, listen to me. I'm the senior officer here. We'll do it my way.' A guard appears. Ward nods at the officer to look faint. He makes a dramatic noise and falls to the floor. Ward shouts out.

'Guard! Look, my man is ill. I need help.' The guard waves Ward away and walks toward Monty. Monty and the guard are in conversation for a short while. Then the guard unlocks the cell and lets all of Monty's people out. Monty then directs the guard to unlock all but the officers' cell. Ward is amazed. 'Hey, what just happened?'

'Oh, like I said, I had a deal. No scones, no deal. He let us out because he knew otherwise we'd try to break out and kill anyone we liked.

'Monty, what about us? Get him to let us out.'

'Sorry, can do not, old boy. The guard thinks your chap has the Norovirus. He heard about all the disease on board the Dogger V – Plague ship and all that – doesn't want to infect the island.' Monty marches out, shouting 'I'll see what I can do for you later, old boy. Meanwhile, I've got a revolution to stop! Governor, come with me.' The released Governor marches out with Monty in preparation of a showdown.

Trev and Dave are on the beach with the rebels, filling the back of the flatbed truck with cans of boiling Fosters from the baking hot container on the beach.

'Paradise, Dave mate!' Dave is nodding and opens a can, spraying it at General Gaz who laughs in a jocular fashion that would suggest a rage within. Then they spot another rebel jeep coming towards them. 'Dave, mate, look who else has joined the rebels – it's Mr and Mrs Jitters.' Jane and Jack are on a tour of the island with their rebel hosts and are having a lovely time. 'Mr and Mrs Jitters – over here!' As they get close, the Jitters couple wave joyfully from the back of the truck. Then joy turns to horror. The pirate boat which troubled Spirit of Dogger V comes into view in the cove. Worse still, the rebels abandon the truck and run for cover, leaving Jane and Jack at the mercy of the pirate rump of four still at large.

'Why did they run away?' asks Trev. Gaz shakes his head.

'We've got no bullets. The pirates have.' Jane and Jack are led to a hut at the far end of the beach and locked in. The pirates return to their boat and start looking at what booty they acquired from Spirit of Dogger V.

'We've got to help them, Dave mate.' They discuss the options for a few minutes and come up with a plan. 'So that's settled then, we'll sneak up at night and cut a hole in the side of the hut and get them out.' As they say this, there's an explosion from the hut, and the pirates run away unarmed from the hut and the boat, which collapses on the craft, causing a secondary explosion that causes the vessel to burn mercilessly. Jane and Jack appear from the smoke, and walk gently towards Dave, Trev and the rebels. They meet them half way. 'Mr and Mrs Jitters, are you alright? Why did they try to blow you up?' Mr Jitters shakes his head and runs his hand through his hair.

'That wasn't them, that was me. I found the things needed to make an I.E.D. - that's an Improvised Explosive Device - in the hut. Even some batteries.' Trev's amazed.

'How the hell did you know how to do that!

Jack looks over his shoulder. 'Off the record, the bomb thing, it's just something I know about. Ack sure, I grew up in Northern Ireland, sure enough.'

'And if you've got the guts to make a bomb how come you're so scared of being on a ship?' challenges Dave. Jack considers this question.

'Aye, now I'd accept that's not rational on my part, right enough.'

Moments later, and after the recovery of some random items from the now deserted and fractured pirate boat, Trev and Dave, Jack and Jane are travelling back towards the town in the back on the open truck with the rebels. The sun beats down and they've got guns and a lot of lager to drink.

'This is fantastic, Dave mate! When we get to the next port let's sign up for some more of the tours.'

'Yeah, I'm lovin' it!' Trev and Dave converse in nonsense language with the other rebels, who have also started drinking cans of Carlsberg. Someone pipes up with a Prole language version of the British National Anthem, and they all join in using their own words. In a funny kind of way, it does feel revolutionary. At the end they clap and cheer. Dave shakes his head a bit.

'I'm thinking, we shouldn't disrespect the Royals. We always watch the Royal thing on Christmas Day. I quite like it.'

'Don't worry Dave, mate. They'll not find out about this.' Although technically what Dave and Trev are doing is still treason, punishable by death. Under the circumstances, it's probably just as well they don't know this as it would undermine their enjoyment of the afternoon. By contrast, Jack does know this and it's making him feel very nostalgic.

Back in town, Monty is on the war path, looking for Peckham Man. Nobody seems to know where he is. Eventually, and in desperation, he goes with his 85 or so fellow guests to the town square. Someone asks 'what do we do now, Monty?'

'We sit down and sing we shall overcome.' There is muttering and uncertainty. 'Oh for goodness sake, watch me and do the same.' Monty sits in the middle of the road and begins to sing 'We Shall Overcome,' accompanied initially only by the Governor who is standing stiffly to attention. Others join in. Eventually, all of them are blocking the road, so that no traffic can pass. This has an unintended consequence. As traffic stops, the occupants are exiting their vehicles and joining in the sit down demonstration. Eventually, hundreds of people are there, all singing along. A carnival atmosphere develops. Some are dancing. Steel drums appear from one of the bars, and play along. The smell of cannabis wafts across the throng, and joints are being passed freely from one person to the other. The island's only policeman turns up. He stands at the perimeter of the demonstration and – helps to park the cars in a more orderly fashion.

At the far end of the street, three large open trucks of Prole rebels are suddenly seen to round the corner. The square silences as these well armed men drive slowly up towards the demonstration. The men dismount their vehicles. There are 40 of them, all in camouflaged fatigues and with bands of bullets in a cross across both shoulders. The guests in the square stand up to face the armed militia. Eventually they're only 10 paces apart. The rebels raise their guns. Some take aim nervously. There's a commotion from near the centre of the rebel pack. Two men jostle their way to the front. They speak in the incomprehensible tongue unique to this odd little uprising. Then they hand every rebel a Fosters, say something else and all laugh. Monty continues to sing 'we will overcome,' and now a few rebels join in, swaying from side to side to the rhythm of the steel drums. Two of the rebels approach Monty. Initially he raises his fists in defence, then recognises them.

'Trev! Dave! I didn't know you had anything to do with this rag bag revolution!'

'We didn't but, well we kind of got involved by accident.'

'Was any of this fading of support amongst the rebels your doing?'

'Well, sort of, Monty. The thing is, we're all hammered and they're our best mates ever! And Mr Jitters made a bomb!'

'Did you really Mr Jitters.'

'Well, technically it was an Improvised Explosive Device, but I suppose you could also call it a bomb. It depends how precise you want to be. But I don't really want to talk about it all that much, if you don't mind – you being in the army and all that.'

'Let bygones be bygones,' exclaims Monty, 'but all the same, jolly well done old boy! One man's terrorist is another man's freedom fighter, eh?' Mr Jitters looks down and mutters:

'That's right Monty. No surrender.'

Trev turns and says something in 'Prolean' to the rebels. Monty raises his eyebrows.

'What on earth did you say to them?'

'Oh, nothing. It's all in the tone, happy or sad, peaceful or angry. They're actually really, really nice lads, most of 'em. General Gaz here comes from near Chorley.' General Gaz raises his can in salute to Monty. Suddenly the singing stops, as the crowd of rebels parts in two. Behind them stands the ring leader – President Cox. Monty and Cox happen to be facing each other, far apart. President Cox shuts instructions in an angry tone, but Trev responds immediately in a very calming tone. In the confusion, the rebels do nothing.

Cox apporaches Monty. He has a gun. Monty only has his medals – a record of past valour. Eventually, they are only a few metres apart. The town is silent. The wind ruffles a tattered British flag on top of the Governor's residence. Tumbleweed inexplicably blows past. Cox speaks first.

'You can't stand in the way of progress, old man.'

'And you can't stand in the way of tradition, Peckham Man.'

'People don't need a royal family. They need a leader.'

'They can have both, but not with a bounder like you. Look around you. You've as much hope of running this island properly as the Labour party in Britain has of counting to 100. Come on Cox, you've had your fun. Can't you just grow up a bit and do something useful, like running a pub or getting them to speak proper English instead of that gobbledegook the Governor tells me you've conjured up?'

'It's a real language.'

'Real?' snorts Monty. It's about as legitimate a form of communication as farting.' Monty walks forwards towards Cox. 'It's over Cox.' Cox raises his gun. 'Cox, don't be rash.' A shot rings out and Monty falls to the ground. Trev and Dave look at each other in horror.

'Are you thinking what I'm thinking, Trev, mate?'

'What are you thinking?'

'That we should run away mate?'

'No. Come on mate.' Trev and Dave walk past Monty towards Cox who raises his gun again. 'Go on then you twat. You've shot an old man. Why not finish the job and kill us too?' Cox lifts the gun higher, and then higher. He pulls the trigger and a shot rings out again. He hits one unopened can of lager flying through the air which sprays in all directions like a lager grenade, but he's struck by half a dozen more in the forehead, face and chest, causing him to fall backwards to the ground, as the rebels cheer and give each other high fives. Trev and Dave run forward and grab the gun, and kick him very hard for a few seconds.

'I demand justice' yells Cox.

'Bollocks to that, mate,' says Trev. 'You're going down.' After they have suitably restrained Cox, with various guests from the ship guarding him, Trev and Dave return to the lifeless body of Monty. The look down at him somberly.

'He did talk a lot at dinner, but he didn't deserve this.'

'No he didn't deserve to die.' Monty opens his eyes.

'Well, then it's just as well I didn't then isn't it my boys!' Trev and Dave are stunned. Monty lies on his back in the dust a little longer and points to his medals. 'I was damned fortunate to have these fellows on. This whopper here appears to have taken the bullet. What are the odds, I ask you?' Trev ventures a guess:

'On this ship, it was probable.' Monty laughs gently, and slowly sits up, to the gasps of those a little further away, some of whom assume that Captain Bladder has such mystical powers as to resuscitate the dead even when he's not present himself. Monty continues. 'Give me a hand up, would you. And as for talking too much at dinner, I'd say you owe me a Harvey's Bristol Cream for that injudicious comment. You should have at least checked I was dead before speaking ill of me. I'd love to stop and chat but I have a little unfinished business to conduct over at the prison. '

As President Cox is forcibly restrained, Trev and Dave start a new chant: 'Cox out! Cox out!' Soon everyone has joined in and the carnival atmosphere has returned.

When Monty re-enters the prison, followed by Trev and Dave, the officers are still planning their escape. Ward sees Monty's associates.

'Oh no, Monty, how many others have mutinied too?' He walks up to the door.

'These two? They're not mutineers you madman – they saved my bloody life – and indirectly yours too I should imagine. Monty unlocks the cell door.

'Eh?'

'Oh Ward you've missed so much. While you've been lounging around here planning your escape, I've been whipping this miserable island back into shape!' Ward is completely confused.

'Monty, the guests? How many down?' Monty smiles patronisingly.

'No need to worry, Ward. All present and correct.'

'How can this be?'

Monty offers Ward the short version as they walk towards the square, where Cox is now battered, bound and gagged. Ward looks down at the wretched state of Cox. 'Has he been treated fairly?'

'Captain Ward, Cox has been treated according to the rules of engagement as they pertain to a bloody idiot from Peckham with the audacity to suggest this island should shun the Commonwealth. And you also owe a great debt to these two young lads who bravely infiltrated the rebel forces at their secret mountain hideaway, and proceeded to teach them the skills of traditional warfare.' Trev and Dave nod, with Dave adding:

'Yeah, we got them pissed and showed them how to chuck cans at people.'

'And Mr Jitters made a bomb!' Dave feels a hand on his shoulder. It's Mr Jitters who speaks to him quietly.

'I'd be grateful if you stop telling people that, if you would be so kind, son.'

That evening there is a great party in the Jolly Roger bar, attended by the rebels, Trev, Dave and Monty with his Mrs Major plus the Jitters duo. The Friends of Dorothy are also in attendance together with some of the guests who have been imprisoned during the day. Late on, other guests who paid some rebels to give them a tour of the island join the party too.

'What lovely people,' says Jane, 'but I really couldn't understand a word they said.'

'Nor could they,' suggests Jack. He looks around and lowers his voice. 'And that business on the beach was quite something, wasn't it? I always wondered I could make a proper bomb. At school we only ever just talked about it, so we did.'

Chapter 27 :
Taking stock

Monty and Mrs Major awake in a humble bedroom in the centre of the main – and only – town on Little Epsilon South. The yellowing net curtains waft lazily in the stifling morning draft. Flies buzz dutifully overhead. It's a big day for Monty and Mrs Major. In a few short hours they will rise from their modest bed to make the final 2 mile journey back to the cruise terminal in port. After a tumultuous day overthrowing the local revolutionaries, Monty slept like a baby and, for the first time in years, didn't talk about Frogs or Nazis in his sleep. His only two outbursts in the whole night were 'we lost the quiz because you went to a comp school' and 'Peckham needs a Berlin wall.'

Moreover, after years of planning their on-going retirement, they have finally secured their dream solution – the presidency of a small banana republic in the Bermuda Triangle. Nor does he now take lightly the choice of ship for this passage to their future. Monty has spent no less than six months fully researching all the options, the ports of call and the technical specifications of the various vessels. His judgement was that Spirit of Dogger V combined all the places he wished to visit with a good price. Yet it took an unscheduled visit to an island which has never been previously visited by a British cruise ship for everything to become clear.

'Oh Mrs Major. I wake up as if from a dream into a dream. I can hardly believe so many foreign people are being so nice to us. It almost makes be believe that, with the right approach, we may be able to civilise them to British standards.' Mrs Major's impressed.

'You mean that possibly, they might be able to function as proper citizens even though they are coloured?' Monty, missing the sarcasm entirely, continues.

'Yes, that's the gist of it. With the right education, and some kind of a stick and carrot approach, I'm beginning to think it's just possible that we can actually shoehorn them into an active role in what's left of our Commonwealth.' Mrs Major makes a calculation in her head.

'Monty, I'm not sure an island with a handful of residents whose main economic activity is growing lychees - and those things we still don't know the name of - is really going to compete with trading links between Britain and, say, Australia.'

'Why not?' responds Monty indignantly. 'Australia is a very good example. All they've got is a dusty outback with a few kangaroos and descendants of convicts. WE'VE got gin, lychees and me. And I've never been in prison.'

'You were yesterday, dear.'

'Well, yes but that doesn't count because I broke out and stopped the revolution. And winners write the history. Just think about it – a letter assuring this island's continued membership of the commonwealth to our Monarch. We could be guests at Buckingham Palace. You could wear a hat! The Governor recorded it all in his notes and will back up every word. That's why we have this accommodation to enjoy.'

'If this is a reflection of his feelings then it's he's only marginally less angry with you than he is with Cox. Oh Monty,' she considers her true feelings. 'I have to tell you that I'm – well – really proud of you. You give those bad revolutionaries a good seeing to and then made them apologies to everyone. I just hope they've learned their lesson.'

'You underestimate me dear. I don't intend to leave anything to chance. I have a plan to use them as a perfect example of British justice and values. Yes, Mrs Major, I intend to give Mr Cox a fair trial, on television and with a proper opportunity to defend himself... and only after that to hang him.'

Trev and Dave have finally left the Jolly Roger, and are briefly blinded by dawn's early sun beaming in from the East.

'What a night, Trev,' mumbles Dave, holding his hand before his bedazzled eyes. 'What time is it, mate?' Trev makes an ineffective effort to read his watch – which has become a seething caldron of dials and hands which he can't focus on at all.

'It's, um, it's roughly the morning, mate.' Dave isn't listening to Trev, because he's still staring at some kind of movement in front of him. The vague form crysallises into Dorothy from the health spa and a friend of hers. She puts her arms round Dave.

'How can we ever thank you, Davey? Me and my girls are so happy that you help the Monty Gentleman to save the ship. We are your real friends now. We want to be REAL friends.' Dave looks across at Trev, who's receiving the affections of Dorothy's other close working colleague. Dave and Trev sway gentle in the breeze of flirtation in which they now find themselves.

'Dave, mate, what do you want to do?' Dave turns to Dorothy.

'What time do we sail, love?'

'Six this evening,' she replies in her seductive Romanian accent. Dave straightens up.

'That's great. Hey, Trev, we've got the time for a couple more with the others!' Dave turns to his would-be beau. 'Hey love, I'd like you to meet some friend of ours who worship you they do.'

'Really?' she says cautiously.

'Sure, they your friends – Friends of Dorothy! Come on, I'll show you!' And with that the four of them enter the Jolly Roger for an unfeasibly raucous morning.

Jack and Jane wake to a knocking on the door. Jack puts on a robe and answers cautiously.

'Yes?'

'Hello, as the cruise Director I'm sorry for coming round so early. It's just that, now we've regained control of the ship and all that, we're trying to put everything right. And I notice you've had a number of complaints about the ship over the last weeks, many of which were only drawn to my attention in the last couple of days in the er, prison. I've been reviewing your case and, all things considered, I can't really offer you a refund without higher approval. However, given your pivotal role in the outbreak from the prison, I was wondering of you'd accept a counter offer – namely instead of getting off in Havana, that you spent the remaining few months as guests at our expense on the cruise?' Jack looks at Jane with surprise – then back at the Cruise Director.

'But we haven't made any complaints.' The Cruise Director looks at his notes. 'Mr Bitters?'

'No. We're Mr and Mrs Jitters.' He stalls again – and realises with delight what's happened.

'You're the Jitters not the Bitters? How divine! Welcome aboard for the rest of the world cruise. I can even offer you a balcony – with a sea view!'

And what of the Bitters?

'Just think of the compensation we're going to get for this,' gripes Mr Bitters in his most monotone Brummy accent, turning the fish on the fire with his stick. 'I mean, it's hell on earth. Compare this to what we had in Solihull.'

'Mrs Bitters looks ruefully into the distance.'

'I'd give anything to get back there. I mean, imagine if the last people we ever see is each other. It would be a fate worse than death. That's what I think.' Mr Bitters looks at her coldly.'

'You don't really mean that, do you?'

'Of course I do. All you ever do is complain. You're doing it now, just because we caught a – whatever that is instead of a cod. Can't you see we've got it made?'

'No I can't.'

'Think about it! The longer we're here, the more compensation we'll get. If we spend the rest of our lives here we'll get a fortune when we die.' Mr Bitters thinks bout this for a long while before responding.

'Actually, I've never thought of it like that before. I suppose you're right. In that case, we need to do all we can not to be rescued.' Mr Bitters burns the fish and his wife begins a mental checklist of things she, in turn, might be able to sue her husband for when they get back to civilisation. Unfortunately for them, the island doesn't appear on any map as the only people who might have reported its existence have been eaten.

However, Mr and Mrs Bitters don't need to worry. The literal translation for the name of the island they're on is 'faecal relic' – and it has been used for centuries to imprison local rejects and outcasts whom cannibals wouldn't eat in case they digested misery themselves. They believe this island will one day be inhabited by beings which convert hope and courtesy into despondency and pessimism. With the arrival of Mr and Mrs Bitters, this prophesy has been fulfilled.

There isn't much to say about Susan and Douglas. They spent the entire coup in bed. By the time they left their room looking for food, order has been restored. They meet Casper the steward.

'Could we have breakfast?'

'Of course – you not only have the freedom of the ship, but also of the island. Simply show your key card and the breakfast will be your oyster.' Susan looks at Douglas.

'What would you like to do, darling?' They stare at each other in that superficial way newlyweds do.

'I'd like a bacon sandwich. What about you Susan? ' She looks at him aghast.

'But Douglas, you know that's going to make you fat. How could you even suggest it! She turns round melodramatically and storms back into the cabin, leaving Douglas and Casper in the corridor alone.

'What do you think of that, Casper?' say Douglas bemused.

'Sir, in my experience that is a record.'

'What? Just 13 days for our first argument since we got married?'

'Yes, sir. It normally takes merely three.'

In the late afternoon, as guests raggedly return to the ship, Acting Captain Ward is informed all the repairs to the propeller are complete and that the ship is once again in full working order. Ward is pleased about that, but not pleased about waiting for Monty to turn up on the quayside. He's in his Officer whites and has a team of 5 people with him, similarly dressed to greet the man of the moment.

An hour passes. No Monty.

Another hour passes. Still no Monty.

The guests are aboard now, milling around on the decks, watching the curious collection of Officers standing on the quayside for reasons they don't fully understand.

Eventually, three hours later, Ward sees a procession of some sort approaching the quayside. As it approaches – he realises two individuals are being carried on ceremonial chairs towards him. It's Monty and Mrs Major.

'I don't believe it,' he mutters under his parched breath. 'It's really them.

A few minutes later the chairs are lowered in front of Ward and his officers. Almost the entire compliment of guests and crew are now on deck and spontaneously applaud the return of the hero. Ward feels obliged to salute, and is followed by the officers who do the same. He is about to speak.

'Wait!' commands Monty, raising his hand. Microphones and battery powered speakers are installed in front of him and the Acting Captain. Monty checks the sound. 'Testing, testing, one two, one two.' This draws cheers from the crowd, causing Monty to bow his head humbly. However sick makingly self-promoting the whole pretence of the moment appears to him, Ward judges that he can't delay any longer.

'Sir, I cannot tell you in words how grateful I, my crew, my guests and all of the A&G Line are to you for – well, saving the day.' More applause. Monty feigns humility.

'No, no, my Captain, the honour is all mine. I went to prison on this land for a reason. After all,' he lets his words echoes agians the side of the ship and into the balconies and decks of the vessel's vast expanse – and gestures with his hand in an emperor like way, ' if doing what is right for my country was my crime, then, Sir I am guilty.' There is cheering and applause once again. Monty waves up at his audience, on deck and also on the balconies. Ward decides to cut it short.

'Sir, we thank you once again and when we return to Britain, we will make sure your contribution will be honoured in an appropriate manner.' Monty lowers his hand to his heart.

'Captain, I shall not be rejoining the ship. These islanders are my people now. My duty is to them, to civilise them, to teach them the ways of British law and justice and to ensure the perpetrators of the attempted coup are hung for their crimes, whether of not they come from Peckham. I, President Montefiore of this fair isle also extend the hand of friendship to all British registered cruise ships from this time forth, but not, obviously to the Germans or Frogs. As a token of the strengthening bond between our peoples I have also dedicated a street to my English wife, without whom I would surely have failed to find the gumption to play my part in our recent and noble struggle for liberty. I invite all tourists to visit her street – the Rue de la Majorette – to sample the delights of all that is best in colonial Bermuda, and also to buy shoes from her new shop. And with that, dear Captain Ward, fare thee well all speed on your on-going cruise.' All aboard erupt into deafening applause and cheering – culminating in the chanting of 'Montefiore! Montefiore!' Ward salutes the new Presdient of the island one last time and marches up the gangway as quickly as feasible to escape the spectacle.

Trev and Dave have returned to their cabin to clean themselves up after a pretty raucous couple of days. Their double bed has gone, replaced by two single beds.

'Hey this is amazing. I wish they'd got these for us earlier,' says Dave excitedly.

'Yeah mate. Then we'd have been able to have just - ' Trev stops. In fact, it wouldn't have made any difference at all. Apart from today, they've had no luck at all in the female department. 'Well, anyway, good.'

As they leave for dinner, with what's left of their table 64, Trev and Dave bump into their steward.

'Hey man, thanks for getting us the two single beds.'

'That is no problem sirs, in fact you have always had them.'

'No, we had a double for the whole cruise.'

'No, it is made up of two singles, but until word was spread about your interest in the health spa ladies I had believed you had interest in each other.' Trev and Dave's jaws drop. Dave asks the terrible question:

'You mean, we could have slept apart all along? Bollocks!'

Back on the bridge Ward looks down to where Monty stands with his entourage and wife graciously waving them off.

'What's gone wrong with the world?' He muses to nobody in particular. A junior shows uncharacteristic courage, perhaps emboldened by the revolutionary events of the last days.

'Actually, Sir, I think something's just gone right. Cometh the hour, cometh the man. He saved our bacon, Sir. I think we should be grateful.' Ward at once feels ashamed and moved.

'You're right. Take the helm.' Ward trots out of the Bridge to a high point on the ship where he knows Monty will be able to see him. Acting Captain Ward salutes Monty with formality and sincerity. Monty – already looking up towards the bridge sees him immediately. He responds with a salute embracing all the decorum of his military days; and in those moments they are bonded by a salute to courage and sacrifice in the service of others.

As clear blue water widens between the hull and the quay, the

Cruise Director signals for the ship's band to shift from the music they have been playing for the Sailaway to their pre-arranged score. In a departure from tradition, they play the British National Anthem – and all on deck stand to attention in honour of Monty. As the refrain echoes out, Monty stands proud and moved to his very soul, knowing that even if this island empire and its people last for a thousand years, this is their finest hour.

Chapter 28 :
Close encounters

Spirit of Dogger V is finally and safely back at sea, and order has restored itself amongst the guests and crew. There's no time to stick around in Bermuda without falling further behind on the schedule. Ward has agreed to meet up with the Line authorities in Cuba. The flights are easier to organise there, and he will have been able to make a full inventory of anything that's damaged or missing in the vessel by then. As it is, there seems to have been little or no damage at all. The main problem us that the islanders – upon the suggestion of 'President Montifiore' – have piled the rear of Deck 12 high with exotic fruits as 'payment' for Monty and Mrs Major – whim they regard as a prized gift from the British vessel. It will take a day simply to store the fruits below deck, and Ward fully expects the newly empowered guests to assist by secretly stealing the fruit for their personal use in their cabins.

The talent show is one of the highlights of the cruise – and occurs towards the end of each 'leg' of the cruise as people prepare to get off and return to the United Kingdom. This isn't always because of the high quality of the performances. Three factors make the talent show particularly attractive. Firstly, there are always a few truly gifted performers. Secondly, there are always a number of comically dreadful ones. Thirdly, a small proportion of the cheekiest entrants alter their performances without notice – from something which is socially acceptable to something totally shocking and inappropriate to the event, causing universal mirth and titillation amongst more of the guests and all of the entertainments staff, apart from the Deputy Cruise Director who inevitable gets the blame for nudity and swearing.

The weather is tremendous and in a departure from tradition, the Cruise Director has decided to hold it up on the open deck around the pool, on the raised stage. The setting sun is faultlessly well behaved, the sea like glass and those preparing to leave the ship having their customary last hurrah at the bar.

The first act passes off without incident – Geoffery and his wife Juniper perform a tango to the sound of the band and kind applause from the audience. Another couple are drunk enough to try and join in but a steward subtly stands in their way, causing a moment of confusion in the two befuddled minds and they sink back into their chairs to await yet another cocktail of the day – 'Dogger's Surprise.'

The second act is less in line with policy. It's supposed to be a duo musical recital by two elderly people –they promised not to do anything silly but it was naïve of the team to trust them. As soon as they emerge from behind the curtain the trouble begins. They're going to attempt the 'feather dance.' Unfortunately, as the Clare de Lune music begins, it becomes obvious that neither has the agility to conceal their naked persons from the audience. Most applaud vigorously, a few walk out and the team do their best to try and curtail the show as fast as possible. This leads to an embarrassing moment when a male member of the Ents crew ends up smothered between four feathers and two nude octogenarians. The lights are briefly reduced and after a silhouetted scuffle, the couple are no longer on stage, despite calls of 'more!' from the audience.

The newlyweds are up next, with a heartfelt and badly sung rendition of 'I've got you girl,' followed by Trev and Dave with 10 members of the Friends of Dorothy, singing and perfoming 'YMCA.' This brings the entire audience onto their feet, performing all the familiar actions for the letters, in time honoured kitsch tradition. It's a knock out rendition and at the end the dance becomes a standing ovation. Trev turns to the Friends of Dorothy, all laughing and panting after the exertion.

'I love you guys!' Dave agrees.

'Group hug!' Trev and Dave have finally found the sense of belonging they came on board to discover. 'It's a close encounter of the third kind!'

Astronomer Starwalker is having a close encounter of his own. He's standing hand in hand with Mystic Maria. He's getting off tomorrow, and has really had a great trip. Most of the time he's had to explain to people that he's not an astrologer, that he doesn't believe in star signs and that the world will end in five billon years, and, yes 'that is more than twice as long a century.' As the next act mutters on about poetry, Violet Cryer marches up to him and demands an apology.

'You made a fool out of me, right inside my own launderette. I really believed you – about the end of the world. I've always done the stars and all that astrology. Now look at me. Even the Captain looks more informed than I am.' Starwalker looks at her through a combination of gin and adoration for his new belle.

'Why shouldn't the Captain know more than you?' Starwalker asks, genuinely curious.

'Because it's my job to keep the ship posted. I've got to make sure the Officers can't cover up the truth. And I know you're hiding something about what happened to Captain Bladder. What IS the truth, Mr Astrologer?' Starwalker looks at Mrs Cryer and concludes she's being absolutely serious. With a supreme effort, he composes himself.

'Please give me your hand, Mrs Cryer.' Despite her lack of cooperation he repeats his request. 'Your hand, now, please.' She finally obliges. He studies her palm carefully and then looks her in the eye as much as his swirling head will allow. 'Yes, Mrs Cryer, I can say with absolute certainty that you are going on a long journey.' Mystic Maria nods sagely.

'I can see that journey will take you to many places – and that you will become a great person.'

'Really,' says Cryer, visibly puffed up by the prediction.

'Oh yes, there's no doubt about it. Are you an Aquarius?'

'No.'

'Libra?'

'Actually, I'm Pisces.'

'Yes I thought so, that's very important. You will go on a long journey.'

'Your boyfriend has already said that.' Maria looks at Lucas.

'And I agree with him. Have a great life, Mrs Cryer. Now we must go and look at something over there.' She points at a featureless expanse of ocean. They leave her standing there and depart for a more quiet corner and a drink with DJ Christian. Meanwhile the next act in the talent show is a passenger who is trying to hypnotise the entire compliment of passengers with a chant, causing amused mirth around the deck.

On the bridge, Ward is finishing off a meeting about the overall condition of Spirit of Dogger V.

'So, in a sense, that's remarkable. Apart from a few broken chairs and scratches in the paint in one of the lift, Dogger is unharmed by her recent traumas.'

'And the fruit?'

'We said there was going to be a shortage of bananas, mangos and lychee. All the fruit's gone sir, apart from a melon which appears to have fermented.'

'Good. Take the melon to Captain Morgan's cabin. I'm sure he'll know what to do with it.' Ward occupies himself with navigational matters and then sits down to start preparing a report upon the extraordinary events of the last few days for the Line officials.

As Ward is writing, a junior officer calls to Ward urgently.

'Captain, look at this!' Ward instantly recognises the radar signature of a small boat a few hundred feet starboard of them. He goes to the starboard side and peers into the gathering darkness.

'That's odd, no lights. Signal them.'

A flashing morse message is sent to the mystery vessel, indicating the identity of the Spirit of Dogger V and requesting the identity of the small boat. The flashing returns from a torch: '..-/--/..-./..-/-././/.-/-...-/...-/-.-.' and everyone interprets the words at once.

'I'm fine. ABC'

'I don't believe it!' exclaims Ward, summarising the thoughts of the entire bridge. "ABC – it's Captain Bladder. Signal that we'll rescue him.' An equally surprising response returns: '-./---/-.../..-/--./--././/.-/---/..- ./..-./.-/-/...-/-.-.' Again, the bridge crew all interpret this immediately.

'No. Bugger off. ABC' Ward grimaces.

'That's not very nice. We can't just leave him here.' He feels obliged to ignore his former Captain's demand. But before he can act, Ward and his team are exposed to the most unusual spectacle he has seen in 22 years at sea.

A distant light aproaches the approximate location of Bladder's unseen boat at great speed and hovers directly above it. Bladder is suddenly bathed in blinding blue light, and his body is seen to rise up into the direction of what looks like a silver bellied craft.

Down on deck, the guests are watching too. Everyone can see it, just the same. The talent show has stopped as people watch the body rising towards the silver object. Once the body has vanished inside – something shoots down and the boat explodes in a flash of white light, before fading to darkness.

Everyone on deck has seen what the bridge saw. Two thousand pairs of eyes follow the lights until they can be seen no more. Once the illumination in the sky disappears to nothing, there is total silence on board. Everyone looks at the Cruise Director for guidance. The Deputy Cruise Director looks across at the Cruise Director too - who simply gestures for her to say something to calm the nerves. She raises the microphone.

'Er, well, that was quite a show – um, let's, let's hear it for the hypnotist!' The applause is slight, as people try to figure out if the lights and noises were a hallucination, a trick of the light or one of those 'Triangle' events. The Deputy Cruise Director continues. 'Our next act is by Edith Maurice, from Deck 11. Ladies and Gentlemen, she will recite for us an extract from 'The Rhyme of the Ancient Mariner,' to the accompaniment of a xylophone. Please give a big hand for Edith Maurice.' Again, weak applause. As Edith recounts the lengthy poem, a quiet chatter begins amongst the guests, who are now comparing notes about what they saw. Edith clearly has every intention of reciting all the many pages of the piece, the Deputy Cruise Director lets it run as it appears to be having a calming effect on everyone there. The Cruise Director waves to his Number Two to continue and slips off to go up to the bridge.

On arriving there, he finds a crew far more traumatised than the guests.

'Did you see that, Captain?' he asks.

'I saw something – everybody did. Was that to do with the frigging talent show? How are the guests?'

'No it wasn't – er, I don't think. But they also seem sure it was part of the talent Show, skipper. Did it register on radar?'

'Sort of – a lot of interference. Then it vanished when the dinghy blew up.

'What the hell was it, Captain?'

'I honestly don't know. But it was definitely something.' A junior officer asks a question now.

'How are we going to report it, Sir?'

'Well, it's surely going to be the tough one to write up in the ship's log: '18.15: crew and guests observe Captain Bladder raised from water - by a helicopter or alien spacecraft - and rise into dark sky. Dinghy explodes. No further contact.'

'Do you think it was a U.F.O. Captain? I mean we are right in the middle of the Bermuda Triangle. Why don't we ask the astrologer?'

'The astrologer isn't going to be much use on this one I'm afraid – but let's not go into that now. The guests all think it was a U.F.O. That hypnotist at the Talent Show might turn out to have been quite a lot better than I thought. Personally I keep an open mind, but for Bladder's sake I certainly hope they were extraterrestrials. If he has been abducted, it will mean he never has to talk to people again. His dream planet is a world with an ocean of gin and tonic and two islands far apart, where nobody wants to sail for fun everyone on one island wants to eat lamb from the other.'

'Yes, that would be paradise for Captain Bladder, wouldn't it?'

'It would indeed. It would be logical to sink the boat rather than leave it as a danger to other shipping, though perhaps a little tough on the former owners of that particular vessel. Whether he's been abducted by aliens or the U.S. Military – or even a religious sect – I doubt we'll be hearing from him again for a while. He's had his fill of the public.' Ward shakes himself out of his reminiscences. 'Right, whatever that was we can't change it by speculating. So it's time to calm down and get this cruise back onto track.' He clears his throat authoritatively. Set course for Havana.'

'Aye aye Captain.' Everyone returns to their stations. Ward surveys his people, and is satisfied that, within minutes, the crew will have found their focus on their various responsibilities.

The Cruise Director is just about to leave, when he notices Ward looking distant.

'I know it's not regulation, Captain, but fancy a drink?'

'No, no. Well, actually, nothing's been regulation on this trip so, on second thoughts, let's do it.' He leaves the others in charge and steps out with the Cruise Director. They traverse the whole distance from Bridge to stern in silence.

'As they stand on the far back of the ship with two large gin and tonics, the cruise Director opens up the conversation.

'Here's a toast to Bladder.' They clink their glasses into the darkness behind the ship, illuminated only by the long, fizzing phosphorescent wake – the myriad sealife responding to the deep, powerful blades propelling the vessel forward into the night.

'Are you worried about Bladder?'

'Not at all. Whatever happened to him will be pretty much what he wanted. And you know, with all that business with him bringing back Morgan from the dead, and then 'finding' him alive on the island, well, perhaps he does have some kind of mystic powers.' He laughs. 'That sounds crazy, doesn't it?'

'Er, yes, it does, Al. You're beginning to sound as nuts as the guests.'

'Well, all I'm saying is that with his dramatic disappearance this evening, in front of our very eyes, I'm one step closer to believing the truth is out there. Saint Bladder of Bermuda, eh?'

'So you're alright then Ward old boy?'

'I am, Al. I am.'

'Why the melancholy then?'

'Oh it's not to do with Bladder It's just something I have to do in Havana. I just have a little unfinished business there, for a barman friend I used to have - Tony. I need check up on someone for him - for old time's sake.'

'About a girl?' Ward nods.

'Her name was Lola. She was a showgirl - with yellow feathers in her hair and a dress cut down to there.'

'Nice! I hear the dancing's quite wild in Cuba.' Ward nods again.

'She would 'meringue' - and do the 'cha-cha'. And while she tried to be a star, Tony always tended bar across a crowded floor.'

'The hours must have been long.'

'They worked from 8 till 4!' Ward smiles. 'They were young and they had each other: who could ask for more?

'Where did they work?

'At the Copa? Copacabana. The hottest spot north of Havana.'

'Wow, that's so cool!'

'Music and passion were always the fashion, at the Copa... they

240

fell in love.'

'Sounds ominous. Did it go well, Captain?' Ward shakes his head with a melancholy rhythm.

'His name was Rico, he wore a diamond. He was escorted to his chair - he saw Lola dancing there. And when she finished he called her over - but Rico went a bit too far. Tony sailed across the bar and then... the punches flew; and chairs were smashed in two.'

'Oops!' Ward turns to the officer.

'There was blood and a single gun shot.'

'But just who shot who?' Ward looks away again.

'At the Copa... she lost her love. That was 30 years ago, when they used to have a show. Now it's a disco. But not for Lola.'

'What's she doing now?'

'She's still in the dress she used to wear... faded feathers in her hair. She sits there so refined - and drinks herself half-blind. She lost her youth - and she lost her Tony - now she's lost her mind.' Ward looks at his junior officer. 'At the Copa, don't fall in love.'

And so the Spirit of Dogger V steams on towards Havana and we pause silently over the ocean as her bright lights and dance music fade into the distance. The grand and majestic cruise ship steams ever onwards towards further adventures and discoveries creating a wake of phosphorescence which will last for minutes... and memories which will last a lifetime.